The Black Marshes

Emma Barrett-Brown

This book is for Jay

It is also for Tasha and Red

Published independently by Emma Barrett-Brown. 2018
Cover Art by McKinnon Imagery
Cover Model: Natasha Crystal Berry

Copyright © 2018 Emma Barrett-Brown

All rights reserved.

PROLOGUE

1810

A drip of the brightest red blood dribbled from the wound on a child's throat, gathering body as it first tumbled down her tiny white neck and then fell, glistening, into the waters of the marsh. The girl no longer cried, no longer screamed. She was almost dead, so close to death in fact that very little could have saved her. The marshes all around were dark, bleak with the setting of the sun, an event almost enough to make even an old drinker like Sam shiver, despite what that imposing ball of brilliance had already cost him. Another bead of brightest crimson slid from the throat of the child, this one catching in her dirty blond hair, spreading out it's long fingers across the length of each hair and colouring the fine strands with its stain.

Sam gasped and pulled away. The child was dead… no… dying though, at least. He panted twice and then sighed, looking down on that silent little face. Ten years or so of age, certainly no more. Not long enough to have lived on this earth to now be dying. Not for this, not for him. The icy waters at his feet seemed to have grown deeper so Sam moved back to the path and there knelt, the child still slumped in his arms. Inside, something pulled, a memory of another dead child, his own, and of a world

The Black Marshes

long since dead too. He brushed the little girl's hair out of her eyes and shuddered to see the damage he had caused to her tender throat. He'd taken a vow, long ago, not to do this anymore – not the feeding, no, he had to do that – but the killing... especially the innocent. He looked down on her face for another long moment, but then came to a decision. Her life wasn't his to take.

Holding the girl close to him, Sam unbuttoned the top two buttons of his shirt and loosened his cravat. His own hands were cold against the skin of his throat as he loosened the tie. A quick pulse check on the girl confirmed that yes, she was still alive, albeit just barely. The scent of her soap lingered too, especially in her hair and Sam breathed it in, once more reminded of that other lost child.

'I'm sorry for this,' he whispered, then with a pointed finger-ring he kept for the purpose, he pierced the vein in his neck and allowed a few droplets of his blood to fall onto the girl's upturned face. She didn't move, limp as a ragdoll in his arms.

'Come on,' Sam murmured, 'Come on!'

The girl didn't respond, didn't move at all. Sam groaned and patted her face. He'd never normally harm a child, not ever but his coach had thrown a wheel and left him walking for hours, vulnerable in the sunlight. Then there she'd been, playing in the dark, dangerous waters. Sometimes, when things got tough, the demon just took over – not so much as it had in his younger years, but it was still ever a risk.

Still the girl lay still, her eyes closed and her body limp. Sam wet his lips, then sighed. 'I have no idea what this will do to you...' he murmured, and then allowed the demon to take his form, shifting so that he was holding it a prisoner, rather than letting it take over and simply finish off the last of the little girl's blood.

'Please, God, protect this child from me and don't let this turn her,' he murmured aloud, and then reopened the wound at his throat and allowed the blood to flow again down onto her face.

This time, the child responded; there was little that could resist the demon's influence.

'Heal, don't destroy,' Sam murmured, 'God, please?' and then pulled away. The colour was coming back to the little pink cheeks already, her little throat working to take in the evil sustenance. Sam laid her down, leant against a fence post where hopefully somebody would find her, and quickly checked her eyes, her lips. She wasn't turning – his gamble had paid off.

Out in the distance, a dog's bark sounded and then a voice shouting.

'Frances! Where are ya gal?'

That was his cue to leave! With a final kiss to the girl's forehead, and a whispered apology, Samuel Haverly turned and fled into the rapidly falling twilight of the day, hoping he'd not been seen.

1

Frances Quinn.
June 2016

The basement was cold, cold enough to make even Frannie shiver, despite the layers of clothing she wore. The darkness was broken only by the odd blue light of the CCTV screens. The feeds came in from tiny mounted cameras dotted all about the vast house above, a ruin in which nobody lived anymore. Even still, Frannie struggled to understand this new tech. She hated it, but then she hated most things lately; Henry Quinn, her lover, was no exception. Henry sat in silence watching the screens in much the manner that a cat stalks a mouse. He, Frannie, and a few of their kin sat around a table in the cold damp room which was at the edge of the long winding basement corridors commonly referred to as the "catacombs" by the group. The room was silent, all eyes on the invaders, tiny and blue as they seemed for the fuzzy screen, watching as they entered the house above; looking for the nest but finding nothing but empty hallways, unused, decaying bedchambers. Frannie could almost feel the frustration they seemed to expel.

'See Frannie,' Henry said, looking up at her, 'This is why I insisted we live underground.'

'Won't help us if they torch the place... especially in the daylight like this!'

Henry's eyes turned to the other people, drinkers like him... like her. He was almost glowing with amusement.

'Ahh, my wife. Always the pessimist....' but even despite the levity of his words, Frannie saw a warning in those blue eyes, still so youthful and yet anything but. His brow was wrinkled too, masked a little by the long strands of his perfectly kept brown hair. Henry had the face of a fox. His eyes shone and his features were a little pronounced, but it wasn't that, it was more the slyness in his gaze, the mischief he seemed somehow to exude.

Beside Henry, a dark-haired drinker guffawed, he was one of the rare ones Frannie actually liked. His name was Terry, or Tony, something like that. He seemed always to have a laugh or a smile – a rare commodity in the household. On the other side was another of the older ones, mousy hair and rather a pointed face, which was probably the feature which led to the dubious nickname of Rat. Henry liked him for all the things which Frannie found abhorrent: cruel sense of humour, relentless malicious streak, eyes which lingered too long several inches below the face of whichever girl he was speaking to before moving to make eye-contact. His victims suffered, Frannie just knew it.

Frannie turned her eyes back to the screens, four in total, each showing a different feed. Absently she put a strand of hair to her lips but the taste of the dye she used to colour the white locks to the bright purple shade they now held flooded her system, causing her to grimace. The changer in focus on the closest screen had returned to the front entrance of the house whilst the rain hammered down on the little group of invaders who waited without for their comrades. A second ambush perhaps – the old one was fairly cunning – shame Henry had known that and taken it into account really. As the old changer on the screen seemed to dither, Frannie wondered if the lack of any resistance had been dubious in itself. Maybe that's why he'd left a group outside in the rain.

'That's him,' Henry said, pointing out the taller of the men, 'Haverly.'

Hugh Haverly was a name that every drinker learned early to recognise – and to fear – and yet Frannie found herself looking upon the man with new curiosity. This was him, this was the man who had killed her husband, James.

Hugh himself pushed open the door again and Frannie saw a younger man take his elbow. The two men spoke briefly, but the cameras had no sound and so despite how Frannie wasn't half bad at lip-reading, she could not pick up their words for the blurring of the images. Just a few words spoken and then a nod.

'The fool, he's bringing them all in,' Henry said, indicating where the ragtag band of changers – five or six of them, some in form and some not, all suddenly moved forward to meet those inside. Henry switched the picture on that particular screen to the next camera, the one in the hallway, giving the group a good view of the carnage which was to follow.

A small buzz on the table and Henry leaned to pick up the small smartphone which lay there.

'Yes, I think so,' he said after listening for half a moment. 'Kill the bastard.'

Frannie's heart thudded as, on the screen, the door swung closed behind the invaders, the lights went off, and her people attacked. The man Frannie had seen with Hugh was at the rear of the pack and when he saw the carnage he backed away. Frannie glanced at Henry but he hadn't noticed, eyes too intent on Haverly's form, heaving and fighting. As Frannie watched, the man slipped away and then moments later a large tan wolf padded out. The man-wolf dispatched two young drinkers with ease as they tried to pass him, ripping their chests open to destroy the hearts. Inwardly Frannie cheered for him. Any love she had for her own kind, for her own nest, had died many years earlier.

The fight continued: Henry leaned in so close to the televised chaos that Frannie almost believed that he would somehow be sucked in, become a part of it all. She glanced back to the wolves and saw that Haverly had stopped fighting. He wiped his mouth quickly, wet his lips and then Frannie saw the silver in his eyes, even through the crappy blue and white images.

'Stop,' he commanded; Frannie could recognise the order even without sound, 'Just... stop!' and then suddenly the fight was stopped. Just like that. Haverly was shaking with the exertion, Frannie could see it in his hands, the way his chest moved. Frannie watched as another, a female came to his side, putting a hand on his arm.

'Come,' she seemed to say.

Haverly shook his head and then another of the changers who was in human form took the girl's arm, pulling her away. Hugh Haverly had a mate too then? Interesting. Hugh fell to his knees, even through the CCTV Frannie could see the strain that he was under, the confusion of the younglings as they found themselves backing away.

'Fools – they have him!' Henry hissed.

'No, no, I don't think they do...'

'What do you mean?'

'I mean... look Henry, he's doing something to them...'

Hugh stood again and backed towards the door, then through it. Then chaos reigned – obviously whatever the old changer had done was broken when the barrier was between him and them. Somewhat incredulous, Henry flicked back to the first camera on that screen, just in time to see Hugh snatch up the frantic girl who'd pulled his arm earlier and flee into the night half-dragging her with him.

The Black Marshes

Henry glanced at Frannie with an almost concealed glimmer of worry. 'Erm… what just happened?'

'I have no idea,' she said, shrugging.

'Nor I… Rat?'

The other guy just shrugged, then stood 'I'll go find out,' he said.

Henry shuffled in his seat, 'They must have some way of controlling drinkers…'

The dark-haired man, (Tony – Terry – or was it Tommy?) nodded. 'We sent in only the new ones. Maybe the old wolves are too strong for them?'

'It looked like mind control,' Frannie agreed, feeling she ought to say something, 'I've heard rumours about the old wolves…'

Henry nodded again and then picked up his phone. 'One-all I suppose then,' he mused, and then dialled a number on the phone.

'Rat?' he muttered, when the phone was answered. 'Did you find out what the hell happened?' he listened carefully for a moment, then nodded to himself, his eyes flitting across his companions before coming to meet Frannie's again.

'All right,' he murmured. 'Bring it in, but for god's sake clothe it first…' He paused, laughed again, and then hung up the phone. 'We got one,' he said, eyes bright, then slid an arm around Frannie's curvy waist and pulled her to him. She forced a smile and held him back. To the outsider they must look like a well-suited couple. She'd been turned at just twenty-one years of age, Henry had been eighteen. He had long hair which fell loose to his shoulders and dressed all in black. He wasn't ornate but a modern tongue would describe him as "alternative" in style. Frannie was much the same, her clothing often dark, and generally not "mainstream", her hair was always coloured some strange colour and she had a couple of piercings in her face: the bridge of her nose, her septum and her lips twice. Henry had put those in for her, but still, she didn't mind it. Henry kissed her twice but then pulled away and went back to the CCTV screen again, glaring at it as though the system was to blame for what had happened above.

A chill blew through the room, making the hair on Frannie's arms stand up. Before, in a previous life, she'd whiled away time by listening to the ticking of an old clock which had stood outside of her chamber, but there was none here to tune into as they waited for Rat to bring in the changer, just the buzz of screens, now barren of any life, and the sound of Henry complaining. Frannie zoned out, it was easier not to heed him and he certainly didn't want replies – in fact, to reply could mean a beating later and Frannie wasn't willing to risk that for anything, not anymore.

At last the door opened and in they came. The changer was back in human form, naked but for a pair of old jeans. His long red-blond locks lay on his shoulders in a matted tangle. The man who led him had had him bound in a silver line, and his skin there was blistered from the precious metal. It was the man Frannie had seen speak to Hugh, the man whom she'd watched sneak away to turn feral and then to fight by Hugh's side. She swallowed her disappointment in silence, no need crying over spilt milk – or soon to be dead changer. How had they caught him, though? Had his pack left him to rot? Frannie doubted it, wolves were well known for sticking together.

'Here, Quinn,' Rat said, then tittered as the changer staggered, almost falling, into the room.

Henry looked up with cold blue eyes but did not respond. He was eyeing up the changer like a kid about to start ripping wings off a fly, or legs from a spider. Frannie shuffled forwards, not wanting to prolong the encounter; she was tired and wanting her bed.

'What's your name, changer?' she asked.

Henry glared at her but he wasn't quite hot-headed enough to show his anger at her in company. The wolf looked up, his grey eyes cold and defiant. He did not reply.

'Wolf, where are your manners? The lady spoke to you!' that was Rat.

'You're an old-blood, aren't you? I can see it in your eyes. Tell me, who are you?' Frannie said again, trying to sound gentle to coax the beast into speaking.

Still the wolf remained silent.

'What? Cat got your tongue?' Henry asked, speaking for the first time since the changer had entered the room. His companions sniggered; not Frannie though, she took the opportunity to stand and back away a few paces whilst Henry's attention was shifted.

'All right, just give me your name,' Henry said. 'Just so I know who I'm talking to.'

'William Craven.'

'Craven eh? An old name indeed. I hear tell that hereabouts the Craven family are the remains of a grander family by the name of Haverly... but I'm sure you wouldn't know anything about that...'

The wolf looked stunned. 'I have no idea,' he said, more cautious this time. 'I am an orphan, never met my folks.' His voice was fairly rich, his eyes darting from Henry to Frannie and then to the other two.

Henry eyed him long and hard. 'Really? Cos that looked an awful lot like Hugh Haverly you were running with?'

Frannie caught William's eye and silently pleaded with him not to anger Henry more so; it really wasn't worth it. He seemed to see the look and Frannie saw confusion flitter through his eyes.

Henry eyed him up a moment longer and then sighed. 'You know,' he said. 'I actually don't give a damn who you are, wolf, you failed and if your pack comes back, they will fail again...' he turned to Rat, who was still grinning like a fucking idiot. 'He's a changer. Take him downstairs and teach him what we think of his kind. Keep him alive though, for now... I want to send a message back to Hugh Haverly.'

'Henry, must we?' Frannie began but a look of pure malice stopped her in her tracks.

'We must. Go to bed, Fran, I'll come ravish you when I'm done here...'

Both the other drinkers laughed, but another wave of disgust ran through Frannie, she grabbed for it and locked it away with the rest of the similar feelings. If nothing else, she was very, very patient.

2

Hugh Haverly,
2016

The little room in the inn was small, damp and dusty but tidy enough. The scent in the air was of mould and the dregs of the previous occupant's scent, all covered over with a good dosage of Pledge. The curtains were of cheap cream and red cloth, and the bedspread coloured to match, although mismatched of pattern. Hugh glanced about quickly from the open door and then stepped inside, a little black and white dog at his heels and Ella on his arm. The light was a good 100 watts, bright enough to cast off the shadows which were forming with the dying of the day, enough also to make him squint against it. Hugh could barely speak for worry. His hand hovered over his blade as Ella detached herself and moved to sit herself down in the chair by the little desk which was up against the window.

'What happened, Flower?' he asked, the first words he'd uttered since she'd pulled him away from the house. 'What the fuck happened?'

'It was a trap. They knew we were coming!'

'How?'

'I don't know. One of ours talking too much? Spies in our house? I just... I don't know... for them to have been up in the daylight hours... something must have alerted them! Somebody?'

Newton, the little black and white spaniel who was ever at Hugh's ankles laid himself down on the rug in the middle of the room and closed his brown eyes. Hugh wished he could relax so easily. Ella simply sat, never one for a lot of words, she merely watched him and then put out a hand.

'It was supposed to be an easy clear-out,' Hugh said, taking the offered hand and sitting beside her, putting an arm around her shoulders. 'It wasn't supposed to go this way.'

'I know, Hugh, but sometimes things don't go as planned.'

'This has never happened to me before, not in five hundred years!'

Ella's eyes seemed to skim over him. 'I know,' she whispered.

'Who did we lose? Other than Will?'

'Gareth went down, I think, when the trap was sprung, and Lizzie was injured but escaped.'

Hugh put a hand to his forehead, trying to control his temper. Hugh was the first, the pack-father, and he'd sworn never to lead them into danger. The crusade was his, to rid the world of those of his and his brother's kind who turned on humans. His crusade, his alone, with his brother Sam's guidance. Only once or twice before had he taken others in with him and every time the thought of worrying about the lives of any other than himself had caused more stress than it was worth. It had been William who had suggested they join him for this one – a good training opportunity he had said. The Orchard Estate was vast, and there were only about ten drinkers in there. It would be easier to get them all if they took in more bodies and the newer recruits could do with the nest-clearing practice. Normally Hugh would have declined, or just taken Sam as he sometimes did for drinker jobs, at a push maybe even Sam's blood-child Reuben who was one of the strongest fighters he knew. With Ella home though, after an estrangement which had lasted centuries, and William – his distant descendant – at his side, suddenly it had seemed a good idea. Comradery, a band of heroes. It hadn't been anything like that though. The trap which had been laid for him had snapped about them all and it was only though his influence that they had escaped.

'I don't think I even know who Gareth was,' he said at last, 'Lizzie was one of the older ones?'

'One of Sam's girls, I think she was turned by Jonathan? Gareth was new, 1980s perhaps?'

'Fuck! Such a waste!'

'It's not your fault!'

'I shouldn't have asked it of them. I should have just stuck to the plan!'

Ella moved so that her head lay on his shoulder. Hugh leaned in and kissed her, tried to ignore the tears on her face. For years he'd held her at a distance for fear of her succumbing to some danger, only to pull her into it now, and to nearly lose her. To lose William. Hugh put up his hands to release his hair from its tail and retie it, an old habit which showed his nerves.

'Do you think William is still alive?' Ella seemed to read his thoughts.

'I don't know, Flower.'

'They wouldn't just kill him, would they?'

'I don't know.'

'If they are as clever as they seem, they will understand who he is and how valuable a hostage he is! Surely?'

'I said I don't know…' he snapped but then checked himself and muttered an apology for his sharpness. It was not going to do anyone any good for him to take his annoyance and frustration out on the sweetest girl he knew. Hugh glanced down to Ella's face. Other than himself and Micah, her own child of the pack, William was probably her best and only friend. He couldn't find the words to tell her that the man was probably already dead. This little bastard, Quinn, was a mean one. Not only did he kill indiscriminately, but he seemed to revel in it. Reports of missing wolves had begun to trickle in over the years, growing in number as time passed. Hugh hadn't put that together with the arrival of this new nest until recently. It wasn't the first time he'd cleared out the Orchard estate, either. Back in the early 1900s, Ella had fallen into their hands and had nearly become a prisoner of the drinkers who had settled there then. He'd gone in, with company again that time, and he'd taken out as many as he could, fury fuelling him to their annihilation. He'd missed the leader though, Henry Orchard – known to him as the boy drinker. With an appearance of an eighteen-year-old boy, the creature was traced back to a very old blood-line, Hugh's own in fact, in the form of his brother Sam's blood. This new threat, Quinn, was likely the same man, if not a close offspring, and he'd defeated Hugh without even showing his face. Hugh had underestimated him exponentially.

Hugh sighed again and pulled Ella in closer to his form. At least he'd got her out. If anything had happened to her, he didn't know what he would do. A love born in the witch-hunts of fifteenth century Germany, and still burning bright. He might be the leader of them all, *the powerful Hugh Haverly* who his pack followed blindly, and his enemies feared even a mention of... but if anything happened to Ella... that would likely be the end of him.

'Will we go back for him?' Ella finally spoke again, 'To bring him home if we can, or to be sure he's dead, if that be the case?'

'Hush, of course. William is family, as well as pack,

there's no way I'm leaving him to die there if they haven't killed him already.'

'I just pray he's still with us,' she whispered.

'He is either alive or dead, Flower. If he's alive, then that means they don't want to kill him and if they didn't need him alive then he's already dead and there's little we can do…' Hugh took in a deep breath and then pressed his lips to Ella's forehead.

'Come, try to sleep flower, you look exhausted and I need some time to think of my next steps.'

3

Frances Quinn.
June 2016

They tortured the wolf for hours. As midnight came and then passed, his screams grew so loud that Frannie could hear him even from her chamber in the catacombs. It was dark, stiflingly so for the lack of windows. Both a blessing and a curse, as far as Frannie was concerned. The air smelled earthy too, being so far underground. Frannie tossed and turned but she couldn't sleep. Usually the drinkers kept funny hours rising at about four pm and then remaining awake until dawn but with the intel on the impending attack, Henry had kept them up all through the day, leaving Frannie to try to sleep at night in order to catch up. Another scream sounded, half-human, half-feral. It was bad enough when they tortured the humans, but at least they could die in the end. When the wolf reached the end of his tether they simply laid off long enough for him to heal and then started again.

'Shut up! Shut up!' she moaned aloud, 'for god's *sake*!'

A warm trickle of water left Frannie's eye and tickled its way down to her nose and then onto the pillow. She often cried at night, in the dark where nobody could see her. That was when Henry was good enough to leave her alone, which was more often now that it used to be at least. Frannie never cried where people could see it – as the co-leader of the nest, she had to maintain an image of strength at least.

Even with that thought, though, the sound of footsteps approaching the door made Frannie's heart pound and sure enough there was the sound of the key turning in the lock. Only two people had a key to Frannie's chamber, Frannie herself and Henry. She rubbed her eyes quickly as he entered and sat herself up in bed.

'Can't sleep huh?' Henry asked.

'No. That wolf's been screaming for hours this time, hard to sleep through.'

'I know. I can hear it too. Wonderful isn't it? He's a hard bastard but he's cracking!'

'What are you trying to get out of him? Hugh's location?'

'Nah, I know where they are, they're not exactly secretive… I'm just playing with the beast for now until I find a use for it. Training the dog!'

Frannie didn't reply, sometimes she could tolerate Henry but other times he just made her feel ill. It hadn't always been so, once she'd loved him back but time had twisted that, along with his temper. Frannie and Henry had been together since James had died, aside from a small amount of time in the 1980s when she'd escaped, loved another man – her Russian, Andre. Henry had put a stop to that quickly enough! Henry moved to her dresser and poured himself a drink from the whiskey bottle he'd left there last time he'd visited her. He slurped down the fiery liquid and then climbed into the bed. He was warm, his muscles taunt and his body ready for hers. Frannie cringed as their skin touched but forced herself to stay calm and let him hold her. It wasn't worth the repercussions of trying to push him away. He'd gotten worse too, over the years.

Any misdemeanour could send him into one of his rages now, even a misspoken word and lately, it didn't even have to be directed at her for Frannie to feel the brunt of it. Sometimes she wondered how many times her body could mend, how many times she could gel the broken bones, vanquish the bruises.

Henry pulled her to him and kissed her nose, his eyes shining. When his face was this close to hers Frannie could almost imagine her lost James was there instead of Henry. As brothers, they had shared features and their eyes were so alike, but never, ever, could James have even imagined the atrocities which his brother committed. Frannie tried not to think of James, but it was difficult, the two brothers had merged almost as one in her mind as time passed and it was hard to separate them. Frannie wondered if somewhere out there, the spirit of James still watched over them. She hoped not; the creature his brother had become would have destroyed him.

'Penny for your thoughts,' Henry asked, he still looked like the charming but mischievous youth he'd once been when he smiled and it was that stab of nostalgia which made Frannie bite down on telling him exactly what she was thinking. Often, stupidly, she would get riled and do just that but Henry was far stronger than she was. It wasn't worth it. With a deep breath, Frannie steeled herself and smiled up at the psychopath she was tied to. She knew that one day she was going to kill him. She just had to wait for her moment.

'Nothing, just listening to the wolf's cries.'

Henry seemed satisfied with that. 'Love you Frannie,' he whispered and she forced herself to smile again. She never said the words back; they'd both have known her lie if she had. Henry pulled her down onto the bed, his fingers slid down her body and Frannie thought that one day she would have the strength to push him away for good, instead, as always, she closed her eyes and pretended he

The Black Marshes

was somebody else. As Henry peeled away her clothing, the screams of the wolf started up again. Frannie froze at the sound. Henry just laughed and pulled her body into position to receive. As he slipped his teeth into her neck, Frannie let go of her tensions and let him taste her, shuddering at the arousal in his thoughts caused by the screams of the wolf. She never bit back either, not anymore.

Frannie awoke from a cat-nap some time later and groggily glanced to the clock, it was only just gone 2.30am. Jesus, the night was dragging! At least at this rate she would be able to sleep out the day and sort out her routine again! She rolled over in the bed and found Henry's side cold and unoccupied but even before relief could settle he spoke from across the room.

'The wolf stopped howling about an hour ago, I thought I might go pay him a visit.'

'Good morning to you too Henry.'

Henry scowled, 'get up.'

'In a minute, I'm still sleepy.'

'It's the middle of the night! Get up!'

'Gimme a minute to wake up, Henry,' she grumbled.

'You have exactly one minute.'

Frannie sighed, she would go upstairs, she thought, into the house where she wouldn't be able to hear the howling anymore, especially if Henry was going down. Besides, she loved the old house still, a reminder of happier times.

'Ok, ok,' she whispered, 'you go, I'm going to head up…'

'Erm, no Fran, you're going to do as you are fucking told and come downstairs with me,' Henry said, eyes flashing, 'It's about time you assisted and actually earned your place in this nest.'

'With more than just my body you mean?'

'Don't be a bitch Fran, get dressed.'

The lower basement was very cold, dim and peaty. It was a level down below the catacombs, making it two below the house, in what used to be the old cold storage back when Frannie, James, and Henry had all been human, hundreds of years before. The lower basement was now divvied up into cells and it was there that Henry kept his prisoners. Mostly just human, food. The whole level smelled like shit, piss and despair. From the side rooms, the odd snuffle or cry could be heard but for the most part, it was eerily silent. How many had died down here? Frannie couldn't count any more. Stupid, docile humans. Vampire-fetishists, mostly, worshipers of the drinkers. They came, pulled in by whispered invitations in darkened clubs. They'd come for the sex, for the experience, sometimes even to be bitten, but they'd never leave.

As Frannie and Henry walked down into the freezing cold tomb, a whimper sounded from the far door. Henry called it the wolf-room. Specially kitted out for holding one of them. For torture. Henry's fingers gripped hers hard as he pulled her into the room and obedience forced her to raise her eyes and look at the wolf they'd caught.

The man was haggard and tired. Blood soaked his bare chest, matted into the hair there as well as dried in little rivers down the front of his blue jeans. His hair was long and dirty blond, falling to about half-way down his back. He looked up as they entered and Frannie saw the grey hue of his eyes. The beast looked intelligent, wise... and tired. The evening before, there had been fight in his eyes but that was all gone now, lost in his agony. He was, limp too, hanging from the silver chains which sapped him and prevented the change.

'Quinn,' the wolf spoke the name through dry parched lips and Frannie had to fight an overwhelming urge to tell Henry to bring the poor creature some water.

The Black Marshes

'William Craven,' Henry replied. 'I see you are enjoying my hospitality.'

Frannie pulled her wrist away and sat herself down in the old wooden chair by the table in the corner. She couldn't take her eyes from the wounded creature in his silver bondage. Henry pulled up the other rickety chair and sat down on it backwards, surveying the bound wolf. Frannie allowed her eyes to take in her lover. He looked young and foolish, easy to underestimate. She prayed that William didn't do that.

The wolf, William, didn't speak a word and Frannie could see that his silence was making Henry even angrier.

'Nothing to say for yourself?'

'I have no idea what you expect me to say,' William said in that same dry, cracked voice.

'Nothing, I expect you to say nothing…'

'What do you want then?'

'I just like listening to you howl,' Henry laughed. 'Do you think Hugh Haverly will try to come back, to rescue you? I'd like to see that man in shackles…'

'If he does, I'll ask him to let me drive the blade though your heart, you stupid boy.'

William's eyes were defiant again and Frannie's heart went out to him. Henry didn't like to be reminded of his youthful appearance and his temper was unpredictable. Even Frannie had no idea what Henry was capable of when in full swing, but she'd been on the wrong side of his temper too many times to want to see it expelled on a person he didn't claim to love.

Henry stood and came to the table. His fingers moved over Frannie's shoulders, touching the skin of her neck and then trailing up to her ear. This was really turning him on, she thought with a shudder. Henry chuckled and then picked up a handful of silver spikes from the box next to her. The spikes were about two to three inches long, bound in leather at the ends to allow drinkers to handle them without the blisters silver bought on prolonged contact. Henry's own creation, designed for the express purpose of causing pain.

'Now I hear that you wolves are a little bit more allergic to silver than we are…'

The wolf, William deflated a little at the sight of the shining metal. He was frightened of it, she could see that. Henry walked up to the man and looked him in the eye. Frannie enjoyed the fact that he had to look up to do so, Henry had never been great of stature and the wolf was a big man.

'William Craven,' Henry said in a quiet dangerous tone. 'Ask me to kill you, and I will. I just want to see you beg before you die.'

'Go to hell.'

Frannie allowed her eyes to flutter closed; she didn't want to see Henry torture this brave, beautiful creature. The man's cry echoed around the room and Frannie opened her eyes to see Henry slowly inserting the spike into his chest, all the way down until the flat circular part at the end was flat on his skin. There Henry gave it a final push with one finger, down into the flesh. The man's face was screwed up against the pain. Even as Frannie watched, the break in the skin began to heal over, essentially trapping the silver inside of his body. It was a cruel instrument, and one well-designed. Henry could have been a master inventor, in another life.

'Let's try that again shall we? Do you want me to stop all this and let you die, William?'

'Fuck you!'

Henry took a second of the spikes, slow and deliberate in his cruelty. He ran it over William's cheek, causing the big guy to flinch in terror and pain.

'Stop it Henry,' Frannie knew her words were wasted but she had to try. 'Please, stop it, I can't stand it!'

Henry glared over at her, as did the wolf, shock written

on his face.

'Look into his eyes Frannie,' Henry said softly, 'and remember my father, my brothers, my sister... even your beloved James... these creatures are worth less even than humans Fran. Destroyers of lives, abominations before god.'

'What does that make you then, drinker? I never tortured a man,' William hissed but Henry didn't even look at him.

'Just think Frannie, it was this creature's family who stole them from us, he is Hugh Haverly's clan. Hugh killed James, killed Phina... and this... this monster runs with him...'

Henry ran one of the silver slivers down William's quivering chest, and then drove it into his flesh, between the ribs. William howled again and Frannie felt the tears welling up in her eyes. Angrily she blinked them away, Frances Orchard didn't cry in public! Especially not for some changer that she didn't even know.

'Henry, stop it. This creature didn't kill James, or Phina. It's Hugh you want, not this one.'

Henry didn't even glance at her. The next three spikes slipped easily into William's collarbone and Frannie felt sure that soon he must break. That much silver inside his body must be agony.

'It's not a great thing you know,' Henry said almost gently. 'To beg to die, just one little sentence William Craven, and then I will end it all.'

'Why not just kill him?' Fran whispered as William just stared at them defiantly. 'Why this stupid game?'

Henry's head shot around again, 'You want to go up there next to him, Frannie?' he asked.

Frannie shook her head and sat back down, looking at her hands.

'Good girl, now watch.'

Henry took another of the little spikes and pushed it

into William's navel, just where his belly button was exposed above his jeans. The wolf clenched his teeth in an attempt to bite back his scream but as Henry pushed the object right inside of him, the beast roared again.

'Henry, please… fine, do as you will but I want to go upstairs now, I can't watch…' Frannie whispered, pleading with her eyes as well as her words. Hesitantly, she stood again.

'Sit there and shut up, or join him up there. Those are your choices. Don't make me lose my temper, Fran.'

William's eyes were glazed, his teeth clenched in agony. Henry paused for a few minutes, letting the man writhe, and then lifted his blade and made a cut about where the spike had gone in. He fished around and pulled it loose. The spike pulled free with a bloody slurping noise and Henry dropped it back onto the metal tray with a clang. This he repeated, and then again and again until William's skin was free of the spikes. He waited a few minutes for the wounds to heal, and then placed the last spike he'd removed back on William's chest.

'Shall we try again?' he asked.

'Henry, I need to feed,' Frannie said, a desperate attempt to stop the carnage.

'Plenty of blood right there,' Henry nodded at the wolf.

Frannie shook her head and looked down at the table. 'Never mind.'

Henry laughed and for a moment Frannie half-expected him to force her to feed from the wolf. It was the ultimate indignity. He didn't though, and simply turned back to his prisoner.

'If you can withstand this, you know I'm only going to step up my game, right?' he said. 'There is more than one way to make a dog yelp,' he nodded towards the old burner in the corner. 'Frannie,' he said, turning to her. 'Go and light a fire will you my dear? There's plenty of wood and kindling in the cupboard in the corner,' he turned back to William. 'I normally reserve fire for misbehaved drinkers but I'm willing to give heat a try on you, wolf. Tell me, which one is your good eye?'

This time the wolf really did cower. Frannie saw the fear in his face. *How much can you withstand, beautiful creature?* she thought, *you'll crack eventually*. His fear stoked her courage again and with defiance she didn't know she possessed, she shook her head.

'Are you saying no to me, again, Frannie?'

'I am!' her voice didn't even shake, she realised, 'I'll have no part in this, Henry. String me up if you like but you can light your own damn fire!'

With that, Frannie stood, ready to flee, but Henry caught her about the waist and threw her down onto the floor with a thud. He might look like a scrawny schoolboy but he was far stronger than she was. Henry kicked her fallen form with his heavy boot twice and then lifted her by her purple hair. Angry and humiliated, she let her own demon show and snarled at Henry. He just laughed and turned to William.

'Women eh?' he said with a laugh. 'All right Frannie, all right. Go back to your chair… but I warn you, get out of it one more time and I really will make you regret it.'

Frannie skulked back to her chair and sat trembling as her ribs rebuilt themselves within her thin frame. She glanced up at the wolf and saw him watching her with sympathy in his eyes. *He's the one bound and bleeding, and yet he looks at me sympathetically.* It was with that thought that Frannie made a decision. There was nothing she could do for now, but later… more towards dawn when the others were beginning to retire… then maybe, just maybe…. She'd have an hour or two before Henry came to bed – he never turned in until gone five when the first dregs of sunlight showed, and the cells weren't guarded – nobody would dare tamper with Henry's prisoners. Nobody would ever expect Frannie to turncoat. Maybe the wolf would even take her with him.

Henry finally got the fire going in the rusty old grate in the corner. A small bed of crumbly coal topped by a tumble of kindling and small wood. Just like before, in the old days. The sound of the crackle and the scent of the earthy smoke brought a wave of nostalgia to Fran, making her want to weep. Henry blew gently onto the flames, forcing them to take, and then closed the little rusty door to let the heat build, being sure to slide open the little oxygen hole. Most drinkers were scared of fire, even she was pretty wary of it, but not Henry, he almost seemed to want to toast his hands over it. For a few minutes Henry was quiet, watching the flames build and begin to devour the coal. If nothing else, Henry was a patient man. Frannie glanced at the wolf again and found his eyes on her. After a quick glance with just her eyes to ensure Henry was still facing away from the fire, she mouthed the word *Change*.

'I can't!' he mouthed back 'Silver!'

Frannie glanced back to the silent Henry and pressed her lips. Another few long minutes passed and then Henry turned back to her. 'Pass me my bag Frannie?'

Frannie picked up the rucksack and threw it at him but Henry just laughed as the bag cluttered to the floor. Inside he had his various instruments for torture. He rummaged, coming up with a silver stake.

'If you heat that up it will just soften,' Frannie said.

'I know. I was thinking the same. Molten silver might be a nice gift for our guest, don't you think?'

Even William balked at his words, his skin blanched almost as white as theirs was and Frannie wanted to whisper to him to be strong, that she was going to help him but she was too frightened that Henry would see.

'This is pure silver,' Henry said, turning to William again. 'Nice and soft, the heat here should melt it down nicely...' and with that he placed the rod upright in the cup and buried it in the hot embers of the fire, right in the

The Black Marshes

now bright red coals. Frannie felt as though she were trapped in one of Henry's sick fantasies, in a way she supposed she was. She knew Henry wasn't bluffing, he'd take the eye and there was nothing she could do about it. Her fingers trembled and she fought angry tears.

Henry moved back to William's side and stroked a hand down the side of his face. 'Last chance, wolf. Tell me now that you wish to die, tell me I have broken you and that you are scum, that your whole breed is scum, and that I have crushed you beneath my boot.... tell me that or I will put a real sparkle of silver into those old grey eyes.'

Frannie's gut clenched, she felt sick and knew that if Henry forced her to witness this, she actually would vomit a cocktail of blood and the dinner she'd eaten the previous night.

'Go to hell, drinker,' William managed. 'Do your worst.'

Frannie wanted to cry but she held back the tears. Henry looked incredulously at the changer for a few long moments but then smiled.

'You're a brave old bastard, I'll give you that,' he said, and then moved to the old burner. The fire was roaring merrily and Frannie watched as Henry prodded the silver rod in the cup with a pair of fire tongs.

The silence lengthened but finally, after about ten minutes, Henry pulled out the cup to look at what remained of the silver rod. Mostly it was intact but the end was softened, hot beads of the precious metal dribbling lose. Henry moved back to William's side.

'Sure you don't want to beg like the dog you are?' he asked, as a drip of molten silver dripped to the floor from the edge of the cup. William clenched his teeth and Frannie saw him take a deep lungful of air. Henry moved behind him and took a fistful of his hair, wrenching his head back so that the taller man's face was level with his own, and lifted the cup. Then the screaming started.

Frannie couldn't watch but she smelled the burning of his flesh, the sizzle of the silver as it touched the wolf skin. William's screams were like the agonised squealing of an injured animal and for half a second Frannie thought the pain might have thrown him into his other form. It hadn't. The skin of the old changer's face had exploded into a splatter of molten silver where Henry had poured it into his eye. Silver liquid dribbled down his face, burning a path into the skin there. Blood and gore poured from the wound.

William howled again and Frannie forced herself to look at the eye. It was gone, the whole socket swelling up around where the silver had gone in. Even Henry looked a little shocked as William suddenly stopped screaming and slumped down, hanging from his bindings where his legs gave out.

'My god, he's out cold,' Henry laughed.

As Frannie watched, the body began to push out the silver. With a clink, the main chunk fell from the eye socket and hit the floor. Then the next bit, and the next.

'He's healing it,' Henry turned to Frannie and still she saw that interested wonderment written all over his features. 'It'll scar though, don't you think?'

'Scar? I thought you meant to kill him?'

'Oh no,' Henry laughed. 'No, this one is going home, I have a message for his pack-leader and when I find more ways to damage that resilient form, the scars I leave on him will carry that message well enough. Maybe Hugh Haverly will be kind and put the creature out of its misery. I won't be persecuted by these damn creatures anymore Fran, I won't.'

'Then why are you telling him to ask you to kill him?' Fran asked. 'That doesn't make sense Henry.'

'Oh Frannie Frannie…' Henry laughed. 'That's just for my own amusement.'

'Is he unconscious?'

The Black Marshes

'I think so... That'll do for Now eh? Now that I know the silver works, I don't need to rush. I bet I get him to break tomorrow!'

4

William Craven, 2016.

The room was silent for some time. Dark, completely, and still. William's body twitched, and another heavy chunk of silver felt from his face to the floor sounding a loud clang. William didn't move, didn't even moan, still completely without consciousness. Another clink, and then another. Suddenly his eyes snapped open. At once the pain flooded him and he had to bite down a groan. The wound in his face was still leaking, pus and blood and god-knows what else. William groaned and tried to cover another gasp of pain. In his life, he had never felt true fear before, never felt like death was close even when his human form had been dying – at least then he'd been delirious with fever! He moaned again and pulled on the chain, it was tightly clasped and too strong for his weakened arms to break. Tiredly he closed his eyes, hope beginning to dim. Even knowing it was hopeless, he pulled for the demon within. Nothing happened. He thought of his pack, of Hugh, and of the rescue which must be coming, but even as he tried to cheer himself, he knew that the chances of them ever finding him were slim. The boy had him well-hidden enough, below the earth by at least two flights of steps. His thoughts turned then to Quinn and a shudder of fear and disgust pierced him, how could it be that the drinker who looked so much a teenager could have such cruelty in him, such power? William sighed and closed his eyes again, when the boy came, he would give in, he decided. Death was suddenly so much more appealing than the humiliation and torture he was living in.

It seemed like hours passed but it could have been mere minutes for all William really knew. His body was healing but still he was in agony. He was sure there was still a spike or two under the skin and his vision in one eye was completely destroyed, along with his spirits. As the hours passed he was seriously contemplating the idea of just calling for Henry, and letting the boy finish him. He almost did it when the door finally opened again. William tensed at once but then saw that it was just the little purple-haired girl. He looked up at her tiredly, fearfully, but she was alone.

'Let me guess, Quinn's coming to torture me some more?' he growled, trying one final burst of bravado. 'Or did he send you to do it in his place this time? Get you to...'

At once the girl raised a finger to her lips to shush him. William pressed his lips closed mid-sentence. The girl glanced about her and then came to his side. She had to stand on tiptoe to whisper into his ear.

'I never tortured anyone in my life, wolf, and I risked my own neck to try and save you too... more than once... have a little gratitude!'

She had, William remembered, but he refused to trust her too much, to trust any of them. He moved so that his weight was back on his feet, giving his arms a well-deserved rest but making his calves scream. The girl eyed him with worry as he shifted his weight.

'I thought you creatures could heal? Like we do but...' Her hand went to touch his burned, oozing face but he jerked back like a frightened animal and she desisted.

'Silver,' he said simply when she had withdrawn. 'It burns, it scars.'

'It is wolf's-bane,' she murmured but there was no amusement in her tone for the jest, then she looked up at him, her vampire eyes glowing with compassion. 'Your eye is intact again, but pure white. Can you see anything in it?'

'No, the working parts are gone. The sight there is gone forever I'll wager.'

'I should have stopped him. I'm sorry.'

'You tried...'

'I did. Can you shift?'

'I don't know. Not bound and there's still silver in me too, I'm almost sure of it!'

The girl sighed. 'Then rescuing you isn't going to be easy...'

'What?'

'You didn't think I came in here for the conversation, did you? This is... there are no words to describe how wrong this is,' her fingers went up to the silver threaded ropes which held William's hands as she spoke and he could feel her trying the sturdiness of them, she hissed as the rope burned her hands. 'Damn. I won't be able to break these.'

'I know, I've tried.'

'Indeed, but I'm older than you... but that's by the by. You need to change!'

'I don't think I can! For real. Your... friend knows that.'

'If you regained enough strength, then you could probably break the ropes?'

'Out of form?'

'Yes.'

'I don't know...'

The Black Marshes

'Oh come on! I know you creatures are stronger out of form too, one of you almost snapped Henry in half once! With all your strength, could you? I daren't go out looking for a saw…'

'Perhaps. I mean, perhaps I could!'

'Then we need to strengthen you up, don't we?'

'How do you expect to do that when they're going to keep coming back? Keep torturing me?' Williams's voice wobbled in fear but the girl did him the honour of not noticing.

'You seem to be misunderstanding me. We're going now.'

'Now? I'm too weak…'

'No, no you're not. Stop it… look, I have a drink for you, I can see you are parched, but then you just have to… have to just suck it up and help me.'

From her pocket, the girl produced a can of soft drink and, after snapping open the can, she put it to his lips. William drank greedily.

'Nectar,' he muttered between gulps. Her common sense was bringing him out of his terrified self-pity and inside he felt his spirit hardening again.

'I wanted to bring you pure water but the can was easier to hide,' she said. 'This at least is better than ought?'

William nodded. 'Aye,' he tried a smile for the pretty little thing and she returned it wryly. 'Won't you be in danger for this?' he asked.

'I'm quite used to being Henry's punching bag. One more beating is nothing to me. Besides, I was hoping you'd take me with you?'

Brave lass William thought silently but to her he nodded. 'I can do that.'

'If humans drink our blood it strengthens them – does that work for your kind?'

'I have no idea, I've never heard of it…'

'We can try but…' The girl broke off as from without

suddenly came a creak and the sound of a door opening and closing. 'Shit! We have to speed this up!' Another noise out in the corridor and she stepped back. William's heart thudded again, almost willing her not to retreat whilst knowing that she had to.

'Lass…'

'There is somebody without,' she said and he saw that she was scared after-all. 'Look, I will come back, I swear, but I daren't risk this now. Better we wait and make a clean break than get caught on the way out and lose our advantage.'

William knew she had the truth of it. He nodded.

'Be strong,' she ordered. 'I'll be in there,' and nodded to the antechamber.

'All right lass… and if they do finally kill me, who is it that I should tell Jesus tried to be my saviour?'

The girl eyed him warily and then spoke. 'Frannie,' she murmured. 'That is, Frances… Frances Quinn. I'm sorry wolf, I have to go.'

William's eyes widened, *Quinn's wife! That sweet little maid is Quinn's wife! H*is mind screamed but he forced impassiveness to his features. Then the door opened and Quinn strode into the room. William searched his mind for something, anything to say as diversion but the man didn't even look at him; he instead strode to the little door to the antechamber. The girl cried out in pain as Quinn dragged her from her hiding place by her long purple hair.

'You?' Quinn spat, dragging her back into the room. 'Of all the people who could have betrayed me… you!' he pulled Frannie's face up so that her eyes were looking into his, then he hit her. The girl's lip exploded and William saw the stainless-steel ring she wore there fly free from her face. William pulled at his bonds, begging the wolf-form to start to come through. He was damned if he was going to stand by and watch this man beat his wife in front of him.

'Even think about it changer and I'll rip her bloody

head off and feed it to you,' Quinn said sharply, spinning about. William believed him and stopped his struggles, losing his head would not help Frances. He looked at the girl; she was neither sobbing, nor did she look frightened, instead she just glared up at Quinn with fury in her eyes as he struck her again and again. Her lip pissed blood, as did her nose and the beast within him churned again to watch as she just gazed at Quinn silently. The poor mite was used to this, he thought, she was fucking *used to it*.

'Why Fran?' Quinn asked of her. 'Why?'

'Because you're losing it. Torture? For god's sake, is there anything of my Henry left in there?'

'Oh, spare me the moral debate, how honest is it to turn on the man who loves you and go behind his back to betray him?'

'I just couldn't let you do this…'

'Don't give me that crap Frannie. Nothing you have ever done has been for me, don't try to fool me into thinking you care now. You were James's through and through and then you were that Russian's bitch! You've never been mine.'

'Damn right,' she hissed, anger flaring on her features. 'Andre was ten times the man you are, as was James!'

Quinn stuck Frannie again, his face contorted with youthful-looking rage. Frannie whimpered as he threw her against the wall and for the first time William saw her hands come up, trying to save herself from Quinn's fury.

'You live here Frannie, you live by our rules…'

'I would give anything not to, you know that! …and I will not be a part of a group that condones this,' she replied, spitting blood. Quinn stood above her, his eyes thick-lidded and cast down and his lips slightly parted.

'I could kill you in a heartbeat,' he threatened.

'You think I don't know that? You think I am scared of death? It's more appetising than this life with you!'

Henry kicked the girl again, so hard that bones must

have broken. Blood bubbled up to her lips, and she gasped, almost folding double. William's blood boiled. Despite it all, he ripped at his bonds with all the strength he could muster but it wasn't enough and only served to make his arms scream. Frannie looked up at him and, bless her, she shook her head. Don't interfere! William's heart hammered in his chest, his wrists burned and his head was hazy with helpless frustration.

'I should have killed you years ago,' Quinn said to the girl, his lips twisted like a bully in the schoolyard. 'I should have just done it!'

'So you keep saying – so do it, if you're going to!'

The look on Quinn's face was pure malice and William thought in horror that he was angry enough to take her up on that. He didn't though and eventually he stepped backwards. His expression changed and for a moment William thought he saw the ghost of regret in those eyes. If it was there, it was covered quickly.

'You want your freedom that badly?' the boy asked of Frannie, 'Then fuck it, go on, go…'

The girl stared up at him and William saw both shock and hope light up in her eye. 'What?'

'Get out of my house Frannie. Now, go, or by god I actually will kill you this time.'

The girl's eyes flew to William and he could see the regret reflected therein, regret that she had failed to save him. He wanted to tell her it was all right, that she had done her best for him and she should escape now that she had the chance, but he didn't dare speak, instead he just nodded. The girl welled up again but forced herself to her feet and all but fled the room. Quinn turned back to him.

'With the mood I am in, you'd better be frightened, William Craven,' he snapped and then picked up his bag again.

5

Frances Quinn, 2016.

In a sudden frenzy, Frannie bolted up the stairs and, pausing only to grab an already packed rucksack which she had kept for years hidden in a cupboard under her dresser, she bolted out of the house. The rucksack had been her lifeline, her goal. Inside were a few items she'd never part with, her letters to James, written in the aftermath of his untimely death, along with his gloves and the shirt he'd worn to marry her. A pack of cards which brought back fond memories, and some old brown and white faded photographs. She had no mementos of her second love, not even a photograph to remember his face. Henry had seen to that. As far as Henry was concerned, James was before him, and so a memory she was allowed to keep whereas her second lover had been a thief, stealing her away and so had destroyed anything she might have kept to cherish. Along with the memories in the bag were two hundred in cash, a knife, a fake ID card and her passport, also complete with fake name, albeit a different one to the ID card.

As she approached the front entrance, Frannie heard a

voice behind her, calling her name but she didn't pause, just kept running until she was at the gate. Outside, the rain was falling hard and a gale was blowing all around, whipping at her hair and turning it into sodden tentacles around her head. She was terrified, frantic and certain that Henry would regret his decision and would now come looking for her. In a million failed escape attempts, never had she ever thought to hear him tell her to just go. A heavy gust of wind almost blew her from her feet and she grasped the trunk of an old gnarled tree which stood near what had once been the gatepost to The Orchard Estate. Suddenly all of the intent left her. She had no idea where to go or what she was going to do with herself. Her father's house was gone, long gone and in its place, was nothing but a broken down old ruin. She frowned and tried to come up with a plan. She had her money, a handful of scrunched up old bills which she had squirrelled away ten pounds at a time from Henry's clothing when he went out to piss in the middle of the night. Just a little here and a little there so that he would not notice it: her emergency fund. Besides that, she had nothing else but the clothes on her back, the shoes on her feet. Day would break soon, it was about 4am, and she had nowhere to go, nowhere to hide herself.

'Shit,' she swore to herself, trying to bite down on panic. She was free, that was all she really needed! Her freedom! Even that seemed more frightening than empowering though, when had she ever had to fend for herself entirely? Not ever!

The wind pulled again and then a noise behind Frannie startled her. For a moment she froze, stock-still, and then, fear overcoming her, she ran from the gate of the house which had once been her favourite place in the world, and out onto the road into town. The rain was torrential and, even walking on the newly tarmacked roads Frannie could feel the peat of the marshes all around her soaking into her

The Black Marshes

thin leather boots. Stubbornly she pushed on, her mind lost in trying to think up a new way to save the wolf, of how to find his people perhaps, of where she was going to find shelter for the night. The thought slipped through her mind to go back, to go home and beg Henry's forgiveness but the very idea of that made her feel ill. She was free at last! She couldn't give up her one chance to escape. Her mind tried to give her the last time she'd escaped, the nightmarish month locked in a closet, bound in a manner that her broken bones could not heal. He'd done that on purpose, just to prolong the agony. With difficulty, she repressed the memory.

All around her were tall bushes which flicked rain down upon her from long, leafy fingers but Frannie barely felt it. Her skin was soaked, her jeans drenched right through to the skin and her shirt clinging damply to her form. At least it disguised the bloodstains, she thought wryly. The sound of the wind crying over the open moors on the other side of the hedgerows was mournful and eerie but to her it was the most liberating sound she'd ever heard. She needn't be afraid of the monsters preying beyond their limits, Frannie thought wryly, she was the monster, and she was very firmly on the road.

Eventually, the old thoroughfare began to branch off, leading into the town and Frannie followed it, past the old mill on the edge of The Orchard Estate which had stood there back when she was a girl, and then down into the town proper. For a moment, she paused, then saw the old inn at the edge of the town square, another familiar landmark. She turned her feet in that direction, hoping that they would have a room spare.

The building was dark, the inhabitants still sleeping. Frannie paused but then knocked on the door, an almost panicked pounding. Nothing at first, but then a light shone in the room above and a head looked out.

'I am in desperate need of assistance!' Frannie

whispered, 'Please? Can you give me a room?'

Despite the strangeness of the situation, Frannie found the little balding man who let her in to be kindly enough. Obviously put out at being woken up, he was placated by the idea of a paying customer. Frannie bartered a little, and eventually settled on the sum of £60 for a day and a night.

'Room's the first at the top of the stairs,' the old man said, handing her a key. 'If you want to dry off, there's towels and such in the bathroom at the end. It's shared, mind.'

'Thanks,' she said again and took the key.

'Try to be quiet – I've got another couple in the room opposite you and I don't want 'em disturbed…'

A little hunched, and with darting eyes, Frannie walked up the dusty old staircase, leaving the owner to lock back up downstairs. The carpet beneath her feet was cheap and looked like it could be nearly as old as she was but a pretty red pattern adorned it making it cheery. The corridor was narrow, the old walls uneven and painted white. Frannie was just fitting the key into the old lock of her door when another door swung open behind her. At once, she was on alert. Drinkers did not have the sharper senses of the changers, but Frannie knew well enough to notice the subtle signs on the face of the man who opened the door. His eyes were the same shade as those of the wolf, William, and yet somehow, she knew that this one was older. His hair was dark, a rich deep brown with a hint of grey at the temples, it was just long enough for a tail, pulled away behind him with a band. His clothing was plain, a white shirt worn over black jeans and a simple long overcoat thrown over the top. He was bleary eyed but the sleepiness was fading out of his expression quickly, more so for his seeing her there.

Frannie's hand trembled as she recognised the figure from the CCTV; Hugh Haverly. Behind the man, she saw

The Black Marshes

the face of another person peeking out, another changer by the looks of it: the female with long fair hair and a pretty face who had tried to drag him away. Both of them glared at her and she at them.

'Drinker!' Haverly snapped in a tone harsher than she would have liked. 'What are you doing here?'

'I am of The Orchard Estate,' Frannie spoke quickly and saw the man's eyes darken. 'I was of there, anyhow. No more. I have a message for...' for a moment she paused, wondering if she was really about to do it, then she spoke again. 'I have a message for Hugh Haverly.... That is, for you?'

At once, the man leapt forward to grip her arm. 'What?' he asked sharply. 'What did you say?'

'I have a message...' she trailed off, her fear was building and she realised that even if she weren't outnumbered, this old creature was much, much stronger than she was. With an abrupt movement, the wolf changer dragged her into the room he'd just been leaving, a hand over her mouth.

'Ella,' Hugh hissed to the girl behind him who had jumped back at his abrupt movement. 'Get me my knife.'

Frannie squealed and tried to pull away, but the man was too strong. It was with ease that he dragged her through the doorway and slammed the door shut. The girl, Ella, handed him a silver knife, the handle of which was bound in leather. The weapon looked very old and Frannie began to breathe heavily as he placed the blade over her heart. She kept her resolve though, pulling her lips into a defiant line and thinking of William and how brave he'd been. From behind her she heard a dog growl and all the hairs on the back of her neck went up. Then the animal moved around to stand at the man's side and she realised with relief that it was just a normal dog, a spaniel by the looks of it.

'Now when I release your mouth, I want to you spill it

all,' the man said. 'Whatever message Henry Quinn has sent to me, I want to hear it now and if you lie to me I will end you, drinker. I am at the very limit of my patience now.'

Frannie nodded slowly, her heart pounding. Slowly he lifted his hand from her lips.

'Speak!'

'You *are* Hugh Haverly, aren't you? I've only ever seen you at a distance or... or on a screen...'

The man nodded.

'Good. I am Frances Quinn,' Frannie said, deciding at once that the truth would best suffice. 'Henry Quinn's... lover, I guess, the message is from me though, not from him.'

'All right. Out with it.'

The little dog beside Hugh snuffled at Frannie's leg, making her feel even more uncomfortable. She swallowed deeply and then nodded and began to speak. The words spilled almost unheralded from her lips.

'I've just fled from the man I have called my husband these past hundred years. I seek refuge, protection.'

'Keep talking, I'll ponder it when I hear what you have to say.'

'I understand, I'm not easy to trust.'

'Indeed.'

Frannie wet her lips again, 'I'll tell you all I know...'

'That's all I ask.'

'Henry captured a changer... a man named William Craven, when you attacked us. He's... he's still alive... William is the reason I'm here...'

'William is alive?'

'I.. yes... yes he is! I... you see Henry doesn't actually intend to kill him but...but... but...'

'But what?'

'But... but Henry is... is torturing him. He means to return him to you useless and broken so that you are forced to… to end his suffering.'

'No!' Ella's cry startled Frannie, echoing out from behind Hugh. Hugh bit his lip and Frannie saw his eye go to his companion briefly. Something flashed between them but then the girl nodded. 'I'm all right, Hugh,' she whispered.

Hugh turned back to Frannie. 'What information is he trying to get out of William?'

'N…none.'

'None, that makes no sense. Why torture him for no reason?'

Frannie looked down at the knife again; the silver was beginning to burn where the point of it had torn the thin cloth of her sodden shirt.

'Because he can… because he is wicked and cruel and because he hates changers more than anything at all… Henry, that is Henry and I… we have both lost loved ones to your kind, and to your pack. Henry is lost in a need for revenge so strong that he is not himself anymore… He has taken over the nest at the Orchard House and was already preparing to wreak his revenge on you people, luring you out to the house was just his first trick. He wants you all dead… not just you… but all your kind!'

'How badly is William hurt, thus far?' Ella asked softly, tears standing in her eyes.

'Hush Flower,' Hugh said, shuffling uncomfortably. 'I'm not even convinced whether or not I believe this…'

'Hugh, calm down and assess the situation,' Ella replied. 'Smell her. She's covered in her own blood and…'

Ella was interrupted by the sound of footsteps in the corridor behind them and then a knock at one of the doors without. The spaniel barked twice but Hugh shushed it, sighed and passed the knife to Ella, who held the point of it into Frannie's back, hidden from view. Hugh opened the door and smiled at the innkeeper, suddenly amiable and friendly. 'Hello?'

'Hello, is everything all right? I heard voices… I hope the new guest didn't disturb you?' The barkeeper looked in through the door with some confusion. Frannie forced a smile and waved, playing her part.

'Leave and go about your business,' Hugh's voice was low and Frannie saw a glint of silver begin in his eye. 'Forget what you saw here. In fact, forget any of us even were here…'

The proprietor nodded like a marionette, his eyes glazing. Frannie gasped – that was essentially what Hugh had done at the Orchard Estate too. Hugh closed the door and turned back to her as though the encounter had not happened.

'So why would you, Henry Quinn's woman, come to tell us all of this? More so, how did you know we were here?' he asked as Ella handed him back his knife.

'I had no idea you were here. I came here because it was the closest place after Henry let me go.'

'Let you go?'

'Thing between us were not… harmonious, not ever, but then I… I… tried to rescue your friend and…'

'You tried to rescue William? And why would you do that?'

'Because he was in pain and I … I … Henry has gone too far this time. He's insane I think… has been sliding out of sanity since Phina and Jamie, that is, his brother and sister, died,' once more the tears tried to bubble but Frannie pushed them back. 'Henry has always told me that you changers are evil, that I should hate you… but… but… William was so brave, so proud and I … I don't know… I …' the tears finally fell. 'Henry is torturing him evilly, he's trying to find ways to scar him… to cripple him and…'

'Impossible,' Hugh said but with more compassion, lowering the knife. 'We heal as well as you do.'

'Not when somebody pours molten silver into one of

your eyes, you don't…'

Ella gasped, her hands going to her face in shock. Hugh's jaw tightened but his concern seemed to be for the blond. He put his free arm around her and allowed her lean on him.

'Oh god,' Ella moaned. 'Oh god no…'

'The sight is gone,' Frannie whispered. 'In that eye at least and god-knows what else Henry has done to him since he threw me out… please, you have to get him out of there.'

'This could be a trap,' Hugh said.

Frannie could have screamed at his cautious manner. 'How can I convince you? What can I do or say to make you believe me?'

Slowly Hugh ran an eye over Frannie, still clutching Ella with his free arm. He seemed almost indecisive for a long moment, but then sighed.

'You can't. Trust has to be earned. If you are serious in wanting to help, then you can give me directions of where to go once I get into the house, unseen if possible.'

'Just the two of you? There are twelve drinkers there…'

'I'm going alone. Ella will stay here,' Hugh said, his grey eyes moving down to the woman whose tears were drying on his chest, then moving back to Frannie, surveying her carefully. Frannie forced her face to remain neutral and not show Hugh how terrified she was.

'But don't worry…' Hugh added, 'I have ways of getting in and out, so long as I am not swamped again.'

'Fine. Inside the house, if you go in by the back door, there are two flights of stairs directly in front of you, go down one floor and you will see another flight and a door. On the other side of the door is a wall with a tapestry on it – it looks bare, like a larder but it isn't. There's a door behind the tapestry. Go through it and you will be in a corridor with four rooms each side, two more corridors going off. That's the catacomb. There is a door at the end.

Be quiet when you go through that corridor, and don't deviate up the smaller corridors. That's where we sleep. Usually the nest is quiet from about 5am so by the time you arrive most will be abed. You can't take that for granted though, Henry kept us all up in anticipation of you all day yesterday.'

'How did he know we were coming?'

'A drinker named Daniel – he is one of Henry's offspring. You gave him shelter a couple of months back…'

'Daniel?' Ella murmured, 'I know him!'

'Well don't trust him, he's your rat. He'll be gone already though by the time you arrive back at Haverleigh.'

'Noted. What next, in the house?'

'Through the door at the end of the corridor where the nest sleep is another flight of stairs, they are rougher so mind your footing. They lead to another line of doors. Those are the pits, the cells. William is in the back one… there are… are humans in the others…'

'Are they guarded?'

'Not especially, but Henry knew when I went down there to help William. He has cameras hidden everywhere too… he's growing paranoid, so paranoid. That's how he knew where you were the other night, something TV he calls it.'

Hugh nodded. 'You'd better not be lying to me,' he warned. 'Because they will not capture me and if I find a trap falling about me, I will come home and rip your demon heart out with my bare hands.'

'I am not lying to you, I swear. Normally Henry would be in our chambers now but… but tonight I don't know… he was angrier than I've ever known him… watch out for him, he might be skulking anywhere, or even still in with William.'

'All right, all right. I don't know why I am trusting you even this much, but… but if you are sincere, then thank

The Black Marshes

you.'

Frannie nodded. 'I am sincere,' she said. 'This is not for you, but for William.'

Hugh looked harshly at Frannie for a moment, and then moved away from Ella to pick up his knife. He made to slip the weapon into a slot on his belt which looked like it was made for that exact purpose, but then seemed to double think and held it in his hand instead. He took a deep breath, and then threw up the hood of his long coat, hiding his face partially. He turned to Ella. 'Watch her,' he said nodding at Frannie, 'And if she tries anything…' he slid the knife into the girl's hand.

'I know,' Ella whispered. 'Be careful out there, Hugh!'

To Frannie's surprise, the big old changer smiled and cupped the face of the tiny woman in his giant paws, kissing her with a kindness that crushed Frannie's heart. For the first time in years, she missed James, really missed him.

'I will be more than careful,' Hugh said tenderly, kissing Ella's nose, and then he was gone. The spaniel sat up from where he'd been lying on the floor and at once began to scrape at the door which Hugh had allowed to swing closed behind him.

'Newton, no!' Ella said and to Frannie's surprise, the dog obeyed, lying down behind the door and whimpering a little.

'Hugh will be back soon!' the girl said with exasperation and then looked up at Frannie, dislike showed in her eye again but she quashed it so quickly Frannie was almost sure she'd imagined it. 'He's not used to being left behind,' the girl murmured, indicating the dog.

'So, you are Hugh's… mate?' Frannie asked after a few moments, unsure of the correct term in wolves.

'I am his wife,' Ella amended.

'I see.'

'Let me be frank, I don't like your kind, you drinkers cause nothing but pain and if you have sent Hugh into a trap…'

'I haven't, I swear it,' Frannie whispered, thinking of her own husband, dead by the hands of that same man. 'You and William are close though? I mean, you seem very concerned?'

'That's none of your business.'

'Ok,' Frannie whispered and looked down at her hands.

The silence deepened. Frannie stood and moved to the dresser. The eyes of the other woman followed, watching her every move. The little dog too seemed to be observing her movements.

'I'm just pacing,' she snapped, 'I'm worried too…'

Time seemed to slow to a crawl as Frannie and Ella sat waiting for the return of Hugh and William in the silence which was broken only by Ella speaking to the little dog. Ella seemed calm, composed, and Frannie envied her emotionless features as she looked quietly from the window, watching the day break. Frannie stayed back of it, the last thing she needed was to allow the sun to drain her. An hour ticked by, and then two, almost three before Ella spoke.

'They are back.'

Frannie stood quickly and knelt on the bed beside Ella to look out. She was just in time to see the side door swing closed. She pulled back again and pulled the curtain too to hide away the bright autumn sun.

'Hugh had William?'

'He did.'

'Oh, Thank god!' a tear formed in Frannie's eye and rolled down her cheek. "Thank god,' she whispered again, 'and if he has killed Henry then I am forever in his debt.'

Ella put a hand on Frannie's arm, her brow was still tight but there was a little more emotion in her eyes.

The Black Marshes

'Much as we are to you, if William was saved by your coming here,' she said. 'I still reserve judgement, but if I have misjudged you, then I am sorry.'

Frannie found a small smile and nodded, despite the hostility of the people she'd found here, she was also starting to see a new beginning.

6

The Man in the Basement, 2016

And now her presence was gone too, gone! Lost! Too far! The man in the basement moaned and pulled on his bindings again. Lost! Gone! Frannie! The man began to cry, she'd gone before, but never like this, never alone. Her scent had been strange too, more like the Frannie of 1812 than this recent ghost of her. Sweet, young, full of defiance and adventure. Better than tears. Better than pain and hurt! But she'd left him. Sometimes he forgot that Frannie didn't know. He sighed, better Frannie gone! Her presence was the key to his sanity, her scent his final hold. With her gone, he could sink into a state of utter blissful loss. Just like before.

But Henry was still here. Not gone. Henry was here and Frannie was gone. Dead? No, not dead! Neither dead! Just gone...

Gone...

The man in the basement began to howl, even knowing that it would not be long before his captor came to administer the punishment again. It always grew back anyway, any piece which was removed but the pain and

The Black Marshes

fear, the terror of it, that remained. The punishment for shouting for Frannie was a tongue... the taste of his own blood bubbling down his throat... the rip as it came loose. The thought was enough to mute him and he crawled back as far as his chains would allow.

A long moment passed, a pause which could have been minutes or hours, he never quite knew which anymore. Safe! Not heard! Safe. The man began to relax. But then footsteps. The man began to sob into his hands as they came closer and closer. Only one person ever came down to his basement.

The door opened.

A figure entered.

The gleam of a blade.

And then the man in the basement began to scream.

7

Frances Orchard, 2016

It seemed like forever between seeing the door below swing closed and the one upstairs opening. At last though, the door did open and there was Hugh dragging a barely conscious William with him.

William's one good eye looked unfocused and he was wearing the coat that Hugh had been wearing when he left, the hood pulled down over his face. With a sinking in her gut, Frannie realised that Henry, or someone else, had had another go at him since she left. William could barely stand. His good eye looked glazed and his limbs shook. Frannie could see fresh blood splattered over the clothing he wore, barely concealed by Hugh's coat. He did not know her, in fact, Frannie doubted he knew anybody at that point.

Hugh nodded briefly at her and Frannie took in the fact that his clothing was spotless; he'd not spilled any blood at The Orchard Estate. With a manner of gentleness that she'd not imagined the man having, Hugh helped the limping William to lay himself down on the bed and then sat down and paid attention to the little dog which was jumping up at him with uncontainable excitement. Frannie took herself to William's side at once, whilst Ella moved to Hugh and embraced him.

'William?' Frannie murmured and his good eye pivoted to look at her. For a moment, he just stared, and then a smile touched his lips.

'Hey you,' he whispered painfully.

'Hey yourself,' Frannie whispered back, touching his hand. William's face was still filthy, covered in blood and gore from his eye. Frannie rubbed a bit of it away with her finger, and then quickly stood.

'I'm going to get some water and a cloth,' she said to Hugh.

Hugh nodded, more relaxed now, and Frannie guessed her information had been useful, that she'd begun to win the trust of the pack. Frannie slipped out of the room and down the corridor. In the bathroom, she found a little pile of white washcloths and beneath the sink was an old washing up bowl which she filled with warm water, adding a little soap, and then walked slowly back down the corridor, being careful not to spill the water.

Frannie's quiet tap at the door was answered quickly by Hugh and, with thanks, she slipped back inside. As she eased the hood from William's tired face, she thought she saw a look pass between Ella and Hugh. She ignored it, bigger things to think about.

William's eyes opened again as Frannie sat down. The right one was completely white, obviously empty of any vision at all and surrounded by deep scarring that he seemed not to have been able to heal. He parted his lips to speak but Frannie shushed him and dipped one of the washcloths into the water to begin to wipe away the gore on his face.

William watched her the whole time but he didn't speak and Frannie was glad of that. Her emotions were wrought and every moment that she spent with him made her feel more and more protective of him, more and more angry with Henry for what he had done. Frannie wiped over the hideously twisted flesh of William's face, removing two pieces of now hard, dry silver which his body had not been strong enough to reject despite how they burned her fingers.

'There,' she whispered. 'Now you are bordering upon acceptable.'

William's lips pulled into a smile. 'Thank you,' he croaked and then moved his hand to open the coat. Beneath it, his chest was still bare and littered with oozing half-closed wounds. She swallowed the bile and glanced up at Hugh.

'We need to cut out the silver – it's inside him,' she said.

Hugh moved back to the bed and probed one of the wounds with a finger, making William moan and clutch his chest.

'Barbarian,' Hugh muttered, but then to Frannie's shock, he handed her his blade. She took it and looked at William's stomach, poised the knife, but then shook her head, 'I… can't…' she said.

'I'll do it, then. Ella, go and grab some clean water from the bathroom?'

Ella nodded and slipped out.

'She doesn't need to see this,' Hug muttered and then lifted the blade. Frannie made to move away too but William caught her hand. 'Stay?' he grunted

Frannie nodded and sat back down, facing away from where Hugh sat with his knife. Once the spikes were removed, William shuffled his body into a sitting position and Frannie was relieved to see that the wounds were closing of their own accord. Ella came back in with a bowl of clean water and Frannie took it with thanks, helping to wash away the last of the muck. Ella said nothing but returned to her spot at the window. Hugh stood up and dropped the silver onto the dresser; his hands were unburnt from the precious metal. He nodded to Frannie and then returned to his wife.

William sighed. 'I need to change,' he said to Frannie. 'I can't heal like this.'

'Do it,' Hugh said from the window. 'I'll keep an eye on you.'

Frannie felt her eyes widen but remained mute. Still she could feel the echo of fear in her gut, and despite how so many years had passed since the massacre of her loved ones by a creature such as these were, still her heart pounded. William exhaled a long breath and then began to let go. He shimmied so that he was out of his jeans and Frannie flushed bright red, averting her eyes.

From the window, Hugh snorted, his normally emotionless eyes gleaming. 'If you intend on spending time with wolves, you'd better get used to seeing us randomly strip off…'

Frannie laughed but still did not look at William's form. Her attention was caught though, when she heard him murmur in pain. The skin was peeling, disintegrating to dust as it fell in flakes onto the bed and floor. He muttered again, biting his lip and then suddenly he began to writhe. She gasped, stepping back. Ella moved to her side and put a hand on her arm but Frannie did not pull her eyes away, letting herself witness the gruesome event. William's limbs began to click and pop and bruises erupted into tufts of fine sand coloured fur from where the skin was tearing away. The wounds bled but, like the skin, the blood disintegrated into powder before it hit the floor.

The entire transformation took only a few moments, but it seemed a lifetime before William-wolf shook itself and then looked up at Frannie. William's wolf-form was larger than a normal wolf, his eyes glowed with that odd light which denoted a changer, and his fur was a mixture of different beiges and sands. Frannie stared at him in wonder. He was beautiful; truly astounding to behold. He moved towards her with a slow ambling gait, moving his head to compensate for his still blind eye. Frannie gasped and moved backwards in alarm but Ella's hand tightened on her arm.

'It's ok,' Ella said. 'He's still William, he still knows who he is and he won't hurt you.' Her voice was kinder than any she'd yet used to talk to Frannie.

William moved closer still and sat himself down at their feet. Frannie put a hand down to touch his silky ears, snatching her hand back like a child to a hotplate at the feel of them.

Hugh glanced over, his lips pressed. 'You are afraid of him, drinker?'

'I'm afraid of all wolves… I have seen the damage you can do and I am not stupid enough to think that I, even with my drinker blood, could ever stand up to one of you.'

'This isn't just Quinn's nonsense, is it? You've been witness to something terrible?'

Frannie set her jaw, pressed her lips. 'Yes, twice. A long time ago, before I was what I am now, my… my fiancé's family were slaughtered by one of yours… The image of that has stayed with me a very long time.'

'You said twice,' Ella said, 'the other time?'

'I was…' Frannie wet her lips, 'I was witness to my husband, a drinker like me, being killed by… by one of your kind.' At the last minute, she drew back from saying it had been Hugh, that would have been too hard to voice in the circumstances.

Hugh nodded. 'Then I apologise, and I am sorry for your loss.'

Frannie's eyes filled with tears. *You are forgiven,* she thought silently and within, a burden lessened. Even as they spoke, William-wolf lay down at Frannie's feet and closed his eyes. Frannie stared down upon him.

'William will never turn on you like that other beast did,' Ella said, 'He is a good man and fully in control of his form – not all, not many in fact, of us are – but he is skilled in control.'

Frannie nodded and lapsed back into silence, looking down at the sleeping wolf, then turned to Hugh. 'Were you seen… when you took him?' she asked.

'Not by any that would remember. Two approached me as I went in but I stole the memory of myself and no others troubled me.'

'You can do that, then? Mind control?'

'I can,' Hugh nodded. 'It comes with practice and time but yes, in fact almost any of us has the potential to possess the ability to influence… even you drinkers, to some extent.'

'So that's why you went alone?

'Yes. Easier to get in and out alone.'

'Why not do that before then? Why attack with a pack?'

Hugh's eyes became guarded again and Frannie was worried she'd pushed him too far but after a moment's pause, he spoke, 'I wasn't sure what the lay of the land was and I underestimated Quinn. I run a… crusade, to rid the world of the evil I helped to create…'

'You…'

'Yes, me. I have in my household several of those like I, who seek to purge the evil ones of our kind. I thought this would be an easy job for them to practice before I set them out alone. It was a mistake. A grave mistake, which if not for you might have led to my losing my best friend.'

'Thank you,' Ella said, turning to Frannie. 'Thank you for helping William.' Frannie was sure she saw the girl prod her husband and then Hugh nodded.

'Indeed, your directions were… spot on… thank you,' he agreed.

Frannie didn't know what to say, so remained silent. William muttered in his sleep, the strange bark finishing with a whimper. Hugh's dog eyed him suspiciously but did not bark.

'How long will he be like that?'

Ella shrugged, 'As long as it takes him to heal… on which note, we really need to get away from here. When Quinn realises William is missing…'

'William is too weak, Flower, and Frances cannot travel by daylight.'

'You will take me with you then?'

'If that is what you wish.'

'Is it,' Frannie's eyes filled up again, but tears of gratitude rather than pain.

'We'll stay here for the day and leave tonight,' Hugh added. 'There I will consult with my brother on what to do next. If Quinn is fool enough to face me here alone, he will regret it.'

'I hope he does come then,' Frannie muttered and felt two pairs of old eyes take her in. She flushed but said no more.

Hugh was quiet again for a long moment, then nodded to the door. 'Go and sleep, if you need to.'

'I do, thank you.'

'When did you last… kill?'

'I don't kill,' Frannie all but whispered, and once more those old eyes seemed to assess her. 'I last fed a day or so ago. I'm good for another few yet.'

'Good,' Hugh said. 'Sleep well, Frances Quinn.'

Frannie walked to the door, but even as she turned the handle William's head jerked up. A little sleepily, the beast stood and moved to her side.

This time Hugh did laugh aloud. 'I think the chances of us being able to leave you behind are lower than you think, even if we wanted to. William, don't you be seen ambling about in form – I'm too tired to put in damage control!'

The tan wolf barely looked up at Hugh, but nuzzled

The Black Marshes

Frannie's hand with its nose. Once they were safely inside the warm room on the opposite side of the corridor, Frannie put her fingers down and stroked William's ears, her hand still trembling to touch him, even knowing that he was no threat. William looked up at her sharply, and then licked her hand, making her smile. He was more like a dog than a wolf, she decided, tamed and docile, despite his hulking size.

Frannie glanced out of the window, checking that nothing lurked without, then pulled the curtains tight closed. She paused before stripping out of her damp, dirty jeans and tight waistcoat, glancing at William. The wolf held her gaze, but then surveyed the room somewhat apprehensively as she undressed and climbed onto the end of her bed, crushing her feet.

It seemed like Frannie simply blinked but when she opened her eyes William was human once more, dressed in his torn and bloody jeans and making tea at the little tea-tray on the dresser. The light spilling into the room through closed drapes showed it to be early evening and the scent of coffee permeated the whole room. Williams hair was long, Frannie noticed, really long, an almost red hue of blond. He had some facial hair too, just a bit of a goatee but enough to see it was more than stubble.

'Morning,' William smiled, bringing her a cup. His voice, when free of the agonies of torture, was as deep and rich as the coffee in his hands.

'Thank you,' Frannie whispered. 'Have you been here all day?'

'Aye. Wanted to keep an eye on you in case that brat of a lover of yours decided to come find you. Snuck back in there for me clothes about an hour ago when I woke up and then came back here and read the paper somebody shoved under the door. You snore by the way, you know that?'

Frannie stared. She'd spent so long under Henry's iron rule that the jest was a shocking deviation to normality.

'Says the man who growls in his sleep…' she managed weakly.

William laughed again and sipped his coffee. 'Ha, I guess you're right! Just struck me as funny,' another mouth full of coffee, 'a drinker who snores…'

Frannie laughed with him. 'I suppose, but we do breathe, you know, not like in the movies…'

'Aye, Aye… I know.'

William smiled again and Frannie let her eyes scan his hairy chest, there were a few odd scars but that was it. The same could not be said of his face. His long hair hid the worst of it but his right eye was still pure white and obviously sightless. The scar from where the silver had spilled ran all the way down the side of his face, puckering and twisting the skin there. Frannie wondered if he'd wear that scar for the rest of his days. Unlikely with his wolf's blood, but not impossible.

William caught where Frannie was looking and Frannie saw a guarded look come into his good eye. 'Hideous, isn't it,' he said. 'But then, I've never been the pretty type…'

'You have no sight there at all?'

'Nope! Nothing. It's… disorientating but I suppose I will get used to it.'

'You're being very brave about it…'

'What else can I be? At least I am alive. At least I still have the other eye. I am just thankful that Quinn didn't completely cripple or blind me.'

'I'm so sorry,' Frannie whispered.

William moved to her side, putting a hand on her arm. 'Don't you dare apologise for that monster, Frances. You are the reason he didn't! You are not in any way to blame for his actions!'

'I wasn't! And I know that, but still – I am sorry.'

William nodded too and finished his coffee, then

The Black Marshes

smiled again. 'You're all right Frannie,' he said.
'I know… I mean, I think I will be…'

8

Frances Orchard, 2016

The drive from the inn to Haverleigh House, deep in the Devonshire countryside was quiet and sombre. The group waited for darkness to fall completely before setting out and the night was deepening as Hugh drove through the silence. Ella and William too were strangely quiet, stuffed into the back of Hugh's car with Hugh's little spaniel curled up between them. Frannie sat in the front seat, gazing out of the window at the passing countryside. Nothing felt real anymore.

Upon arrival, it was a relief to depart the car and to Frannie it seemed the others were feeling the same, not least the little dog who bounded about on the lawn barking and making her smile despite herself.

'Well, he seems happy to be free of the car,' Hugh smiled. 'Stupid mutt.'

Frannie nodded but Hugh's attention was already gone as his wife moved to his side. Together Ella and Hugh wondered off into the shadows with the barking puppy and Frannie could hear Ella laughing as she played with the dog. The sound filled her heart with joy; other than

Henry's sadistic cackle, she wasn't used to hearing people laughing so openly.

It was too dark to get a proper look at the house but Frannie could tell it was old and in the daytime, she knew it would be a beautiful building. She might even brave the sunshine for a minute or two to come and have a look, she decided. A few moments out in it wouldn't hurt – not any more.

William joined her as she drank in the old stones.

'Magnificent, isn't it?'

'It is. Does it belong to Hugh?'

'I suppose it does in a way. It's part of the trust and so therefore belongs to us all… but before that, it was mine.'

'Oh wow,' Frannie whispered, and suddenly the house was all the more beautiful. 'You grew up here?'

'Partly. My grandfather was the owner, but for a huge chunk of my life I lived here. When I married, Rosa and I made our home here too with my grandparents, and aunt, and some cousins – there were many of us who couldn't bear to leave. When Grandmother died she left the house to me though.'

'You're married?'

'I'm a widower,' William said abruptly, then very obviously moving away from the subject. 'After the rest of my family were dead, I donated the house to the trust, that is, our pooled resources and so now it is ours, rather than mine.'

'You share everything?'

'Well yes, easier to deal with a trust than to remember to be born and die singularly,'

'I guess so.'

'Come inside,' William said and Frannie nodded, suddenly as shy as she had been the first time she'd entered the house known as The Orchard Estate, some two hundred years earlier.

Inside, Frannie found herself taken through the great hall and into a small room off the side. Haverleigh was very grand, she thought, and so much older than the Georgian "Orchard Estate" with its low ceilings and dark wooden features. The room into which William took her was fairly large and brightly lit by modern electrical lighting. There was a guy with a short dark ponytail sat in the corner reading and two girls playing a board game at a table by a window. All three looked up as they entered but only the girls stared. Frannie gazed around her, blinking a little at the sudden brightness. William entered the room behind her and smiled.

'Frannie, meet Reuben,' he said, indicating the guy with the ponytail.

'Hiya,' she managed. The man just nodded. He was a drinker too, Frannie didn't know how she knew, she just did.

'The girls here, Jane and Susie, are donors – that is, they live here in exchange for blood, to feed the drinkers,' William added, 'and Reuben is of your kind.'

'I thought so.'

The girls went back to their game, although Frannie saw the darker one eyeing her out of the corner of her eye. The man glanced up again, half-smiled and then went back to reading his book.

'Make yourself at home here,' William said. 'I need to put on some new clothing and find out if we have any made-up rooms upstairs. If not I might have to put you in the attic, if that's ok? I know there's a room made-up up there next to Ben's, but it'll be cold. It'll only be until tomorrow though.'

'Anything,' she murmured. 'Even a sofa will do.'

'I'm sure I can do better than that,' William said and slipped back out of the room.

Frannie stood awkwardly in the doorway. The room was warm and she could feel tiredness setting in. This

The Black Marshes

must have been an entertaining room, she thought to herself, back in the day. Although the ceiling was low, shot through with black wooden beams, the room was too big to have been a cosy family room. In the centre of the room were two long sofas, between which sat a narrow wooden coffee table. The furniture looked modern, new and not overly expensive. Both of the sofas were of the same soft leather material, grey in colour and were of the type that are often seen in coffee lounges or student bars. On the wooden table was a beer bottle, empty, with the cap next to it, opposite which sat a half-drunk cup of coffee. Towards the back of the room Frannie saw that there were actually two other sofas but they were surrounded by heavy wooden furniture and didn't look so worn and used as the ones in the middle of the room. The room was devoid of people but for those to whom she had been introduced but Frannie guessed from the subtle clues that if the hour were earlier, the place would have been a hive of activity. She wondered how many lived here. At Henry's place, there were seldom more than ten or twelve and even then, they struggled to get along. What would it be like to be pack, she pondered, was it like being in a nest? She hoped not, she was tired of the hierarchy battles and petty squabbles.

With a level of timidity not like her, Frannie moved into the room and sat down on one of the sofas. The night was chill and she shivered, goose-pimples running up her arm. She wondered grimly at the practicalities, she had no clothing other that what she was wearing, did not even have a warm jumper to put on over her dried on purple shirt. She had nothing now, and very little money to make a new start with. She worried how drinkers who did not kill were supposed to make money, to get on in the world. She could not imagine working, especially in the daytime, although she supposed that there must be drinkers out there doing just that, playing at some masquerade of being human until the hunger took them. Not all drinkers were lucky enough to have been rich like Henry and James had been. She glanced over at the guy with the ponytail, Reuben, he looked old, she thought, older than her at least. What of the others, were they newlings or was this whole pack ancient too?

With a sigh, Frannie dipped her hand into her pocket and pulled out the wad of notes she'd stolen from Henry. There was less than two hundred pounds all told, not enough to do much with at all. Frannie sighed and put the money away. At least she didn't have to eat, she thought grimly, although she would still feel the hunger.

With a small cough, William indicated his return, Frannie turned and smiled at him almost shyly. He looked tired, she thought, haggard and ill but then, he had been through hell in the last two days and it was no wonder really. He had dressed himself in new, un-bloodied clothing; a black sleeveless shirt thrown on over a long-sleeved t-shirt, jeans and boots. His hair was tied in a tail down his back and about his neck was a little faux silver chain. Frannie decided the look suited him.

'You all right, Frannie?'

'Just worrying… I have a tendency to work myself up over little things. Did you find a room?'

'Yeah,' he nodded. 'Actually, the room next to mine is free. Ella's pup, Micah, sleeps there when he's about but he's with Sam these days… trying to learn control, he's very young.'

'Sam?'

'Yeah, Samuel Haverly: Hugh's brother – he's a drinker like you. Keeps a house a few miles down the road. He has more patience than Hugh so the young'un's go there.'

'I see,' Frannie smiled, she could imagine Hugh not being the most tolerant of people.

William held a hand out to her. 'Come on,' he said.

The Black Marshes

'Come upstairs and get settled in.'

Frannie nodded and stood, taking his hand and allowing him to lead her up the stairs. Her mind still raced as they walked in silence up to the top of the house. William seemed so kind, so open, and she didn't want to take advantage of that. She was no use to the pack, just another drinker, and soon she'd have to feed too… she sighed very softly and felt William's good eye rest upon her, he didn't speak though and she was grateful for that.

At the end of the corridor, William pushed open a door and Frannie peered around the frame as he clicked on the electric light. Her caution melted as her eyes took in the beauty of the room. At the rear was a large window, below which a deep wooden ledge served as a window seat. There was a table near the back of the room with a folded towel on it and a dresser against the other wall with a large mirror and a softly cushioned stool there. The curtains and carpet were blue, the wall panelled in dark-coloured wood at the bottom, green wallpaper above. The bed was a four-poster, fashioned in dark wood and made up with green bedding.

'Oh William,' she whispered. 'What a gorgeous room.'

'It's a bit sparse, but it'll do. If you like it then it's yours for as long as you want it, I doubt Micah's coming home anytime soon and if he does I can move him elsewhere.'

'I promise I won't impose any longer than I have to…'

'It's no imposition. You are welcome to stay as long as you want, and don't even think about leaving until that brat Quinn is out of the picture. I don't know why Hugh didn't finish him off when he came back for me… but until he is dead, the streets are not a safe place for you. I am offering my protection and that of my pack.'

'Thank you,' Frannie smiled and to her horror, she felt a little choked up. '…Thank you, William, you are a good man.'

'I do try to be, and Frannie, if it weren't for you, I'd

probably be a dead man, or blind, or... or god-knows what..'

'I doubt it, Hugh and Ella were coming back for you anyway... and... and Henry wasn't going to kill you... not even if you did beg him to...'

William's lips pressed together but he remained otherwise serene of feature. 'You have done more than you realise, Frances Quinn,' he said. 'Now, let me loan you something to sleep in?'

Frannie looked down at her grubby clothing. 'Thank you.'

William left the room with a nod, returning moments later with a handful of clothing. 'Are you all right sweetheart?' he asked. 'You look a bit lost.'

'Overwhelmed is probably a more apt word,' Frannie replied, placing the clothing he'd handed her down on the dresser,

'Overwhelmed, how so?'

'Well... I don't know how to explain... it's been a very long time since I could say I am a free agent of my own will... if ever. For so many years, I have had Henry barking orders at me, telling me what I should and should not do, when and when not to do it... I... I don't know what to do with myself.'

William didn't speak, just pressed his lips together.

'Makes me sound pathetic huh?' Frannie added, 'I'm sorry, I think I am just tired. I'll be fine in the morning.'

'You're ok now,' William said, taking her hands. 'You can be whoever you want to be now, let your guard down a little. We're not the bad guys Fran. I'm not going to chastise you for speaking your mind.'

'I know that, I'm sorry, you have been so kind and now... I... could you just go? I don't mean to be rude but I can't... can't cope with company right now...'

'It's all right. You don't have to apologise for being tired...' he turned to leave but she stopped him with a hand on his arm. 'I really am grateful to you,' she said. 'So grateful. I was dying in that place and you saved me, I'll not soon forget that.'

'I could say the same to you, and mean it much more literally. Goodnight sweetheart, sleep well.'

'Goodnight William… and thank you.'

9

William Craven, 2016

William sat heavily on the old couch which was closest to the fireplace in the room he used when he was situated in the house. It wasn't a bad place, a bit bare, but despite how he'd grown up in the house, it wasn't home. Not anymore. The green damask curtains at the old wooden window frame weren't his own, nor were the heavy wooden furnishings or the few scattered ornamentations. The dressers were filled with his clothing, but still they felt borrowed, alien. He could not help a sigh, and allowed his eyes to wonder back to the door, thinking of Frannie. The girl was wounded still, indeed the more time he spent with her, the more he saw it. He wished there was more he could do for her; she had a home here for as long as she liked and he'd ensure her safety, but he already knew that nothing but time would put a gleam back in her eyes, or a smile at the edge of her lips. He pushed the thoughts aside and looked instead to the darkness pooling behind the nets at the window. He knew Hugh was probably expecting him below. It was early, and there was much to be discussed. For now though, he wasn't content to leave

The Black Marshes

Frannie alone, unprotected.

A tap at the door, and then it's opening made him catch his breath but it was just Ella's blond head which appeared.

'Hello William. I thought you might enjoy some company.'

'Hugh send you?'

'No, he's gone out…'

'Not running with him?'

'Not tonight. He's… pensive.'

William nodded. His pack-leader was a bit of a loner when he was stressed, and despite how obvious his adoration for his little wife, he was a man who needed solitude from time to time. William could relate but still he smiled to Ella and nodded her towards an armchair by the window which she took with a graceful smile. William returned the smile. He'd known the quiet little changer only a year or so, but already she was a firm friend.

'Is he going to call in Sam?' William asked.

'I think he's going to have to. Rogue drinkers are more his territory than ours.'

'He won't interrogate the girl too badly, will he?'

'He'll do what needs to be done. You know that, Will.'

'I guess I do,' he agreed, then, 'I don't think she's sleeping. She went to bed but I keep hearing her moving about.'

Ella's lips pressed a little tighter but her eyes showed none of her emotion. 'It's early for a drinker, they don't usually sleep at night, do they?'

'I guess not.

'I'd not be surprised if she's traumatized too, in part at least. You know I don't like… them… but she's… well she just looks like a little girl.'

'As do most of them, sweetheart.'

'Why is that? Why are so many of them so very young?'

'I've often pondered that myself,' he replied, 'there

does seem to be a pattern for them being turned young and it's getting worse now that what they are is so romanticized. I wonder if it's the essence of youth which they find so appealing.'

'Perhaps, and the beauty so often found with it. I suppose love factors in too, it's easy for one who is tinged with evil to crave and desire some form of innocence.'

'True.'

'It does not help though, when ending their lives, if they all look like children – but then sometimes I think I must be one of the oldest living beings on this planet.'

William chuckled. 'I guess by the time you've seen half a millennium, almost everybody must seem young?'

'I suppose that is true. Still, physically I was above five and twenty when Hugh took me. You must have been gone thirty?'

'I was. Closer to thirty-five.'

'And yet that girl looks what? Twenty, if that? As did most of her siblings in the blood. Not even fully-grown humans, let alone anything else. I wonder if their minds are mature, or if they remain forever at the age they were taken.'

William sat up a little straighter, he enjoyed debating with Ella, she had interesting insights.

'It might explain the way they behave,' she mused, 'Sam is a drinker too, but he was a man before the curse and he has no malice in him whatsoever.'

'This is very true. Drink?'

Ella nodded and William dug out a bottle of scotch and two glasses from the cupboard in the dresser beside his bed. He poured one for himself and then handed a glass to Ella. She sipped it and screwed up her nose slightly.

'I'm sorry, I don't have any wine.'

'It's well,' Ella said, and took another mouthful. Her eyes moved back to the window. Her pale hands were folded in her lap, the glass held lightly between them. She remained silent for some time, but then spoke again.

'William, I am sorry for what they did to you. I know you won't want to talk about it now, but when you do, you know that I understand... I was tortured too. So very long ago now I suppose but I don't think it is something anybody simply forgets.'

William closed his eyes. The flurry of events since his rescue had helped to keep his mind clear of dwelling on it, and he wasn't ready to go there yet.

'I know... I know something of your past,' he said, 'the witch-hunts?'

'Indeed. I was declared guilty of witchcraft in my human years... My lover who took the form of both man and wolf was somewhat condemning evidence, even above the other accusations.'

'Hugh?'

'Of course. They arrested me whilst he was absent and tortured me, condemned me to die. If Hugh hadn't returned and found me, they would have burned me alive, just as they burned my sister before me. Here, in England, they at least hanged most of the victims first but not in Germany. We were a cruel people back then.'

'Don't think of it!' William commanded, remembering how just a year earlier, Ella had attempted suicide by fire. 'Hugh did find you, and so you are saved.'

'Just as Frances saved you...'

'Aye, just as she did.'

Ella took a long swig of the amber liquid in her glass and then put it down on the dresser. She was silent again for some time, but William was used to that.

'I was pondering,' Ella said at last, 'Before... when I was desolate, I wrote out my life story; for my child, Micah, and for Hugh. It gave me time to really reflect upon what I had suffered, as well as to put things back in their place, within me. Perhaps, if Frances would do the same it would save her the discomfort of being interrogated by Sam, and also it might help to lay her demons to rest.'

'That's not a bad idea,' William agreed. 'I'll put it to her in the morning. She has nothing though... would you loan her something to write it on?'

'Of course. I have some clothing for her too, not mine, mine wouldn't fit, but some of the girls have offered up some bits and pieces...'

'Thank you, and thank them for me – that is very kind of you all.'

The girl stood, and William did the same. Ella was tiny, the frame and size of a person from five hundred years gone. She could not have stood more than four ten, and wore clothing which might well have been worn by a fifteen-year-old. In contrast William, born in the early twentieth century, was a bigger guy, standing at six foot and fairly broadly built; his hug almost engulfed Ella, and he had to bend to kiss her cheek.

'Goodnight William,' she whispered, 'I'll send up anything Frances needs before morning.'

With Ella gone, William moved to sit in the chair she'd vacated so that he could look out onto the world below through the now completely dark window. As he did so, he caught sight of his face again as a reflection. The scars were distinct, even still, and he knew his wolf-blood would never fully undo them, even with its potency. His dead eye was pure white, hardly formed, but even despite that, he hoped for its return to working, telling himself it was starting to see again already. His life was a dangerous one without good vision. Too dangerous. He took a deep breath and nodded.

'I guess this is what you look like now, Will Craven,' he murmured to himself. 'Could be worse.'

On the other side of the wall, she stirred again, and William was sure his enhanced senses gave him the sound of crying coming from her room. He stood and moved to the door but there he paused. She'd not thank him, he was sure, for intruding. Just as he was about to force himself back to his seat, the movement came again from the next room, and then footsteps. Her door opened, clicked shut, and then her footsteps came again in the corridor, pausing outside of his room. Without even awaiting her knock, he opened the door.

'I can't sleep,' she murmured. 'I'm not used to sleeping at night and my thoughts…'

'Come in, then.' William said, ushering her inside the room. The girl was dressed only in his shirt, which was massive on her, and her blood-soaked jeans. She was calmer now though, despite the redness of her eyes.

'Do you want to talk? Or…'

In response, she stood on her tiptoes and put her lips to his. William closed his eyes and allowed the kiss to ripen, savouring it, but then pulled away.

'That's not a prerequisite for your staying here,' he said, 'Nor do I want to become some sort of bandage for the hurt you have felt.'

Frannie nodded, pulling away. 'I'm sorry.'

'Don't be, just don't think that is what you need to do here.'

'Ok,' her voice was barely above a whisper as she turned to leave. William put a hand on her arm, reluctant to thrust her back to her loneliness.

'My bed is large enough to sleep two, if it's just comfort you seek?' he said. 'I could do with a body to hold too, tonight.'

'I guess… I guess we already did sleep together once,' she smiled, casting his mind back to the night before, of how he'd slept in form at her feet.

'Yeah, I guess we did. Come on then, climb in.'

10

Frances Orchard, 2016

Frannie awoke alone in William's bed the following morning. The room was bright, too bright where the curtain wasn't quite covering the window. It wasn't enough to have rendered her feral, as too much sunlight could, but was enough to have started up the pangs. Frannie pulled it and clambered back into bed. The sheets were now stained with the blood from her jeans and she felt a twinge of nerves in her belly to now have to locate clean linen and washing machines.

With a glance to the door to ensure it was staying closed, Frannie slipped off the jeans and looked about the room for a shower cubicle. Like in her own room, there was a door which led to a tiny closet which contained a modern plumbed on-suite, just big enough for toilet and shower – just. Frannie squeezed into the room and stripped off the rest of her clothing, then flicked on the shower and climbed under the jet. The hot water was bliss as it poured down, running off a little blue for the dye in her hair, but not enough to stain. Frannie had begun dying her hair as soon as dyes were available. Beneath it was white, sheer white, for the shock she'd suffered at witnessing the murders of her family, and of Henry's back in her human life.

The shower was hot on Frannie's skin, and the only soap she could find was William's, which smelled somewhat of the sea. The scent engulfed her, soothing and musky. As she inhaled it in, Frannie at last began to relax. Once clean, she stepped out and picked up William's towel. It was still a little damp and an odd thrill went up Frannie's spine to think he must have dried his naked form with it before she awoke. She smiled at herself and then wrapped the towel about her. She really didn't want to get dressed again yet, not in her old clothes. Those jeans really were fit for a wash, if not for the bin. Just as she stepped out of the bathroom, though, William returned to the room, two coffees in hand. He paused and despite it all, Frannie saw how his eyes lingered. She blushed, thinking of how she'd tried to kiss him the night before.

'I'm sorry,' she said at once, 'I'm... I hope you don't mind...'

'Mind that you wished to wash my blood from your skin after saving my life?'

'I suppose when you put it that way...'

William smiled and put down the cups, moving to her side, to put a hand on her arm. He took in a deep breath and then kissed her forehead.

'I'm... I'm having trouble finding anything to wear,' Frannie said, 'I only have my jeans and they're... well fit for a wash anyway if not the bin... and that shirt isn't smelling too great now either.'

'I'll find you something... Ella has had a whip around but god-knows what she's acquired,' he smiled, 'Might be better to buy in new...'

'Do you mind going for me, I... I have money... I just don't want to go out, and it's day and Henry...'

'Of course, say no more. Keep your money, too – I'll

shout for this. I'll find you something here for today, and later I have to go out anyway so I will find my way to a shop and grab you some essentials. The least I can do...'

Frannie's heart thudded and suddenly she was overcome again, 'Thank you. You are the very best of men, William Craven,' she whispered.

William coloured and indicated the door, 'I'll find you some stuff for now,' he said, then vanished.

William was gone no more than ten minutes or so, but returned with an armful of clothing.

'That was fast!' Frannie observed, standing from where she'd been sitting pensively looking out at the brightness behind the curtain. The need to satiate that hunger was growing.

'Thank Ella, not me.'

'And I didn't think she liked me...'

'Ellie doesn't like drinkers in general – don't take it personally. She'll warm up as she comes to know you.'

'Ok, I'll thank her later.'

'Later... she also gave me this...' William held out a lined rule book and a clear pencil case full of pens.

'What... what for?'

'Get dressed and I'll explain!'

Frannie retreated to her own room to finish drying and then to dress. As the morning was fading, the air had grown warmer, more comfortable to let the towel slip and stand naked for a moment. In the pile of clothing was a white shirt, black jeans and a black sleeveless frock coat. Frannie put these on, and then braided her hair. She paused to add a little powder from a pot which was in amongst the clothing, but refrained from the thick makeup she normally wore, leaving her skin as it was. She glanced to the mirror. Contrary to the Hollywood depiction of her kind, the drinkers still had reflections, and Frannie was rather pleased with hers. Not Fran Hodge, the little girl

The Black Marshes

who had loved a man named James, and who had fallen into the arms of a drinker as her family were murdered, to be given his immortal kiss. Not Fran who had damned them all. Not Frances Quinn either, garish, over the top vampire extreme – Henry's bride. No, this was just Frannie, Frances Orchard, who dressed for herself and no other, who smiled again, and who stood in the home of the first people ever to give her herself, with nothing in return asked.

Frannie took in a deep breath and moved back out into the corridor. William stood awaiting her at the door to his own room. He smiled when he saw her.

'Pretty.'

'I scrub up pretty well, so I'm told.'

William stood aside to allow her in, and then ushered her to sit down and drink the now lukewarm coffee. She took several long sips, then nodded.

'So, what now? I suppose I am to speak to Hugh? You'll all have questions for me?'

'Not I, so much, but yes, I suppose Hugh and Sam will want to know much of you.'

'I thought as much.'

'It is unavoidable, especially if Henry is to be disposed of, you might have an insight which could ease the whole process and save lives. Hugh and I are going today for Sam's We'll be gone a day or two – maybe three…'

'Ok, and I am to stay here?'

'Yes, I have a task for you, should you feel up to it?'

'Of course.'

William picked up the book and pens from where they'd been discarded on the dresser. 'Ella suggested it – write down your life story. Write down all as you remember it, and perhaps Sam will be less… imposing… when he arrives and wishes to talk to you…'

'That's fair.'

'You are happy to do this?'

'I am. What if Henry comes here, whilst you are away?'

'He won't. If he knew where we were, he'd have come before.'

'He told me he knew…'

'And he wasn't bluffing?'

'I don't know. Maybe.'

William paused. 'Hmmm, I'll tell Hugh, see you're helping us already. He won't get in though, if he does come. There's a lot of security and he'd struggle to get in, let alone past the changers who reside here.'

'Are there many of you?'

'Eight, with Hugh and I gone, plus two drinkers too, and all know that there is a danger. Reuben, you met him, is a damn good fighter – he's probably one of the oldest and strongest of your kind living. He's looking after the house for now so you will be safe.'

'And if Henry does get in?'

'If he does then I want to you leave by any route possible and run out into the forest. Follow the path north and then east until you stumble onto a cottage. That's my place, my actual place, when I'm not here… go there and run into the basement, at the edge of the room is a large tapestry, pull it aside and you'll find a door with a set of stairs. Those stairs go down into a large chamber. This should be a hiding place enough but if you are still not comfortable, then there is another hidden door at the back set into the rock, into a cubby there, go there and wait for me.'

'Mysterious…'

'Not very. The Haverly family, way back, were poisoners and alchemists. Those rooms are the remnants of that life.'

'The Haverly family, but I thought this was your home?'

'It was, but I am a descendant of them. I am Hugh's brother's god-knows how many times great grandson.'

'Oh, I didn't know...'

'Indeed. I don't know much of it, but Hugh once told me that the curse we all carry, is born of bloodlines which stem from this vey estate. The house as it stands now is more modern, but Hugh once lived in a house which stood where that old cellar now lies. The cellar once beneath it. You might see strange things down there, but ignore them...'

'Such as?'

'Phantoms, echoes of the past. If you are of a mind to see them, then you might. I know that I saw enough of it before the wolf-blood, but very little since. It might be that the blood dulls them.'

'Perhaps,' Frannie whispered, her mind on another ghost, from so long ago. No phantom though, that one, but a real and corporeal being.

'When do you leave?'

'In a minute.'

'So soon...'

'I know, but best to remain in motion than to sit on this and allow Quinn to get his plans back in motion.'

'I suppose,' Frannie said, then smiled and shuffled closer to William. He put an arm easily around her and she laid her head on his shoulder.

'Before you go, I just want to say something...'

'Yes?'

'It was... was an honour to save your life, William Craven. I look forward to coming to know you better in the future.'

'Aye, and you too. Frannie. I'll be seeing you when I get back – write up that book, if you can?'

'I will do. I promise.'

William kissed her forehead again, just softly, and then stood and moved to the door. With a wry smile, he waved and then was gone. Frannie stood and stretched. Feelings, definite feelings happening. It was nice, just like it had been before. Emotions without the promise of pain and destruction. Frannie smiled to herself and picked up the writing pad. It's very whiteness, it's smooth newness was daunting. Frannie couldn't remember the last time she really sat and wrote. Not for years, not since the letters she'd once penned to a dead husband, a wrought and troubled attempt to try to somehow keep him alive. She wet her lips and then took the book back to the bed and sat down with it. She paused a moment and then curled her long fingers about a blue biro.

'Ok, then,' she said to the empty room, 'let's do this…'

11

The memoirs of Frances Orchard, Devon, 1810-1817
(Ghost)

This is the memoir of Frances Ann Hodge, Nee Orchard, Nee Quinn. I dedicate it to those who lived throughout these pages, and who live no more. I've never written anything like this before, so to you, William, Hugh and any other who puts an eye upon it, forgive the feeble writing, the stumbles where dates don't quite tally. 200 years is a long time to try to remember and, as ever it does, memory plays tricks, swapping one event with another, rendering the day to day faded and obsolete whilst the moments of event suddenly once more find colour and vividness. Firstly, I suppose I should state who I am, or more truthfully, who I was – despite how, in a way, before it all I was just another nobody. I was born in the year of the turning century, 1800 to a farmer and his wife on some land which became home to breeding mares. I was the eldest of their children, aside from Charles my half-brother from my father's first marriage, and I was, as much as ever a young lady was then, educated. My father owned our farm so we were not tenant farmers, but landowners. We had not a great deal, but we had enough. There are no tales of suffering and hardships for me, as there were for so many others of the village, there was just life. And what life it was, a bustle of activity, a busy house and the noise... the animals... the glorious stink of it all.

I digress though, and am stepping ahead of myself. I suppose the first event of note, and my earliest childhood memory to boot, is of him.... of the "ghost". I was about ten, certainly no older. I had escaped the farm by means of a broken gatepost and was out in the mires by my home, enjoying the exhilaration of what my father called bog-hopping. A dangerous pursuit indeed, where one literally hops, from one tussock to another across a feather-bed mire. This was something sometimes done by the village boys as a sport, and occasionally by the men of the farms if they had to move across the edges of the mire in a hurry. I however, was but a ten-year-old girl and I knew well I'd be in for a whipping if my father caught me. Up ahead, too far ahead now to see me, was Charles. He the scrap who had enticed me into such play, being somewhat older at fourteen. I idolised Charles, I adored him and when he died, a year later, of the pox, I was inconsolable for so long.

Just for that moment, though, all that suffering lay before me, and I was carefree, lost in the feeling of exhilaration as I hopped across the waterlogged grass and after-all, I told myself, it was only a little bog; waist deep at the most. Further down the road, after our turn-off, there were bigger, more dangerous bogs which hid beneath the tall grass, and not even Charles and his buddies would have dared try to cross one of those, they could easily swallow a grown man whole. There were two types of bog in the mires surrounding the town where I lived, the big peat blanket bogs and the smaller but more lethal 'feather beds' which hid deep ponds beneath the crust of vegetation. In the winter, when the rains filled the ditches,

The Black Marshes

the wetter ones would just take you and you'd be gone, vanishing from view in an instant. If you were unlucky, you could find yourself stuck in one of the peatier ones closer to the edge and even more terrifying in my ten-year-old mind, vast quicksand-like mires which would drag you down to oblivion slowly. Suckling, hungry beasts they were, to my childish imaginings. My father told me often that at the centre of the mire, the bogs were more than twenty-foot-deep and even the outskirts were enough to take down a whole carriage completely if you could get one out past the shallow edges. This idea terrified me, yet in some ways it was thrilling, filling me with an odd, youthful curiosity, especially to consider the age-old bodies which must lie beneath the waters where I paddled and hopped with my brother.

After ten minutes or so of jumping from tuft to tuft of grass, I found myself back on the dry path and my heart-rate began to slow at once. I loved the feeling of being back to safety almost as much as I loved the thrill of the danger. Charles was so far ahead that he seemed just to be a speck, running for home that he might choose the best scones from Mama's cooking. That was if "the girls", my younger sisters, hadn't already pilfered them. I was about to switch over to the path which led up to the farm when I suddenly heard a voice. It sounded very close, almost as though it were behind me.

'Little one,' it whispered, 'Little girl.'

Chills ran up my spine and I spun around quickly. All about me were mires, ponds, grassy tussocks, the odd tree, but at first, I couldn't see the owner of the voice.

'Who's there?' I demanded, my high-pitched child's voice echoing in the emptiness.

'I'm in the mire.' The voice replied, still sounding like somebody was stood right beside me. 'Why don't you come closer?'

My heart pounded but to my horror, I found myself

walking back down onto the main path and toward the gate which marked the edge of town. I began to cry, I could not understand why, but I could not stop walking.

'Good girl. Good girl,' the voice whispered on as I walked, and suddenly I saw him. A man stood motionless in the dusky light of the late afternoon. He must have been in his forties; his hair was cut short, his skin very pale. He had a beard, and old, ancient grey eyes which seemed to shine. He held out his hand to me and I moved forward, against my will, and took it. The man kissed my chubby hand, and then lifted me up into his arms.

'Shush now, don't be frightened, child' he said softly, and I felt my body relaxing, despite my terror. I raised my eyes and saw that his face was changing, the lips lifting to reveal sharp teeth which looked like the teeth of a wild beast. His eyes too were different, silver and shining with ethereal light.

'What…' I murmured, frightened but still unable to fight, to move.

'I am a dream,' he whispered, 'and when you awake, you won't remember me.'

I shuddered but could find no response. The man put his lips to my throat.

'Don't!' I murmured, but I still could not move, not even to flee from the man, to save myself. Tears ran down my face as the man bit down hard and then put down his lips and drank deeply from the wound. It hurt and I wanted to scream but still, I was mute, immobile. The man drank greedily of my blood and I, prone in his arms, was suddenly certain that I was going to die, right there at just ten years old. The monsters Charles teased about were real and one of them had got me!

Consciousness wavered and the man showed no signs of letting up. My chest closed up, my breathing restricted and the sound of my pounding heart became louder in my ears, ringing and echoing. I gasped, my heart beat

The Black Marshes

irregularly and I realised with horror that death was close. My eyes tried to close but I forced them open again, watching the swirl of greens and brown as the world spun around me. The man gasped too and pulled his lips away, he stared down on me with shock and horror registering on his face.

Painfully, I let my eyes slip closed.

And that was how I met the man I came to call Ghost. I did not see him again for five years. As such a child as I was, I couldn't, then, fully appreciate what had happened, and I had no idea the events it would lead to, the stain it would put into me. In some ways, my turning to what I am now, began that day, but I will speak more of that later. And so back to those early years...

My father retold my story over and over, a little ghost story to scare the locals and to keep my sisters away from the marshes. To me, it was no mere tale, but a retelling of a horror which still chilled me to my very marrow. As time passed, I gave up trying to make people believe me, but that didn't mean I forgot it; it was just that nobody believed it had really happened. I'd awoken, hours later in my own bed at home after being found by my father, fast asleep by the gatepost. There had been no blood on my clothing but I'd been unwell for some days, an illness, my father said roughly, born of my falling asleep outdoors in my wet clothing. The men had gone out to search for the stranger but had found nobody anywhere close. More so, when I had examined myself, I had been shocked to see that there were no marks at all on my throat where he'd bitten me. It was an anomaly, a scary memory but one which faded into the monotony of our existence.

I could talk now of the mundane, of everyday life during my childhood but I fear that to do so would be to wallow in nostalgia. I could talk of how my brother died, and how we mourned. The wake, the black cloths at the mirrors and the tears which seemed never to abate. That event, I think, was what really took away the memories of Ghost, for in truth it overrode all. I could talk also of how we moved from cattle and sheep – stupid things which seemed incapable of not falling into the mires in droves – to horses... good horses, well, somebody had to breed them! In a world of carts and carriages and where riding was our only real mode of transport, horses were vital, and ours were strong! I could talk of all of that, but the relevance to this tale is low. Maybe if you ask, I will tell you more of it. Instead, I will be concise, and I will move to the next time I was to meet ghost, three months into my fifteenth year.

The day of Ghost's return was overcast, drizzling, but I was hot despite the rain. I had been working for the last hour, helping the grooms to feed and muck out the horses and had just begun with the saddle breaking of a young colt. This might seem strange work for a young girl, but on the farms, this was actually fairly normal... would have been more so, had I been a boy perhaps but my father had all girls so we too had to learn the trade! My clothing was simple: a cast-off old pair of trousers and a tailored riding jacket which was actually a part of a new riding habit that my father had bought for me. The britches were old ones which had belonged to my brother, and which I had appropriated from his rooms along with several other pairs after his demise. My boots were sturdy, comfortable and well-worn, breaker's boots, and I lived in them. My blond locks were pulled tightly behind my head, coiled and braided to keep them out of my face. The horse I was breaking was one of last season's foals; I had been working tirelessly with her for almost two weeks and finally the time had come for trying an initial mount. The sport was a dangerous one, but I persisted, it was my passion. I was good too, even the men on the farm agreed: 'If you can't get a cob to cooperate, give it to Miss Fran.'

Finally, I felt the saddle slip onto the little horse and snapped the leather straps into place, the thrill of winning over-rode all other emotions; nothing in this world, even since those days, can beat the thrill of a first saddling. It is a feeling I still miss, even now so long past. I laughed in triumph and patted the little horse.

'Good girl!' I said. 'Good, good girl!' and then rummaged in my coat pocket and found a handful of chopped carrot to treat the young horse with. As she nibbled them up, I looked up at the clouds. The rain was stopping, thinning at least, and the sun prying from behind the big grey clouds. My jacket was soaked through from the thin drizzle, and I thought wryly that my father would certainly have something to say if I caught a chill. I eyed the now-saddled horse and felt my lips twist into a smile. I'd have one go at mounting, I thought, the horse seemed calm enough now that the saddle was actually on. If she panicked, then I'd give it up for the day and come back to it tomorrow.

On the fence was an old rag and, even knowing the mess it'd leave my hair in, I quickly ran it over my head, drying my face and hair as much as I could, and then drying my hands off, I'd need a good grip.

After all the protests the horse had put up to being saddled, I was somewhat surprised at how easily she submitted to a rider. I'd not expected to even be able to mount, let alone to ride. The colt was still flighty, and it took all of my skill to remain seated but I found myself grinning as I began to get the beast under control. Suddenly, though, something in the trees caught my attention. I stared and the face became clearer. Piercing blue eyes. Watching me. The man was dressed in a warm grey overcoat, blond hair being blown about by the wind. There was no doubt whatsoever of his identity. My eyes widened and my breathing became laboured.

'Ghost?' I whispered. My heart pounded as I looked onto the face of my nightmares. I shuddered, frightened, and my hands loosed on the reins just as the skittish horse reared. I cried out and tried to grip harder but already I could feel myself falling.

The sound of something breaking as I hit the hard dirt was unmistakable, a loud crack as I landed and a cry escaped from between my lips. My hip! Agony – that came afterwards, somehow, after the realisation of pain.

At my falling, the man came forward, out of where he lurked. He knelt beside me in the dust and laid a hand on my forehead.

'No pain, chid,' he whispered. 'Do not be afraid of me.'

A silver glow gleamed in his eye as he spoke, pulling me back into that other, hideous memory. I gasped again, and then wriggled to be free.

'Where are you hurt?' he asked.

'Hip.'

'His eyes moved down and then a hand rested on it. 'How the devil...?' he muttered, 'it's healing already...'

I lay still, half-convinced I'd fallen into a dream again, unconscious on the ground. Ghost put a hand to my forehead again, then frowned.

'I saw you... before...' I managed to sit up. Somewhere, deep within me, I knew I should be afraid of this man. He'd nearly killed me in my girlhood, and yet there was no fear whatsoever. I suppose Ghost, whoever he was, had a power similar to Hugh's, that he could command and be obeyed. In truth, I begrudge it not, for had that terror taken me, I could not have come to really know him, as I was to.

'Here, stand,' he said, doing the same and holding out a hand for me. I took it and allowed him to help me to my feet. after a few flexes of my limbs, I found a smile.

'I am well, I think,' I said, then glanced back at him. 'What business have you here, sir?'

The Black Marshes

'You.'

A moment of fear began but was easily repressed by whatever influence it was he held over me. 'Me?'

'Yes. Do you remember…'

'Yes.'

'I'll come, tonight, meet me outside? In the barn? Midnight?'

'Why should I do that?'

'Because I need to explain, and I need… just, just come? Yes?'

I nodded.

I suppose at my age, living such a life as I did, many girls might already have learned the safest ways of sneaking out to meet with young men in the night. In truth, it wasn't something that had ever crossed my mind. Nor did it then, in that sense, as I slipped out of my bed, careful not to wake my sister who slept in beside me, and tiptoed out into the dark corridor. A modern tongue might call me a tomboy, I suppose, but I did not even consider to think of the propriety of my actions.

Opening the front door gave me another challenge, for it was locked, and so a key had to be retrieved from the hook in the kitchen. Despite this though, I managed to slip out unheard, and made my way to the haybarn which was just across the field. The night was chill indeed. I wore only my nightgown, covered for modesty by a long robe which was actually one of my Mama's, but which I had recently grown into. Inside, the barn smelled of animal, sweat and of course the fresher scent of newly cut hay. Here I paused, still being as quiet as I could. Most of the boys who worked the farm for my father slept not here but in the upper part of the bigger barn, to the south of the house but still, I was terrified of being caught out of bed.

By the by, the barn door opened again and there was

the man. He paused and looked about, then came to my side and put a cold hand to my face.

'Hello child,' he murmured.

'Ghost...'

The man laughed, 'As well it may be. Astute child. A ghost, yes.'

'Have you a name?' I asked, my fear fading a little more.

'Do ghosts have names?'

I paused, and then smiled, unsure of myself. The man – Ghost, as I was ever to know him thereafter – dropped his hand from my face and indicated we sit in amongst the bales. I did so and he draped his cloak about my shoulders.

'I have no intention of causing harm here,' he said. 'So please do not be afraid. What do you remember of me?'

'When I was a child... you... you did something to me...? You hurt me? I... I think you... bit me?'

My heart pounded and my pulse raced but still that strange calmness, that lack of fear held me together. Ghost nodded, his eyes glimmering in the darkness.

'I did, I'm sorry for that.'

In childish naivety, I just stared at him. Curiosity and fear fought, but curiosity was still winning through.

'Miss Frances, may I take a droplet of blood from your wrist?' Ghost asked of me. 'I won't... won't bite you, just prick with a blade.'

'Why?'

'Because you don't have the scent of a human, and out in the marshes, I gave you a gift which might be the reason for that.'

'I don't understand?'

'And you don't have to.'

I felt somewhat as though I was back in a dream, reality blurring. I knew I should be frightened, that this man before me was a creature intended only for nightmares but I could not push myself to feel the fear I knew I should.

'I'm not human?' I said at length.

'I hope that you are, just that you are a little tainted from what I gave you. This shouldn't have happened, but I took a gamble when I saved your life. It must be… come, give me your wrist!'

Ghost, moved to kneel before me, taking my hand and rolling up the lacy cuff of my sleeve.

'Don't be frightened,' he said again, and gripped me tightly. I wriggled a bit but it was cursory, because in truth, I was more curious than afraid even still. From a pocket he produced a knife and from there he nicked the skin, making the blood bubble free. I made a strangled murmur at the pain, and tried to pull away but he held me tight. He dipped his other finger into the cut and then put the blood to his lips.

'You're definitely still human,' he said.

I merely nodded, not sure what he had expected.

The man kissed the wound on my wrist and then sat back watching the gash, as though he were waiting for something.

'Queer,' he said. 'You mend broken bones but not flesh. Here…' he put his lips to his own wrist, tearing the flesh there. I watched in a strange paralysed way as he thrust his own finger into the wound, making the blood splash. His face was normal again, I realised, whatever demon lurked within him well hidden once more. He moved until he was sat behind me and put his arm about me so that I could drink from his wounded wrist. A droplet of blood fell onto my white nightgown, staining it forevermore.

'There child, there,' he spoke softly. 'Just a little. Good girl.'

I sipped the thick coppery liquid, screwing up my nose as I did so, and thinking that the way he spoke to me was somewhat reminiscent of the way I spoke to the horses I was breaking. The man let me drink just for a few moments and then pulled away. My eyes went to the wound on my arm and, to my shock, I saw that it was healing, the edges folding in and making up a network of new skin.

'What?' I gasped.

'Consider it a gift,' he replied, ruffling my hair. 'For frightening you so badly. I'll come and visit you again.'

'You're… going?'

'For now,' he agreed and stood, brushed straw from his knees and then held out a hand for me. 'Come, I'll see you back into the house my dear.'

And so normally encroached again. The seasons changed, as dramatically as they are wont on the moors, with boiling summers followed by winters filled with winds so violent they whipped the very breath out of you. As my normal life carried on around me, as the farm prospered and my little sisters began to grow from children to young ladies, our fortunes seemed ever to rise. Our horses escaped disease and grew in strength and popularity. Often, since, I have wondered if Ghost somehow had a hand in our sudden rise to fortune. The horses were becoming more and more famous throughout the region and Father gave up working altogether, hiring more workers to run the farm for him whilst he enjoyed the benefits of his years of labour. A gentleman farmer at last. I was pleased, my father had worked hard for what we had and I enjoyed seeing him happy and content in his newly acquired fine clothing.

For some months, Ghost stayed away somewhat, but from time to time I thought I caught a glimpse of him, just a flash of colour or a face watching silently through the trees. I ever pondered the oddness of it but never spoke of it to anybody else. He was my secret and I knew that he depended on my silence. As time went on, I began to feel myself looking forward to his visitations, looking out for his face in the trees and always when he did appear I found myself overjoyed, protected.

It was a clear night, warm in the middle of the summer's heat and again, I was in bed, not sleeping but with the lights out, when at last he came to me again. This was just after my sixteenth birthday and thankfully, by then I slept alone.

'Hello Frances,' he said quietly, standing in the doorway.

At once I sat up in bed, clutching the blanket about me. 'Ghost?'

'Is that still what you think I am?' he asked, and a smile touched the corner of his lips.

'Aren't you?'

'No. Will you come with me?'

'Where?' As an almost-adult, I was much warier to follow than I had been as a child.

'Outside, to the barn.'

'I don't think that proper,' I said and again, I saw the briefest touch of a smile at his lips.

'Nothing improper. I just want to talk with you.'

I went to stand but the wariness of encroaching adulthood paused me again. 'I am in just my nightgown,' I said, clutching the soft coverlet about me. Ghost moved at once to pick up my robe and pass it to me. I nodded and put it on, and then reluctantly pulled myself up out of bed and followed him down into the barn.

'I suppose you want a taste of me, like before?' I asked, eyeing him cautiously.

'I need to just check… that you are…'

'Still human, yes, I know, I remember… although I still have no idea of why, or of what you expect.'

Ghost paused, his eyes settling on me and I forced myself to smile. He really did have gentle eyes, I thought, even though they didn't soften.

'I mean,' I clarified. 'What are you? If you are no ghost,

you must be a monster of sorts? A demon even? Why am I not frightened of you?'

'You are not frightened of me because I told you not to be,' he said, 'my kind, we command a small amount of control thus. I told you not to be afraid, and so you are not… and yes, I suppose demon is as good a name as any. I am what my people call a drinker. I have to drink blood to survive.'

'You kill people?'

'No sweetheart, not any more. A sip here and there sustains.'

'You nearly killed me, when I was a girl!'

'I did, but it was an accident. I did something, to heal you… but I, well I think I might have done too much, made you a little like me so now you are my responsibility.'

'And that is why you come?'

'Yes. That is why I come.'

I held out my arm. 'Then do it,' I whispered.

Ghost put his lips down this time, rather than a knife, and what he took was no mere sip, but three gulping mouthfuls from my open vein.

'Thank you, Frances,' he said at length.

'Still human?'

'Mostly.'

'What do you mean by that?'

'I can feel the demon influence within you but it is too weak to manifest.'

'Oh god,' I murmured, inexplicably putting both hands to my belly, as though somehow the demon he spoke of was some unwanted babe within.

'Hush now, nothing to be afraid of, darling. Close your eyes for me now and sleep.'

I could not refuse the order and in moments, I was falling into a deep slumber. I awoke in my bed, wrapped up tight in my coverlet, tucked in as though by an errant father.

The Black Marshes

12

The memoirs of Frances Orchard, Devon, early 1800s
(James)

And so there is how I met Ghost, how I first stepped into this world of drinkers. To this day I know not really who he was, or why fate turned me onto this path. But from that day onwards, my ghost was to become more of a regular visitor. He came again six months later, and then again. I see no reason to recount these encounters, in truth they were all much the same, save for perhaps a more relaxed air to Ghost's manner, and ease which grew with every visit. I suppose James then, is the next thing to recount, my James, my husband. In some ways, I have Ghost to thank for him, too, for if Ghost had not attacked him to feed from him, then I suppose I never should have met him, let alone fallen in love with him.

The sky was darkening as I turned onto the road into the marsh that day in the February of 1818. I'd been into town for the festivities, as much an excuse to show off my father's horses as it was an excuse to celebrate. The day had been long though, and I was tired. Too tired really to

The Black Marshes

have taken up the offer to stay and join in the dancing which had been offered by a blushing young man who worked the fields of Cherry Blossom Farm, on the other side of the village to my father's farm. My father however, had insisted I stay and had taken the horses home with the help of Lily and Jane, the older two of my three sisters, and so I'd been forced to endure it.

The fading of the light had been my excuse and I finally slipped away before the revelry in town became the bawdy, drunken celebration it was like to become after dark. I knew that I shouldn't walk the marsh way in the dark but my knowledge of the marshes was better than that of anybody I knew and I was confident that I would be safe so long as I stuck to the old, half-submerged road. I walked carefully but there was still enough light in the sky to keep me from worrying about stumbling off the path. I smiled and quickened my pace, trying to think of my nice warm home, of how happy with my father would be due to all of the interest we'd drummed up in town that day, of how admired the horses had been.

Suddenly a noise out in the marshes caught my attention. At first, I thought it was just the wind but then it repeated again, a voice, faint in the distance. I froze, a small smile spreading on my lips, surely that must be Ghost's voice? Who else would be out in the dangerous marshes?

The voice called again and the smile slipped away. No, that certainly wasn't Ghost, I realised, a different tone, younger. It called again, crying for help, and then I heard sobbing. My skin prickled and all at once I remembered the stories I and my sisters told, late at night, about the spirits of all the dead people out in the mire.

I trembled, the thoughts of my own ghost were eerie enough but the idea that there might be an actual spectre there were so much worse. I stood, frozen in place, unsure as to whether I should flee or stay and investigate; the adventurous part of me fighting with my fear. Again, I heard the cry and the thrill of adventure won through.

With a pounding heart, I turned from the path up to the house and stepped onto the marshlands. The ground was not too bogged down and I knew that a few steps further out was another old road, half-swallowed but still firm enough to walk on. It had once been the road up to my father's farm but as the winter passed, the months of heavy rain stole the land back for the marsh and despite the hot day, the summer had not managed to push the waters back yet.

Again, the eerie call, like a whisper, came sobbing out from the marshes but I was aware that it was closer, the hair standing up on the back of my neck as I heard it. I was aware too that even the path I was walking on was becoming stodgy and muddy beneath my shoes and I was certain that the voice must belong to a ghost; surely, nobody living was foolish enough to be walking out in Stateman's Pool? Nobody other than my own ghost, I was sure, and it certainly wasn't his voice.

'Is somebody there?' I called softly, not expecting a reply.

To my shock a voice called back. 'Yes! Please, help me! I fell in.'

I thought I was going to be sick, so it was a spirit then. I was terrified but my feet seemed rooted to the ground, unmovable in my fear. The darkness was coming ever closer and I squinted against the pink sunset.

'Please!' he called again. 'It's pulling me down.'

Still afraid, I looked about me in the dim light. There! No ghost but a man, clinging desperately to a tussock of grass. He was up to his chest and his shoulders were under as he was being pulled down.

'Oh god!' I cried. 'I'll get help!'

'Please!' he called back. 'There's no time. I can't hold on much longer. Don't leave me!'

The Black Marshes

'Can't you just pull yourself up?'

'No! If I push on this grass it moves!' The voice was high-pitched with fear and I empathised, I'd fallen into the bog once, not deep but enough to go past my middle. The feeling was frightening beyond belief. The man cried out again as I stood pondering the situation, a wail of pure terror. The weight of responsibility weighed heavily on my eighteen-year old shoulders. The man wasn't even close to the path, I thought grimly, and getting him out alone would be tricky, but then if I didn't do something he could well drown, sucked into the thick, grasping mud.

'Please! Help me!' he cried again and as my eyes were adjusting, I could see that the grassy tuft had partially submerged, tipping him into the waters up to his chest. The poor man must be freezing. To my horror, he began to struggle, the very worst thing he could do.

'Wait, keep still! I'm thinking!' I called out. 'The more you struggle, the faster you will go down.'

The man cried out in fear and struggled more, almost losing his grip altogether.

'Shush!' I called. 'Shush, we'll get you out, I promise, I just need a moment!'

I was almost too scared to think straight but then, as a burst of inspiration, my eyes went down to where my hand rested on the old rusty fencepost which had once denoted the borders of my father's land, before the mire had stolen it.

'Please, I don't think I have much time,' the man called again, desperate.

Frantically, I looked about for something to tie around myself but there was nothing. The man was up past the top of his arms by then, he was right, time really was running out. Suddenly I had a flash of insight, I could make a rope: I was wearing linen petticoats which were strong and durable.

'Ok, I'm going to come and get you,' I called.

'Don't be a fool,' the man called back. 'We'll both end up beneath the water.'

I shook my head. 'I've done this before,' I said. 'And I'm going to tie myself to this post. Just hang on a little bit longer and don't struggle. Peat's like quicksand – the more you struggle, the faster you go down. Keep still!'

'Very well,' he called but I could hear the terror in his voice.

Quickly, I pulled off my apron and then undid the skirts of my white underdress beneath the blue wool I wore. The coarse linen which served as a petticoat beneath my blue dress was as strong and hardy as I'd expected. Hoping upon hope that my father would understand, I used the edge of the rusty gatepost to make a tear in the material so that I could rip off a strip and this I repeated until the underskirt was torn into lengths. As I worked, I glanced up at the man and saw him struggling again, gripping the grassy mound with his fingers. I thought I could hear him praying too, pleas for god's mercy but that was a fact I knew I would be keeping to myself, should I manage to drag him out.

'For god's sake, keep still!' I called again and to my shock and dismay I realised that his prayers had turned to sobs of fear. 'Please... try to stay calm, you have to stay calm.'

The man did not reply but his sobs quietened.

Once done with my makeshift linen rope, I tied it firmly to the rusty post and then put my pinny back on, tying it firmly and threading the rope that had been my underskirt through the loop. Then I took a deep breath and left the path, the water gripped me like ice about my legs, causing me to lose my breath for a moment. I paused, but then pushed on. There was no time for foolishness! The edge of the mire was shallower than where the man clung to his tussock for dear life and I waded a few yards into the icy water before I began to lose the bottom and so

The Black Marshes

climbed up on to my own grassy mound. The man raised a desperate hand to me but I was still too far away.

'Wait, I'll come closer!' I ordered and then, steeling myself, I jumped from one tussock to the next. The rope pulled tight about my waist and I realised that this was all the give I had. The crust where I stood wobbled treacherously beneath my and for a moment, I thought I was going to go in too but luckily my balance won out and I managed to stay above water.

'Here!' I said, holding out my hand. The man's fingers barely grazed mine and I felt the rope straining as I leaned in closer.

'I can't reach!' he said, his voice terrified, and I realised I was going to have to come up with a new plan as he began to struggle again, tears rolling down his face. I looked down at the rope about my waist and sighed, I didn't like the idea of going without but if I didn't take the risk this man was going to die before my eyes. With trembling fingers, I undid my apron and tied the lace of that to the knotted petticoat rope. In my pocket was an apple and I tied the other apron string around that to give it weight enough to be thrown.

'Catch this,' I said, the fingers of one hand white around the rope, and then threw him the apple. For a terrifying moment, I thought he'd missed it but then I saw he had it in his one free hand.

'All right, pull gently until you are grasping the linen part,' I ordered. 'I'm not sure how sturdy that apron is.'

Wordlessly, the man obeyed. I watched with trembling legs as he came closer, an inch at a time until I saw he held the linen. He'd managed to free the other hand in his effort and gripped my petticoat firmly with both hands.

I took a deep breath, trying to remember my father's teaching. 'Right,' I said with more confidence than I felt. 'Right – now you need to try to pull yourself so that you are lying flat on your belly with your body as horizontal as you can over the grass whilst I pull you in.'

Again, he nodded and I could see he was still terrified. Still, he did as I ordered and I took a deep breath, the weight in my chest loosening.

'Good,' I said encouragingly, hoping my tone didn't show my own fear as the crust beneath my feet wobbled again. 'You're doing fine!' I added and tried tugging on the rope. The tussock on which I was standing wobbled far too dangerously.

'Hmmm. This isn't going to work, keep a hold of that rope. You'll be safe as long as you hold it.'

'Where are you going?' the man cried and I nodded towards the path.

'To firmer ground,' I said.

The man's eyes ran over my form and I saw his lips pressed together. 'You have no safety rope though,' he said, worried. 'Last thing I want is for you to fall in too.'

'Sir, I've been bog-hopping since I was a child, I won't fall!'

Quickly, so that he wouldn't see my fear, I turned and surveyed the challenge. The sun had almost set now and the water was very cold around my feet. With a deep breath, I ran a step and then jumped; I landed easily on the next piece of grass and then turned back to the man, he was using the rope to pull himself horizontal as I'd ordered. I had no illusions now of him drowning now, he was safe and I'd saved him. Quickly I jumped again, back into the shallower water by the road. My feet touched the bottom and, thankfully, I pulled myself to the shore. As I stood and went to the rope to help pull the man in I was alerted to the sound of hoof-beats on the old path.

'I can hear hooves!' I cried out. 'They must be looking for you, no-one in their right mind would come down here in the dark otherwise.'

Sure enough, even as I grabbed the rope and began to pull, a black horse skidded to a stop beside me and an

The Black Marshes

older man dismounted. 'Is that you out there, James?' he called.

'Father!' the man cried.

'Here, let me!' the man ordered, taking the rope from my hands. With his father pulling rather than I, the young man was easily brought back to shore. For a moment, he lay gasping, shivering and so dazed that I thought he might be in shock.

'Thank god,' the older man said, pulling his son to his feet and hugging him. He pulled off his coat and wrapped it about his son's body. 'I've been worried sick!'

'Thank god this young lady happened by,' the younger man, James, whispered, turning to me. 'She risked her own life to save me.'

James's father turned his eyes on me. 'I will never be able to thank you enough, Miss…'

'Hodge, Frances Hodge. And I did no more than anybody would have done. I am merely glad I was here tonight, sir.'

'It was a great deal more than most would do,' James argued. 'And I am very grateful.'

'As am I! Where are you from, child?'

'My father is Peter Hodge, who owns Mannaton Farm.'

'Ahh, then you are our new neighbour!' the elder man said. 'I'm Sir Richard Orchard and this young man whose life you have saved is my son, James.'

I bobbed as much of a courtesy as I could manage with my shivering limbs. 'Sir,' I murmured.

'Come, we can get the niceties done easier over dinner,' Sir Richard said amiably. 'Say tomorrow night?'

'You're inviting me to dinner?'

'The very least I can do. Here, you take the horse, Frances. You and James are both soaked through and shivering but you were the one with the good sense not to fall into the mire so therefore, I think you are more deserving of the mount.'

I smiled tentatively and pulled myself up onto the horse. I knew I looked ungainly riding astride like a man, sopping wet skirts hocked up to my thighs, but it was all his saddle allowed for and besides, I was no stranger to riding astride.

'Here, this is your turn off?' Sir Richard said at length.

I nodded and slipped down off of the horse at the break in the road.

'Thank you for the ride,' I said and the older man nodded. James, who'd been remarkably quiet during the journey home, took my hand in his elegant but muddy fingers.

'I owe you my very life,' he muttered. 'Thank you,' and with that, he placed a muddy kiss on my cheek. I blushed scarlet and turned to flee from the two men, back towards home.

I cannot deny, in truth, that the attraction to James was instantaneous. I took up the dinner invitation the following night, taking my father and younger sister with me, and there I spent a great deal of the evening in his company. I found out quickly that his family were in mourning for his mother who had died only weeks before, and that he was one of rather a large brood, three brothers and a sister. James being the eldest.

After supper, my father and old Mr Orchard sat down to a battle of chess, whilst James and I stood in the window, looking out.

'I hope you enjoyed supper, Miss Hodge,' he smiled.

'Very much so! Better fare than on our table, I am sure.'

'Then I am glad, you are a very welcome guest at our table, always. You saved my life, you know.'

'I do know,' I said, no false modesty. 'What the devil were you about, out there in the marsh? The moors should never be underestimated!'

The Black Marshes

'I see that now, but it's rather a queer tale, you see – I think I saw a ghost, out there.'

'A ghost?' suspicion loomed but I repressed it for the time-being.'

'Yes, well, you see I was coming alongside the marsh, having got myself lost looking for the village! I hoped to witness the dancing but I think I took a wrong fork. I went to pass by your farm, actually, and there I heard a voice calling me.'

'A voice?'

'Yes, a man's voice. It really was rather bizarre! I went to follow it, almost against my will, and there a figure stood watching from the very edge of the mire. He beckoned me and I followed. I have little memory then, of what occurred, but... but then a fear like that of the devil took me and I fled, not realising whence I went... I was waist-deep in the mud before I realised what I had done, and I was so turned about that I could no longer sense where safety was. That's when I saw you out in the distance and began to shout for you.'

I blinked and swallowed the fury which began to build in me. This poor man had had an encounter with Ghost, there could be no doubt of that. I could hardly explain thus to him though, and so instead I forced serenity.

'I am just glad to have been nearby!' I said.

James smiled. Now that he was no longer sodden and covered in mud, he was actually rather an attractive young man. His hair was short and dark but fell into feathers about his face, his eyes were blue, a fair contrast, and they shone when he smiled. In truth, that smile was a killer – it could have taken any young lady's heart without any other input from him. Poor James! Even in writing this, he comes back to life for me. A sorrow of loss which I have carried for so long. I go ahead of myself again though, and so will move on. I invited James back to the farm the following day to meet the horses, and from there on in, our friendship was assured.

13

The Memoirs of Frannie Orchard.
1818
(Donor)

I think it was the very same night, or at least in the same week, of my meeting James, that Ghost came to me again. He found me, I confess, in rather a less than pleased to see him state of being.

'Did you lead James Orchard out into the marsh, Ghost?' I snapped, even as he came to take my hand. I avoided the touch, glaring at him.

Ghost eyed me carefully. 'Yes,' he confessed at last.

'Why?' I demanded, still furious.

'I was coming to see that you were home safely from the fair when he stumbled onto my path. I needed to drink and so I did. I did not expect the young idiot to run into the bog-land.'

'You nearly killed him!'

'That was not my intention. I cannot be held responsible for what happened to him, his own feet took him there.'

I stared in shock, anger and sorrow flooding me in equal parts. 'You really are a monster, aren't you?' I whispered.

'I have never denied what I am.'

We were both quiet for some time, and then I held out my arm to him. 'I suppose this is what you want,' I said quietly.

Ghost ran a finger over the vein there. 'No,' he said, 'I don't need to do that anymore, I don't think.'

I frowned and my hand trembled for a moment before I withdrew it. 'So why have you come?'

'To ensure you are well for your adventure, and to say goodbye to you.'

I paused again and wet my lips. As angry as I was, I did not want to say goodbye properly to Ghost.

'Goodbye?'

'Yes. I think whatever shade of myself I put into you is fading so there is no longer any need for my visits. You're not a child anymore, Frances, and only children have imaginary friends.'

'But you are not imaginary!'

'I hope that one day, I will at least seem that way to you. I'm sorry child, sorry for it all.'

'I'll be melancholy if you go!' I whispered, anger fading more so to be replaced by misery, 'I will miss you – you bring me an air of the unknown, proof that the world is not so drab and dull as it seems. Even when you merely lurk at corners and watch – yes, I see you there!'

'And that is all?'

'Yes,' I whispered. 'You are like some strange creature who appears from nowhere and yet you are…' I shrugged and smiled. 'You are… you could be… my friend.'

'Have you need of such a friend? In truth?'

For the very first time, I considered this creature before me not as a supernatural being, but as a person with their own emotions. I put a hand up and touched his arm.

'I have a need of you,' I said softly, 'dear old Ghost. How could I be without you now? You have been with me

The Black Marshes

since my childhood, you have protected me and given me a break from the dull mediocrity of life. I could not very well do without you now. Say you will still visit? Please?'

'How could I decline such a plea?' he said, placing a hand over mine. 'you remind me so much of... of my own daughter...'

'She is dead?'

'A long time since, yes.'

I smiled in a manner of sorrow, and squeezed his hand. 'might I ask a boon of you then?' I asked, 'as one who reminds you of somebody so dear?'

'Of course.'

'I'd rather you didn't... didn't drink from... from the people around here,' I finished.

'Why? They don't remember what I do afterwards, normally.'

'Because they are people. Because it's wrong.'

'Then to drink I'd have to go further afield, and take other people... are they lesser beings than your townsmen?'

'No... no I suppose not, it just feels so...'

'I know. It is a dilemma my people have faced for centuries. None of us want to be the attackers in the night. None of us wish to cause harm.'

'Then take it from me!' I said, holding out my wrist. 'I have plenty, and I am willing. Come to me when you are of a need, and take it – here – take some now!'

'No, no my little angel, you are very brave but I couldn't... not from you.'

'Surely that is better than attacking strangers... stealing from them and then blinding them to the memory of it?'

'I... I feed once a month or so. It would be too much for you ...'

'Then find others, find others who wold offer you the same,' I whispered. 'A donation, in exchange for curing ills, for gifting life where it is about to perish. You don't have to be a monster, Ghost. Be a guardian angel instead, just as you have been for me!'

Shakily I held my hand out to him again, he looked at it for a long time, but then pulled me into his arms and thrust his teeth into my throat. I gasped and my fingers stiffened into his hair. The pain was horrendous and I couldn't breathe. It was a terrifying experience, and one I have never forgotten, not in all the deeds I have committed since.

Ghost drank for a long moment, holding me prisoner in his grasp, and then pulled away again and looked down into my face. 'See what you are offering me? This is no fairytale, Frances, I can't do this to you! The feeding can never be beautiful!'

I shuddered, but pulled his head back to the flow of my blood. 'It is, though, when given in love! Take it,' I whispered, 'and then heal me.'

'To do so, I risk tainting you again, you already carry too much of my blood within you. It is fading now – I don't want to reignite that.'

'And if I care not that I carry such?'

'Then you are a fool.'

'A fool who loves you,' I whispered.

'A child who knows not what love is. Fine, come, I'll taste you and I'll heal you and I will pray to god that he will still take you when you die.'

His lips came back to my throat and there he suckled, drinking of the blood which poured free from my veins.

Here I must pause again, for in writing this, I risk running on over matters inconsequential. I could write for hours of how Ghost and I became closer, of how I became the very first of what your people now call "Donors" for my ghost. I could waffle on too, about James Orchard, and of how matters of the heart turned complicated as I realised I loved him and Ghost both, and how as I blossomed into womanhood, those feelings began to grow into urges I did not quite understand. I won't though, I am sure you get the gist of such! I will suffice to say that as time passed, Ghost and I grew closer, but also that a deep friendship was born between James Orchard and I. Within months James moved from the stranger next door, to being my constant companion. He'd come to visit with me most days and I came to love how he watched me with the horses, sitting on the fence whilst I got them all ready to be sold. He never commented on my attire, nor did he scold me for the danger of my pursuit, in fact, if anything he seemed to enjoy it, calling me *"Milady in Britches"* with shining eyes. Sometimes his brother, Henry, came too and whilst James was happy to sit and observe, Henry was more active and preferred to make himself useful, ducking to tighten the straps under the horses' bellies once I'd thrown the saddle on, grabbing at reins.

I suppose to those of you who have witnessed the angry little creature Henry – yes, that same man – has become, I suppose it is hard to imagine he could ever have been carefree and full of laughter, but once – in those early days – he truly was! Where James was handsome, his brother was fairer, with a hint of copper to his hair and a freckle or two over his nose but with a beaming grin and a nature of playfulness. God, the change in him is horrific.

Again, though, I digress! When the days were drawing to a close, James and sometimes Henry too would come and sup at the farm, or I and my family would go over to The Orchard Estate and dine there with Sir Richard, James, Henry and their older siblings: Josephina and Peter.

So it came to pass that one evening in late July, my father and I were invited to have supper at The Orchard Estate. This was not uncommon, nor was our finding of the family sat at cards in the living room upon our arrival. Other than James, the entire family seemed rather too fond of gambling to me, but then I supposed that that came of being born and bred in the city as opposed to the little town where they now resided. That evening, Peter and Josephina, James's elder siblings, were playing at the card table whilst Sir Richard sat watching. Father sat down at the card table with them, leaving James and I to talk.

'Beautiful evening, isn't it?' James said as I joined him by the window. 'I tell you, the sun never looks so beautiful in the city.'

'It will be setting soon.'

James smiled and took my hand, pulling me to the window to stand beside him.

'The sky will go pink, and then bright orange, purple and then finally dusk will fall.' I added, 'I love watching the sunset.'

'As do I. Especially here. We are so blessed Fran, you've never seen the ugly grey of London so you will never know how much so,' his fingers squeezed mine and I smiled up at him, my heart pounding. James's lips twitched as though he were about to speak but we were interrupted by Sir Richard's voice.

'James! Come and share a hand of cards with your brother and sister, I'm done for I'm afraid, and Henry's doubled this month's allowance already.'

James laughed but shook his head. 'And I will halve mine if I try to better him!'

'Mayhap, but then you could steal your sister's!' Sir Richard chuckled.

'We have no fourth though,' James still protested. 'We cannot play with three!'

'Frannie is good at cards,' my father interjected slyly.

I sighed, 'I do not wish to play!' I said, knowing I'd win again and not wanting to embarrass James who was a dreadful player.

James laughed though, perfectly at ease. 'It is a partner who is not good at cards that I need, Father!'

The Black Marshes

'Do play!,' Henry wheedled, coming to sit at the table. 'Come James, you and Frannie verses Phina and I?'

'I accept that challenge,' James said. 'At least I will have you to cover my hide, Henry, and Phina is a worse player than I.'

Both Father and Sir Richard came to sit beside the players too whilst Peter, the older brother, seemed to lose interest and left quietly. Sir Richard dealt the cards and, with a smile, I played the first move.

The cards flew about for twenty minutes, with much laughter and joking. With me sat opposite him, James's card playing improved immensely and I smiled to think that it must be his wish to impress my which spurred him on. James took Phina out with apparent ease and the girl laughed as I laid down my last card. I eyed Henry squarely across the table and within three moves, he too laughingly admitted defeat.

I raised my eyes to James's face and smiled. 'Just you and I then, Jamie?'

'Indeed, I hope you have enough coins,' he goaded but the words were obviously jest.

I just nodded and played a king of clubs; James played the ace and picked up the cards. The room went quiet and Henry moved so that he could look at both sets of cards, smirking as he looked from one player to the other.

'I think a wager is in order,' Sir Richard said, sitting back in his chair and lighting a cigar. 'I will of course have to back my boy to win, what about it Hodge?'

'Frannie, with ease!'

A flair of competitiveness grew up between the two men and I let my eyes flick between them, no longer looking at my cards.

'What is your wager, sir?' Sir Richard asked. 'Better make it worthwhile, because if you don't I'm going to take another of your fine horses!'

Father chewed his bottom lip, thoughtfully. 'How

about this,' he said. 'If my girl loses, you get your pick of my horses, but if she wins, Frannie gets the choice of your boys as her husband.'

I dropped my cards facedown onto the table, flushing bright red. 'Father!' I gasped, stunned by his impropriety but Sir Richard's eyes lit up. 'I think we can shake on that.'

I felt myself grow redder. I raised my eyes to James's face and saw his gaze burning into me. My face flushed, my hand shook and suddenly the last thing I wanted to do was to play the final three hands. Sir Richard surveyed me carefully and I blushed even brighter.

'Come, play your cards,' James said quietly and I nodded, picking them up. The room was very quiet. With a shaking hand, I played the eight of hearts. James pressed his lips together and then played a four.

'Surely you must have a better card?' I whispered.

Sir Richard smiled, 'Let my son play as he likes Frances,' he said, a hand on my arm. 'I think he is making a point here. Although, I confess, with James you never know.'

There was some polite laughter but I felt my skin pale even further. My hands shook so badly that I could barely hold the cards. My next two moves won the game easily and as I placed down my final card, James was forced to play his own, the Ace of Diamonds to my Ace of Hearts. I gasped and even James smiled at the omen which seemed to be present on the table.

Henry clapped his hands together slowly and Father sat back in his chair with a smile. 'I do believe I won our little wager,' he said.

Sir Richard laughed. 'Indeed. So, come on Fran? Which of my boys takes your fancy? I assure you, they have no choice but if you choose as I expect you to, I doubt we'll hear any arguments either!'

The room erupted with good-natured laughter but I stood up abruptly and, my composure gone, and fled from the room. Behind me, I could still hear my father's laughter.

The garden was dark, only the light from the lamps illuminating the vast lawns. I ran down to the hedge-surrounded flower garden at the back and sat, shaking with embarrassment and ire at my father for putting me into such a position, it was unkind, I thought angrily, unkind and foolish to tease me thus! My thoughts pulled to James, to his gentle smile and easy manner. Of course I was enamoured of him, any girl would be, but we were from different stations in life and it was cruel to taunt me in such a way.

The wind whistled past, and above me, I saw the clouds pulling across the sky, half covering the bright full moon. The weather was chill, very chill and I felt the heat of the tears as they spilled down my cheeks. The flower garden smelled heavenly and even as I sniffed in weeping, I smelled the mixture of heady perfumes. Angrily, I wiped my eyes and wrapped my arms about myself. I'd not picked up my shawl when I'd fled and was now regretting that as the cool air settled upon my skin making the goose-flesh stand.

The sound of footsteps came to my ear and I wished I could just disappear, not ready yet to face any member of the Orchard household, or my own for that matter. A shadow passed the hedge, then paused and James's face appeared around it.

'Frannie! Are you in there?'

In his hands, he carried my shawl and this he draped over my shoulders as he moved to sit beside me on the cold iron and wood bench. 'are you well, sweetheart?'

'No! Far from it. I hate my father, I hate him!'

James looked puzzled. 'Why?'

'For his teasing, thus! For making me look a fool in front of you... of your family.'

'Nobody made you look a fool,' James said, throwing

an arm about my shoulders. 'In fact, the only person who looked a fool was I, when you fled the room.'

I looked up at him, confused. 'You?'

'Yes, I, because now everybody thinks you don't want to marry me,' he said with amusement, his eyes twinkling.

'What?'

'I said, now you have made everybody believe you don't want to marry me, but everybody knows that I want to marry you, so I'd say I am the fool, not you?'

'You... what?' I couldn't take it in.

'I am starting to wonder that too... I suppose I am reading things all wrong and you don't wish to marry me after all, hmm?'

'No, no! Of course, I want to marry you Jamie, I ...' suddenly I trailed off, realising what I was saying.

'Well, we'd best get back inside then and let everybody know that, hmm? Else Henry at least will never let me live this down.'

I gaped at him, lost for words, and then suddenly a suspicion came upon me. 'You planned this?'

James dragged me to him, kissing my lips. 'Of course I didn't,' he said as he pulled away. 'But I already asked both your father and mine. They engineered this... this proposal... on the spot though. I was as shocked as you were, I assure you.'

'So, this is a proposal? You are asking me to marry you?'

'Yes.'

Happy shock caused my eyes to fill up with water once more. 'Then I accept.'

'I knew it!' James whispered and pulled me in for another kiss. 'I knew you loved me too.'

14

The memoirs of Frances Orchard
1818.
(2 months before the wedding.)

Fast forward some months. My wedding was all planned, all ready to go – dress purchased and cake tasted. Church booked and honeymoon to Venice planned. I, however, lay that night in the arms of he, my other love. Ghost stroked my hair out of my eyes. His own eyes were sad and I wondered if it were the upcoming wedding which troubled him so. I put a hand over his.

'Are you well? You seem melancholy,' I said.

'I am somewhat but it was always going to be this way. We both knew that this little tryst had a time limit on it.'

'It doesn't have to have…'

'And yet it does' he said, wiping the remainder of my blood from his lips. 'Just two months to go and then you will be Mrs Orchard.'

'It still seems so alien,' I agreed. 'Will I ever see you again? Once I am wed?'

'Do you wish it?'

'Yes,' the words were no lie, as much as I loved James, Ghost was my closest friend, a bond strengthened in the

Emma Barrett-Brown

months where I had been satiating his blood-lust with my fluids. I rested my face against his pulse, feeling my limbs tremble in his arms. My nightgown was pulled aside to bar my throat and breasts, hocked up my thighs for how my legs had wrapped about him, but despite how more than once he had kissed my mouth, Ghost never took more than that from me.

'You said once that you loved me,' he said, gently wiping away my blood and kissing my throat, 'Do you feel this still?' His words were strained and I looked into those hard, grey eyes, seeing there a flicker of emotion I'd never seen before.

'You are my dearest, most adored darling... my very best friend.'

Ghost held me tightly, 'if that is all, then yes – you will see me again, you to me are as dear as one of my own blood-children. I'll not forsake you if you don't want me to.'

I buried my face in his neck and hid my tears. Things would change, they must, but I was glad that I would not lose him entirely.

'Come,' Ghost said at last, 'Let me take you home?'

I nodded and stood, wiping away the blood with a rag before buttoning my nightgown and taking Ghost's hand.

The following evening, I made my way up to the house which was soon to become my home. James greeted me with the usual kiss to my cheek and then led me inside. The family were playing cards again but I abstained, having felt the brunt of losing all my coins to Henry's sly playing style on more than one occasion. Instead, I sat and took to advising James on which cards to play, much to Henry's chagrin. Josephina and Peter sat on the other side of the room; both of them had already given up at trying to play cards against Henry and I, and were calmly conversing over glasses of wine. Sir Richard sat in his chair looking

The Black Marshes

out at his children, a smile on his pinched face.

'There, and Jamie and I win again!' I laughed, picking a card out from James's fan and placing it on the table.

Henry laughed and conceded the point. 'Again!' He exclaimed. 'Fran, I think I am going to have to ban you from playing cards.'

Together the three of us laughed, I was rather fond of Henry, and he of I. It was a pleasant feeling, a comfortable omen for the future. Henry took the deck and began to deal again, his slender fingers touching mine as he did so, causing him a smile. I smiled in return, I was well aware of Henry's little attraction to me and I never minded it. He was just a boy, in truth.

Henry dealt the next hand, pointedly putting the cards before me rather than James, and then picked up his own. We were interrupted, though, by a knock at the door.

'That'll be Father, I wager,' I said.

James squeezed my hand, I beamed up at him and for a moment we both sat grinning, then James laid a soft kiss on my forehead. Henry groaned good-naturedly and I blushed.

The door to the parlour opened and I looked up with a smile, ready to greet my father. I was surprised then when instead of his appearance, the butler stood there alone. 'A stranger sir,' he said to Sir Richard. 'Begs an audience.'

James made to stand, but his father ushered him to sit and went out of the door.

'How very queer,' Henry said easily. 'Will be some beggar I bet. Wanting charity or the like.'

'Mayhap,' James said absently, then. 'Frannie, I do feel I am ready to challenge you again at a few hands. If you will?'

I nodded and at once the strangeness of the situation was broken up as the family began to chatter again.

Five minutes later, the door opened again to reveal the stranger. The man was soaked through, his hair matted to his head and his clothing stuck to his thick frame.

'Hello?' Henry said warily and Phina moved a little closer to Peter. James took my hand in his but he didn't move, just stayed sat where he was at the card table.

Sir Richard came in behind the man. 'Err, yes,' he stumbled over his words, seeming somewhat confused. 'Let me... let me introduce you to my family. That there is Henry and beside him is Phina, they are my youngest two. Peter is the one in the corner and at the card table is James, my eldest and his betrothed, Frances Hodge.'

'Charmed,' the man said, removing his hat.

'Erm, hello?' James said uncertainly but I was well aware that the stranger's eyes were boring into me.

'My name is Parsons,' the man said, handing his hat to the butler hovering at his arm. 'I was caught in the storm and your father here was good enough to offer me shelter.'

There was something wrong with the man, I couldn't put my finger on it but all of my senses were screaming at me. I wished suddenly for Ghost. This man was like him, I realised, that strange ethereal feeling that I only ever got from him. My hands trembled and I was sure I saw the man smile.

'Come on in then,' James said, standing. 'Dry yourself by the fire, friend,' he seemed not to see the danger and I wanted to scream out to be careful. The man smiled and took the indicated chair. He wasn't quite like my ghost, I realised, my senses were honed to Ghost and I was sure I'd recognise another of his kind but there was something about the man regardless, something which chilled the very marrow of my bones.

The man sat for a few moments drying his scraggly hair and I began to feel uncomfortable in his gaze, twice it seemed as though he was sniffing me too, discretely but definitely. I cowered back into James's embrace and he looked down at me, surprise in his eyes.

'Are you all right Fran?' he asked softly.

The Black Marshes

I shook my head, 'I think I... I think I am going to have to leave,' I whispered.

James frowned and drew me out into the corridor whilst his father began to chat to the stranger. 'What is it?' he asked, kissing my forehead.

'I don't know Jamie, I don't know, I... I...'

Before I could continue, a crash sounded in the drawing room. James and I both stared in shock at the door, Josephina screamed and Sir Richard's voice was distinctly audible, exclaiming in shock.

'What the devil?' James frowned and moved back to re-enter the parlour, only to find the door closed. 'Father!' he called, pushing at the door but there was no response.

Another clatter came from within, and then a smashing sound. I stood trembling in the corridor, not sure whether to run or to stay. James rattled the door again but the old wood refused to budge. He looked at me, his features frightened, almost as though he expected me to know what to do. Then Josephina screamed again and James's paralysis broke. Moving back a few paces, he ran and threw himself against the door. More crashes from within and then Henry's cry.

James ran against the door again, his face terrified. 'Father! Henry!' he called, throwing his whole weight against the door again and again.

'James!' it was Josephina's voice, high pitched and frightened and then suddenly, the sound of tearing and splintering and the door flew open under James's weight.

I felt my knees going weak and even James recoiled. The stranger was gone, but in the middle of the room stood a huge beast. Its shape was that of a wolf but it was monstrously large. Its muzzle showed large, sharp fangs and its eyes glowed bright silver, unearthly. Its muzzle was covered in blood and I saw at once where the blood had come from: Sir Richard lay dead at the creature's feet. Peter too was slumped at an odd angle and I could see that

Henry was cowering behind the sofa, Phina in his arms. I screamed and recoiled as the creature's head swung upwards to look at me.

'Oh god...' I whispered as the animal began to pad closer, sniffing the air. James threw me behind him and it was him the animal stuck as it leapt.

I screamed and ran. There was only one person who could help now and I had to get to him. The animal knocked James flying and sprinted after me. In a panic, I fled through the front door and slammed it on the creature's nose. It screamed aloud and withdrew. I fled out, running down the path screaming for Ghost. I had no idea if he was even close by, but I didn't know what else to do. My feet found the path down into the marshes and, not caring how dangerous it was, I fled that way, still screaming for Ghost. My panicked mind put the creature just behind me. In my mind, it was gaining, and snapping at my heels but in truth the countryside behind me was silent. At last, I felt the sting of cold water on my ankles as I waded into the marsh.

'Ghost,' I cried out again, but this time it was more of a sob than a cry of terror. I'd left Jamie behind, I realised with a pounding, heavy heart. I'd gone and left him for dead. As the waters passed my knees, I realised my danger and stumbled back, onto the path. With a wail, I fell to my knees and began to cry, my hands over my face. A rustle came from behind me, the splash of somebody or something coming closer, through the still waters. I stumbled back to my feet, ready to run again, but then, within me somehow, a voice called my name. Ghost's voice. I fainted.

15

Frances Orchard, 2016

Frannie's writing was interrupted by a knock on the bedroom door. For a moment, it was difficult to pull free from the sea of memories, but then she blinked and called to whoever was there to come in. The door clicked open and Ella entered, mobile phone in hand which she at once offered to Frannie. Frannie glanced at the clock to see it was gone midnight. Mystified, she took the phone from Ella and put it to her ear.

'Hello?'

'Frannie?' it was William.

'William? What's up?'

'Just missed your voice.'

Frannie felt a strange feeling begin in her gut and work its way through her body. She smiled, how strange to have such a feeling when she had just been writing of her and James in the early years. He'd once made her tingle too, although now he'd been gone for so long that Frannie could barely remember his face.

'Frannie?'

'Yes, sorry I… I miss you too. Sorry, I'm not used to

these things.'

Ella smiled and stepped back out, mouthing that she'd be in Frannie's room when they were done talking. Frannie nodded.

'You never had a mobile before, huh?'

'No, just phones in general! I wasn't... wasn't allowed.'

'Oh.'

'It's nice to hear your voice though.'

'And yours.'

The conversation was at risk of going in circles but then William asked about the memoir.

'It's coming along,' Frannie replied. 'I think... I'm probably writing too much but I am allowing it to flow as I remember it.'

'I don't think you can write too much, to be honest.'

'Unnecessary detail about things which don't matter... I...' Frannie broke off. 'Remembering, I suppose, but it's difficult because I am trying to remember people who are better off left locked away, painful memories, and at the same time, whose faces I barely remember.'

'I understand, sometimes those are the hardest.'

'You...' Frannie broke off, not wanting to mention his dead wife over the phone. 'I suppose you do understand,' she finished lamely. 'What of you? How fares the trip?'

'Sam was out when we arrived, he just got in a little while ago but now Hugh is running. This is how these things can take a few days. Hopefully we'll meet properly tomorrow to hash this out. I hope to be back by tomorrow night though. I don't like leaving you there alone.'

'It's well hidden and well-guarded here, as you said.'

'I know but still...'

Frannie smiled and allowed herself to begin to relax. William's voice was bringing her firmly back to the present, and with it, the image of him, his warmth and his big heart. Suddenly she really did miss him.

'It will be good to have you back,' she said, 'I... I look

forward to your company, sweet wolf.'

William was very quiet for so long that Frannie looked at the display to ensure the phone was still connected. When finally, he spoke, it was a little choked up.

'And I miss your company too, sweetheart, very much so. My bed will feel empty tonight. Goodnight Frannie.'

'Goodnight, William.'

A click and then a buzz as the line went dead. For a long moment, Frannie stared at the now blank phone, her heart pounding, and then slipped out of William's room to find Ella next door. The little blond woman was looking out of the window, a little wistful.

'Here, thank you,' Frannie said.

'It was good to speak with him?'

'It was.'

'I can empathise. Hugh and I often fall asleep with this little device still connected. After hundreds of years apart, it seems silly but I can't go a night without him.'

Frannie paused, Ella, who had had trouble hiding her dislike at first, now seemed to be opening up a little. It made her more cautious than anything.

'It must be difficult, with him being so much in danger so often?'

'It is and yet I know there is little which can harm Hugh. He has survived so much. Your husband was something of a shock to him, he is not often bested.'

'Henry isn't my husband,' Frannie corrected, 'He is my husband's brother... my husband, my James, was a sweet and kind man. He's dead.'

'I'm sorry, what happened?'

Finally, it was a relief to say it. 'Hugh, actually, Hugh killed him, back in 1912. He was... he was a part of a nest, like I was, which did bad things. We didn't... didn't know... but that didn't save him. I only survived because Henry pulled me free and dragged me to freedom, otherwise he would have killed me too.'

Ella pursed her lips, her grey eyes darkened slightly.

'1912, you say?'

'Yes.'

'The Orchards?'

'Yes.'

'I… never mind. No wonder you were frightened of us, then.'

Frannie nodded. 'I have been writing it all down, William said that was your idea. I will hand it to you, when it's done, to give to your husband. I hope that my regret is apparent in the pages I write.'

Ella nodded and then glanced back out of the window. 'You have… have my condolences, for your loss,' she said.

Frannie nodded, then spoke words she was dreading, especially to speak to Ella who disliked her kind so intently. 'Ella, I… I have to…'

'To drink?'

'Yes. How is it… I mean, I don't know…'

'Sam has what he calls donors, willing humans who donate their blood to him. There are two of them living here currently, feeding the drinkers who come by. You could probably ask one of them nicely tomorrow?'

'I could…'

'You are urgent?'

'I am.'

Ella took in a deep breath, and then let it out and held out her wrist. 'Take some from me, then.'

'What… oh, god, no – I couldn't!'

'You can and you will. I've been drunk from before, so I know it's possible. Hugh wouldn't approve, I'm sure, but then Hugh isn't here…'

Frannie moved forward a few steps and took Ella's wrist in her hand. Still she paused, though. 'This isn't some test? If I drink am I then homeless once more, and without friends?'

'That is not the way of it here, Frannie, no…'

'I don't want to…'

'Just take it, you won't hurt me, Frances, and I am safer to drink from whilst you are het up.'

Frannie nodded, conceding. That at least was the truth. She took in another deep breath and then as gently as she could, she bit into Ella's wrist. The wolf exhaled sharply but did not pull away as Frannie drank a few mouthfuls of the rich, thick blood. She'd never allowed a wolf's blood to taint her lips before, and it was rich and sweet. Nectar.

'Oh,' she said, moving away, 'it tastes…'

'I don't want to know how my blood tastes,' Ella said, icy once more. 'It will tide you over until tomorrow when you can feed properly.'

Frannie drank again, feeling the wound healing even as she did so. She didn't have it in her to bite again and so pulled away.

'I will never in whatever is left of my long life, forget how kind you have been to me, Ella Haverly,' Frannie whispered, humble. 'Thank you so much for… for everything.'

Ella's expression thawed again somewhat, although her eyes remained guarded. 'You are welcome, now go – finish that book for me as a thank you.'

Back in William's room, Frannie sat back down on the bed and allowed William's scent to come to her, to soothe her. The thought of what was next to record was daunting, but it had to be done. She could skip some, she realised, those early days meant little, really, it was what came later which would tell Hugh and his brother all they needed to know.

16

The memoirs of Frances Orchard
1821,
(3 years later)

The rain was falling as I disembarked from the train. I had been travelling for over an hour. My legs felt stiff and sore from being cramped in the same position for so long and my whole body was damp with perspiration from my confinement in the dusky and hot carriage near the front of the train. In my hands, I carried a basket which contained three items: a bunch of flowers which my employer had given me leave to pick, a fresh baked pound-cake for my father, and my coin purse.

I sighed as I stepped down onto the platform of the little train station at my home-town, the place where it had all happened. Even the sight of the station filled me with sorrow. I straightened my basket and then stepped out from under the old tin roof and into the rain. It always seemed to rain on the moors, cold dreary and windy with rain that was so cold it felt like it was cutting through you like a knife. My heart was heavy too, as it always was on that date: the twenty-seventh of November – the

The Black Marshes

anniversary of the day, three years earlier that my life had fallen apart. I'd not been back since the last anniversary and the memories threatened to flood me as I looked about at the sleeping town. To prevent them I began to walk, ignoring the rain pouring down onto the bonnet which hid my bright white hair, hoping nobody would see me.

As I walked the short distance from the station to the outskirts of the town, I was irritated to see heads turn in my direction. I fidgeted busily with my basket a moment to calm my nerves and then glanced about, forcing myself to smile and acknowledge the people who stopped to stare. There were always stares when I came home. One old man even nodded his head and called out a hello. I nodded back but did not stop. Ever since the murders at The Orchard Estate, and then the subsequent killing of my sisters, the local people had looked upon me with pity. My fiancé had disappeared, my sisters were gone, my horses were gone and my father had become bankrupt six months later, lost in a bottle of whiskey.

Almost as bad as the pity, were the curious stares of the people who remembered the attack, the people who knew that I had been there. In the aftermath of the disaster, before I had left, I had constantly found that voices ceased when I entered a shop, eyes turning to me and of course, taking in my bright white hair. It had been that way since it'd happened, robbed of all its pigment overnight. My father was a drunk, almost insane, and I couldn't blame him, not after what he had witnessed when the creature finally had bounded up to the house. Not after he witnessed the slaughter of his children. Sometimes I found myself amazed that I wasn't lost in the bottle with him, despite that Ghost had saved me from witnessing the worst of the horrific deeds.

I was drenched by the time I arrived at the run-down old

Emma Barrett-Brown

house which had once been the most well-known and respected horse-farm for miles around. The tired creaky old farm building which sat squat and broken amongst the weeds of the yard was now a ruin, a ghost of the rustling, busy hive of activity it had once been. The empty fields held nothing but the broken memory of the horses which were dead and gone, the echo of a whinny and the long-dead peal of girlish laughter from my sisters. I heard in my mind the bark of the old farm-dog, the sound of my father's voice shouting for the hound to be quiet, never knowing that the bark was in response to my sister's baiting. Even as I approached, I missed the sound of my horses bellowing, of their hooves on the path. 'The Ranch,' as my father had once called it with such pride, was now nothing but an overgrown wreck. Weeds poked up even through the driveway and I guessed that my father owned no carriage or trap anymore. As I walked, wave upon wave of sorrow washed over me. I never understood why my father stayed there. He lived alone now, the workers who had quickly abandoned ship after the slaughter. Superstitious to the last declaring the place haunted and cursed. Perhaps it was. I wiped away a tear and then, with a sigh, pushed open the creaking farmhouse door and entered the house that had once been my home.

Inside, the farmhouse was neglected too. Food lay out on the kitchen counter and I was surprised it hadn't drawn rats since it had obviously been there some time. My father sat huddled in his chair in the corner by the fire, seemingly obvious to the decay around him. I wasn't surprised, it was his normal place. Outside, the wind was whipping up and I felt almost on the verge of tears to remember how my sisters had once run around in the wind, pulling the horses indoors to ensure that they were safe in case of a real storm. I dismissed the memory, it was too painful.

'Fran,' my father said with a weak smile as he looked up and noticed me loitering in the doorway, he looked frail

The Black Marshes

and secretly I wondered where the big, beefy old man I'd once worshipped had gone. He looked gaunt, emaciated and ill.

'Hello Father,' I murmured. 'How are you today?'

I took one of the hard kitchen chairs which Lillian, Jane and I had picked out in a different lifetime and set it down next to the fireplace.

'Much the same,' he said quietly. 'I sold another acre last month so there's good whiskey on the counter, if you're wanting a drink.'

'Is there water?'

'In the well…'

I set my lips but took the whiskey bottle and poured myself a small tot. As I did so, my father's aged hand came out from under the blanket he was huddled in and tapped his own glass. I filled it grimly, right to the top. I knew that he'd drink a full glass or more over the next hour, and he did.

After an hour of stilted and uncomfortable conversation with my father, I replaced my bonnet and cape and set off out again, leaving the cake on the side where I knew it would eventually go stale. The Orchard Estate was a ten-minute walk from my father's house, less if you took the mire road but I didn't. Too many memories would have flooded me there, both good and bad.

After the attack, Ghost had taken James and Henry away, Phina too. The others had been dead before he'd got there. More deaths on my conscience; if he'd not paused to protect me, to take me to the safety of his own house, he might have saved them, or at least some of them. The creature had taken every life in its path. Servants, family, even Phina's little dog: Cinnamon. It had slaughtered everything in its path before finding its way from the house and down onto the road. On the way up to my home, it had slaughtered two others, a traveller on the road and an old lady who was outside in the garden of her own cottage. I will never really understand what it was which drew the creature up to my home, but I can only presume it followed my scent.

As I lay in an unnatural sleep, hidden away in the damp basement of Ghost's little house, the creature had murdered my sisters, my horses, two of the workmen, and then it had vanished into the marshes where it had met with Ghost, and, he assured me, he had killed it. He had returned to me in the aftermath, covered in blood and frantic with anger and worry. There he'd pulled me into his arms and whispered a thousand apologies, for what, I did not understand. He kissed my face, kissed away my tears as he explained that he'd been too late to save my family, and most of James's. Then he'd taken me home to my father and the authorities. The following day, he'd vanished with what remained of the Orchard family. Three days later, I'd received a letter from James saying he was gone for good, and that he loved me but he couldn't stay. It took me almost a year to realise that Ghost too was 'gone for good'.

In my nostalgic rumination, I walked in a manner almost dreamlike up to the house, pausing only at the little church to lay down my flowers upon the graves of three little girls. After the church, the Orchard Estate was only a few minutes' walk and so I stood in quiet contemplation outside of the once-beautiful house. I wondered silently what would happen to the old place now. It had been three years and still the house stood empty. The locals shunned the place, they said it was haunted, and who could blame them – it was a prime location to house ghosts. James and Henry had been gone for so long that I could not believe that they would ever return… and why would they? They had lost their entire family there in what the local authorities had put down as a horrendous wild animal attack. Only I knew the truth behind the attack, only I and those others who had survived it, and none of us was

The Black Marshes

contradicting that story. The old bricks were crumbling into decay at an alarming rate, weeds poking up through the path and one window was broken on an upper floor where an unruly wind had blown the bough of an ancient tree though the pane.

With a sigh, I turned to leave, wondering a little why I still came here every year. Was it still for the missing of them? Perhaps more for morbid curiosity or some kind of strange obligation? I knew I should leave but always lingered that ache, that hope.

In silence, I began to make my way back down the pathway but then suddenly an unusual noise caught my attention. Wheels clattering up the driveway, the sound of hooves. For a moment I stood completely still, certain it was a ghost from the past, that somehow the long-lost dead members of the Orchard family had returned from beyond the grave to chastise me for my uninvited visitations to their house. Then I saw the carriage turning the corner and my fears dissolved. The vehicle was black and very grand, but also very modern. In shock, I stood stock-still in my position by the front entrance and watched curiously to see who would alight. Was James finally selling the house – or at least letting it out to someone new?

The carriage pulled up with a cloud of dust. The four horses at its front seemed to have been driven hard and all had foam at their mouths. I watched in some strange dream-like state as the door of the carriage opened and then my heart almost stopped to see James himself alight from it. A strangled gasp pulled free of my lips, strange lights flickered behind my eyes and in extreme shock, I swayed. At first, James didn't see me and I watched speechlessly as he stood and straightened his clothing. Then he looked up.

For a moment, we just stood staring at each other and his expression of shock mirrored mine exactly. I went to speak, but my throat was too dry, my words too fragmented. James's chest heaved.

'James?' I managed but then the door at the other side of the carriage opened and there was Henry as well, followed by Josephina – a family of ghosts.

Henry too gaped at me for a moment and I saw a concerned eye flitter to his brother's face before he spoke. 'Frannie?' He asked. There was surprise in his tone, but happy surprise.

James still seemed frozen in place, unable to speak – his eyes drinking me in.

'Henry, James,' I finally managed to speak again. 'Phina... what are you doing here?'

'Well, one might ask the same of you,' Henry said, but his tone was friendly.

Josephina was the next to break through the shock and I grinned as she ran to me and took my hands in hers. 'Dear Frances! Dear girl!' she said and then I was embraced.

'Frannie!' Finally, James's voice. He was ashen; I had never seen him look so shaken.

'James!' I said and pulled away from Josephina to go to him. He took my hands in his, rather in the same way that his sister had moments before, but he held my fingers tightly, almost painfully.

'Is this real? Or are you some evil spirit come to torment me? Your hair... my darling...' His eyes shone, glowed with a strange light as he looked upon me with concern. Henry took my arm and almost pulled my away from his brother.

'Don't mind him Frances, he will get over the shock in a moment... and what odd coincidence that we should meet you here on our first ever trip home, but then, I suppose it is not so strange – we are, after all, here for the same reasons. Three years! Three long *bloody* years.'

Phina flashed him a look, 'Henry!' she growled and I

The Black Marshes

sensed a warning in her tone.

'Indeed. Three long years indeed.'

James's hand gripped my arm again and, unable to bear it any longer, I embraced him.

'My god,' he murmured into my hair. 'I am sorry Frannie. I just didn't expect you to be here. I thought I was seeing a ghost of my own past when I stood up and saw you there with your white hair and your pale face…'

Behind, I saw that Henry had discretely taken his sister by the arm and led her up to the entrance of the house

'Are you home to stay?' I asked at last.

'Yes, Frannie, we are… for a time at least.'

'I see,' I nodded, but then bitterness crept into my tone. 'And you did not think to contact me? To tell me you were coming home?'

'I did, oh darling, I did. We were going to settle in first though, and then come and get you, if you wanted to come…'

'Truly?'

'Truly. Henry, well, all of us thought it might be better to face the demons alone… just for now but… oh Frannie…'

'I don't understand! I have missed you so! Not a word or even a letter to tell me that you were well, that you missed me? Do you understand how very much that has hurt me?'

James had the decency to look bashful, but he held fast to my hand without reply.

'Will you come in, Frannie?' Henry asked, returning to James's side. 'You were a part of that night too. Do you also have demons to exorcise?'

'I can't,' I whispered. 'I can't… not now! This is too much of a shock to begin with, let alone walking through the rooms where…' I paused, seeing a strange glance go between Henry and James. 'I have to go soon, actually. I work as a maid in a house ten miles by train, I need to get back…'

James shook his head, shock and displeasure showed in his eyes. 'Don't go back,' he said. 'I am home now. I have heard a little of your circumstance and you do not need to demean yourself so anymore. Stay here, stay with me.'

'James,' I whispered, 'I don't think I can…'

'Frannie,' James's voice changed, his jaw tightened, 'Please… consent to stay,' he said again.

Henry stepped forwards too and something in his eye began to make me feel wary. I stepped back but Henry's fingers gripped my shoulder hard and pulled me towards him.

'Stop!' I demanded, beginning to feel afraid and looked to James. His features were miserable but he did not move to intercede.

'Stop, I'm not staying!' my voice was pitched and frightened but Henry was immobile.

'I'm afraid we're going to have to insist,' he said.

17

The memoirs of Frances Orchard
1821
(the day I died)

The inside of the house was musty and damp. I could smell it even through my fear. Henry's grip was vice-like as he drew me into the darkness, into the house which still bore the bloodstains of the dead. I struggled and tried to wriggle free of his grasp, but he held me too tightly.

'Let me go!' I whispered, shocked, digging my nails into his fingers but then I froze. Henry's face began to change, just like Ghost's. My heart raced and pounded so desperately it almost stilled my breathing.

'Don't struggle,' Henry commanded softly, 'or else this will hurt.'

'James!' I screamed, 'James!' but James was unmoving without, leaving me alone with his brother.

'James!'

'James has not the gumption for this, but he knows it to be for best. He won't interrupt – hush now.'

I gasped, struggled and tried to pull away again, tears of terror trailing down my face. What had my ghost done? What madness was now occurring? Surely Ghost didn't know of this? Surely James wouldn't allow it? Again I screamed, calling out James's name in my terror. Henry's eyes filled with that same strange light, glowing silver in the candle-light. His lips moved into a smile, showing me his teeth. They had become long, sharper and pointed and I was sure his jaw had shifted slightly to accommodate them. The canines were the largest, although all of the front teeth seemed to have become sharper too, like cat's teeth.

'Your ghost gave me this gift,' Henry whispered, impounding my terror, 'and now I pass it on to you, darling Frannie.'

'Oh god,' I whispered, 'Oh Henry no!'

Henry lifted me and carried me to the sofa despite my struggles. The hand which held the top of my body roped around under my hair and clasped over my lips. I struggled in his arms and as he lay me down I almost got free. Quickly he pulled himself on top of me, pinning me down with his legs. For a moment, the look in his eye changed and I thought he might try to kiss me, but he didn't and the softening was gone, replaced again by the hard silver gleam. I tried to struggle and scream again but his hand came over my mouth, pinching, as gently he stroked my face with the other.

'Frances, you will thank me for this one day – even if you hate me now. Just try to remember that what I am about to do will tie you to me… to my brother for eternity,' he said gently, brushing my hair out of her eyes, 'Now be shush, and be still. You won't be able to move for a while, and I will have to drain the blood from you which will hurt, but the pain will be fleeting only, I promise.'

At his softly spoken words, I felt my body slump, my lips parted but I could not speak, fear paralysing me. Henry nodded and then put his lips to my skin, his fingers pulled at my gown as his teeth broke through the skin of my throat, making my blood flow. His lips made slurping noises where he suckled, and the sound of that was enough to release tears from my eyes. A warm trickle escaped him and I could felt the tickle as it spilled down over my shoulder. Almost absently, his lips moved down to the top of my breast and there he bit again, his fingers caressing my hips and lower body like a lover. My blood splattered onto his fringe but he paid it no heed as he stole my life fluid. Gradually I felt all of my energy leaving me and when he released me, I slumped back, unable to move. My terror was mounting but there was nothing I could do; my limbs lay still and my vision was blurring. Still I gasped for oxygen but in my heart, I realised the truth, recognised it from a childish memory of Ghost; I was dying.

'Just a few moments of pain my dear,' Henry smiled down at me, 'And then I will make everything all right again. I know what I am doing and you are half one of us already. Stop fighting Frannie, just accept it.'

I could feel myself blacking out. I felt a touch on my face and heard Henry say something else but I could not make out the words, then he lifted my hand and put his teeth to the pounding vein there, tearing open the flesh and letting the blood pump free. Tears ran from my eyes unbidden and he saw them,

'Come now, shush! You will thank me later for this, I promise,' he soothed, running a hand down my cheek, and then his lips were back at my wrist, suckling the last drops from my body.

Even as I slipped from consciousness, James voice echoed back to me, just one sentence.

'Is it time?'

'Yes, come,' Henry replied, 'she's very nearly dead.'

Then oblivion.

My first thought as I opened my eyes was that the room was too bright. My second was that I didn't feel very well.

I caught the scent of James, and then felt the arms about me where he held me close to him. He was asleep but sitting up on the edge of the bed where somebody had dragged me after I'd died. I was disoriented, the events of the previous day still a little hazy, a little lost. I murmured and tried to sit up, a million little sensations stirring my broken body.

James muttered as I moved and I saw his eyes open.

'Hello Fran,' he whispered. 'Are you awake?'

I was so dizzy I couldn't speak. The world spun, my eyes hurt and every sound seemed deafening, even under the rush of the sound of my blood in my ears. I made a strange whimpering noise in my throat, reaching out for James again.

'Horrible isn't it… but don't worry, it's just a part of the change. Once you are fed, you will feel better. Come here Frannie, let me hold you. I will make this better – I promise.'

My limbs were shaking but I pulled myself close to his chest, frightened and unhappy. His heartbeat was immense, a dull but heavy pounding by my ear. Thud, thud, thud, thud, and then I realised I could hear more, the sound of his very blood flowing in and out of that beautiful organic pump.

James stroked my hair. 'Come on,' he said at last. 'Come and feed. Don't worry sweetheart, I won't let you kill. Henry left some sustenance downstairs for us. All this strangeness will go away once you are satiated.'

James unwrapped my trembling form from about his chest and stood me on trembling legs with tenderness. He moved to the end of the bed and pulled out a white cotton shirt which he threw to me. 'Put this on,' he ordered.

I nodded. I had not even noticed my still-torn dress until then. Trembling, I pulled the shirt over my head and James took my hand, leading me from the room. Together we walked down the stairs of the empty house and into the kitchen. In the milk larder was a jug of something and this he took and handed to me.

'This is what your body needs,' he said. 'Drink.'

My trembling fingers shook violently as he handed me the jug. 'What is it?' I managed my first words since awakening.

'Blood.'

'Blood?'

'Yes.'

Tears ran down my face as I put the jug to my lips, James obviously saw them but didn't comment. The crimson fluid was a salve to my wounds. I expected it to taste foul but it didn't, it was sweet and coppery. Greedily I drank of the life-fluids until James took the jug from me.

'There,' he said. 'You should start to feel more yourself now.'

I nodded. I could feel my mind strengthening already. James took a long swallow of what was left in the jug and then put it down on the table. The return of my clarity was abrupt and with it, it brought back the memories of what had happened to me. As I remembered my death, I felt my skin go cold.

James was at my side at once, pulling me close as I began to tremble. 'It's all right,' he soothed. 'It will be all right.'

'How?' I sobbed but he didn't reply.

James turned my body and walked me back up the stairs to the chamber where I'd awoken. I was sobbing painfully, gasping, and instead of going to the bed, I simply slumped down onto the floor. James sat beside me, his fingers stroking my hair and his voice murmuring soft comfort.

'You stay with me now,' James said with the ghost of a smile. 'Henry might have been the instigator but I sired you too, that makes me your protector in my eyes. I said I will marry you, and I meant it Frannie, nothing changes.'

I was about to speak again, to ask more of what I now was, when the sound of a door below made me start sharply again.

'It's all right,' James soothed. 'It's only Henry and Phina.'

I felt the anger building again at the mention of James's brother but I quashed it, waiting to see what would unfold.

Footsteps on the stair, and then a rattle of a door handle. Then the bedroom door opened and there he stood.

'Ah, you're awake?' Henry smiled.

'I am.'

Phina appeared behind her younger brother, pushing him into the room to pass him and come to my side. 'Frannie!' she smiled, taking my hand, and I noticed at once that the smile seemed more genuine than it had been. 'Oh Frannie, you look well. I take it you've fed?'

'She has,' James said. 'I gave her the jug you left.'

'Good, good,' Henry smiled and threw himself down on the bed. He still looked like a boy of seventeen or eighteen years but already I could see the changes the blood had forced upon him, his eyes looked deeper, older.

'Why did you do this?' I asked Henry

'Consider it a gift to you both.'

'My life was nobody's gift to give but my own.' I snapped. 'How dare you presume anything otherwise?'

Henry sat up to view me, disbelief written on his features. 'You're angry with me too?' he asked, surprised and strangely downhearted. 'Why? I have given you only what was already growing within. What is there to be angry about?'

'You have made me a monster! An abomination!'

'You become accustomed to the drinking,' Phina said, patting my arm. 'I hated it too when it happened but it's just what it is… you learn to cope.'

'I don't want to learn to cope,' I snapped, but then,

seeing the hurt on Phina's face, I forced myself to soften. What Henry had done was done and there was nobody to blame but him. I had no right to be rude to Phina.

'I'm sorry, I'm just… overwhelmed.'

'I can imagine,' Phina smiled. Then looked up at her brothers. 'So, what happens now?' she asked. 'We've broken our sire's one golden rule. We'll have to leave here I suppose?'

'I suppose so,' Henry said. 'As soon as possible I'd say. If Ole Ghost finds out what we did...'

'Let me stop you there,' James interrupted quietly. 'I have a wedding to plan first. If Ghost comes, he comes. We can explain something to him…'

Both Henry and Phina stared at him in surprise. 'What?' Henry finally managed.

'I am not just going to snatch Fran away like this,' James said quietly. 'I'm going to honour her properly and marry her. Then we wait for Ghost and we explain.'

Henry laughed aloud. 'If you say so, brother.'

'Best plan the wedding for a cloudy day,' Phina added.

James's lips pulled into a slight smile which he tried to repress. 'I think late afternoon in the winter would be best, don't you?' he said with a nod.

And so it was done. I cannot pause any longer to describe what it was to be newly fledged. I cannot bear to consider the terrible deeds which I committed in those early years, either. The blood in the jug, that was my father's you see, fed to me by Henry, over months, whilst that man lay bound in our cellar. That was the first atrocity, as was my eventual murder of that man. I killed then, like the others did, and I fed as I wished. It was not until later, much later, that I began to question what I was, and if we really needed to behave as we did. Ghost never returned either. No-one knew, or at least would ever tell me, where he went and I half-believe that Henry killed him, thus their return. If not, then he forsook me, after the attack on my home, forsook us all. I leave this chapter here, then, and I move the tale forwards by a hundred years. I cannot bear to remember, thus to tell you, of how I finally claimed my husband, in every way, but I will tell you how I lost him, for that is more pertinent, if indeed it breaks my heart again to tell it.

18

William Craven,
2016

William lay himself down in the hard, unfamiliar bed and put his head down on the pillow. The scent of washing powder clung to the white cotton fibres, strong enough to burn through his changer sinuses. *How do the changers who live here bear this day in day out?* he wondered, frustrated by insomnia. His phone lay on the dresser in case of a call or text but knowing Frannie had no phone of her own and was probably too timid to borrow, he wasn't hopeful. That's if she would text at all… why would she want to do that? She wasn't feeling this burning attraction like he was – or was she? Their conversation earlier had been strained, but despite that she had seemed pleased to receive the call. Maybe she did like him too? William found a smile on his lips to think of her. He'd not had "the hots" for a girl since Rosa had died… had never thought to either, but it was hitting him hard now. He glanced at the clock on the mantle, nearly 2am. Well, she was a drinker, she was probably still up. She didn't have a phone of her own though, and if he woke Ella up again, she'd be pissed.

'Just go to sleep, old man,' he told himself, speaking aloud, 'you'll see the lass again tomorrow, you soft old git.'

That was if he could actually get both Haverly brothers in one place long enough to discuss the Orchard problem, he thought, frustration building again. They really were hopeless, and yet they'd run this operation for years, just the two of them. William sighed again and glanced back at the clock. Two minutes since last he had looked. This was going to be a long night. He forced himself to close his eyes, but wasn't surprised when the image of her face appeared behind closed eyelids again. Damn the girl! William groaned and picked up the phone. He paused a moment and then typed a quick message to Ella, asking if Frannie was still awake.

"Probably, but I'm not!" the reply came.

William smiled, "Can you loan her your phone for the night then?"

"No, in case Hugh calls."

'Dammit!' William muttered, he'd have to get Frannie a phone of her own. Mentally he added it to the shopping list of stuff he needed to pick up for her before he went back.

"I miss her, I want to talk to her!" he typed, an honesty reserved only for Ella.

"You spoke to her two hours ago!" William glared at the handset, trying to think of how to word another text when the little handset vibrated in his hand again.

"I'll go and tell her you miss her, but then I am going to sleep and if the next buzz of this phone is you again rather than Hugh, we will be having words!"

William chucked, "Thanks, Ella" he typed and then lay down again to try and sleep. He half-hoped for a reply, but when none was forthcoming, he finally gave in and allowed sleep to begin to take him.

19

The memoirs of Frances Orchard, 1910 (Nest)

I lay back on the sofa at the back of the family room of the Orchard estate. The young'uns, the new batch of drinkers James and I referred to as "Henry's brood", were being noisy again and that noise was beginning to irritate me. Much had changed in a hundred years, too much for my liking and despite how perfect life had seemed in the early years, now I wished that James and I could just run away, escape from the constant chatter and noise.

The house was now a hive of activity. Phina made the first young'un, a man named Thomas, in 1875; the subject of a love affair between the two of them. That was back before the great change, before Henry had decided to devote our immortal lives to the destruction of the wolf-clans which had bred the monster that had destroyed our families. At first, all three of us were guarded and sceptical about Phina's new playmate. Thomas was a tall man with pretty eyes and sandy hair. He smiled easily and laughed a lot. Henry murdered him in his sleep several months after his turning. I didn't know why, only that his death was the result of a screamed argument between Henry and Phina. For a few weeks we lived like before, just the four of us, and then Henry began to bring people home.

Throughout the years, James and I tried to keep to ourselves as much as possible, avoiding both Henry and Phina, as well as the rest of the world. Living at the Orchard Estate, it was hard to keep hidden; people knew us, knew the family and knew the scandal which had torn us apart. Often, I worried that people knew that there was something wrong, that the family didn't age. If nothing else, bringing in the new drinkers helped a little to stop people from prying. Eventually there were too many of us there for individuals to be recognised. We were careful too though, always keeping the carriage covered if we went out, always hunting outside of our own village.

I sighed and looked up to where James was sitting at the other end of the room, flirting a little with another young drinker who was new to the house. I didn't mind his flirting, I knew that he was mine completely and I quite enjoyed the envy that I saw in the eyes of the other girls when they realised that, despite all his flirting, he was completely enamoured of his wife. James was lucky, I thought absently, he'd been captured in the height of his beauty: mid-twenties, a trim figure, luscious chestnut-brown curls, the very first wrinkles about his eyes. I sometimes wished I'd been allowed to grow a little older before I was stolen from my life. My hair was still white, my frame small and my features still that of a twenty-year-old girl. Henry was the same, his face had never matured to full masculinity and his frame never became anything other than wiry. Phina, like her brother, made a beautiful drinker. Her full head of hair was Henry's shade of chestnut but it was full and thick, falling in waves down her back. As the new century dawned and fashions began to change, Phina moved with them, often looking daringly fashionable and pretty. I tended to stick to what I knew:

long plain skirts with buttoned jackets and white frills to my shirt, it was dowdy but it attracted no attention.

At my fourth sigh, James glanced over and smiled at me, and I smiled back. I beckoned to him and at once, he left the girl with whom he'd been flirting and returned to my side.

'You are melancholy today?' He asked. It was close on six in the evening and we had only been up for an hour or so. The strange intolerance that we all suffered to the sunlight had led to us sleeping later, slipping back into bed in the early hours. The change had been gradual, but seemed to make sense.

'A little,' I replied, taking James's hand. 'I get tired of all the noise, truth be told.'

'Me too,' James said, sitting down and pulling me into his arms comfortably. 'I am apprehensive too…'

'Let's go outside… I worry that…' I indicated the room, hoping that my point would get across. It did and James nodded.

'Indeed,' he said quietly.

Together, we stood and clasped hands, weaving our way between the scattered sofas and tables which littered what had once been a grand parlour. There were fourteen in the house now. I knew this because every bedroom on the first floor was occupied. Up in the attic, James and I had our little nest and down in the dark basements, Henry and Phina tended to reside, hiding away from the sunlight as much as possible. I had my suspicions about Henry and Phina, suspicions which worried me greatly but that I had no idea how to broach.

'So, what is worrying you?' I asked quietly once James and I were outside.

James chewed his lip absently, his eyes clouded for a moment, and then he turned and pulled me to face him. The dusk was falling upon the marshes, and even though I could feel the effect of the remaining weak rays of the sun,

I thought absently that the sunset was truly beautiful. Its orange and pink glow setting over Stateman's pool which I could see the borders of over the hedges, made me think of the first time we had watched the sun set together, the night he'd proposed. The night was chill but my jacket was warm enough, James was in just a shirt and trousers but he never seemed to be concerned by the cold.

'I am worried that our home has become a nest of sin, I am worried that my brother is growing power-hungry, and that he had a lust for killing almost as strong as his lust for revenge. I am worried that his multitudes of children will run riot eventually and if he manages to keep control I'll be bloody surprised.'

James's eyes caught mine and I nodded, I had been thinking the same thing for some time.

'I think that they are committing atrocities too, down in Henry's basements.'

'What?'

'Last night, I heard somebody screaming down there. I... I didn't go down, but I think that they were... that they had another wolf.'

I shuddered and James put an arm about me, leading me over to the pretty rose-garden. Henry had found wolves before, several times and, despite how they frightened me, not even I could condone the treatment such creatures had received. Torture, using both physical pain and terror. I left quickly but James had remained, and when he returned had been the first time he'd talked of leaving. James talked about leaving a lot, just as I thought about leaving a lot, but never did he make a move to do so, even when pushed. Deep down I knew that he was too timid and that he was frightened to break from the fold. Henry handled every aspect of our lives, I had no idea how he did it and I had a suspicion that James didn't know either.

The other issue was James's feeding habits. James

never, ever fed directly from humans, he was frightened to lest he kill and instead he drank only what Henry left him. Sometimes I even pondered if Henry had done this on purpose, making us rely on him but I dismissed the idea. Even if he hated the world, I knew that Henry loved me and James.

'I want to leave here, Jamie,' I whispered, my eyes cold and hard. 'I cannot... I hate this place. This isn't our home anymore.'

'I hate it too. We should leave! I'll ... ponder on it.'

'Like you have before?'

'The timing is never right. We need money, somewhere to live, some means to travel and... and if we just say we're breaking loose, Henry will take it all. You know it as well as I do.'

I frowned and bit back on a retort, sometimes I wished James had a little of his brother's fire. Over the years, James had become more and more placid, Henry more and more forceful. Sometimes it was as though the two were cancelling each other out.

'I'm sorry Fran,' James said quietly, looking out over the lawn at the now almost completely set sun. 'I'm sorry. I know you think me weak but...'

'No!' I exclaimed, hearing the lie in my voice but not wavering. 'No Jamie, you're not weak just... just you are sweet and kind instead of forceful and power-hungry,' I put a hand on his arm and pulled him to me. 'I wouldn't change you for the world,' I whispered burying my face in his throat but on the inside, I made a conscious decision that if James wasn't going to go and have a chat with Henry, I would.

James and I lay tangled together in the rose-gardens. Our talk moved onto kissing quickly enough, and that had led to other things. James clutched me to him, his arms giving me both a pillow and extra warmth through my thin shirt.

My jacket was unbuttoned and I'd torn one of the buttons from his shirt. He'd wriggled back into his trousers but they were still undone, allowing me to caress the wiry hair on the bottom of his belly.

'I love you,' James whispered, kissing my head and I cuddled in close. Sometimes I wondered if his love really was eternal, James never seemed to falter or double-think anything but he was also a terrible flirt and sometimes I wondered if it was loyalty that kept him at my side as much as it was love. I still loved him though, I knew that much and still sometimes I'd look at him and find my mind blown by his beauty, by the rush of affection within. We had grown apart a little, over the years, but my love for him was still one of my driving forces.

James stroked my long white hair, kissing me. 'What is on your mind, my darling?' he asked softly, bringing me back to the present.

I sighed onto the flesh of his neck. 'Wondering if you still love me as much as I love you…'

'What a thing to be thinking! Can you not feel it Frannie Orchard? I love you more.'

Suddenly, I felt an odd feeling of affection and vulnerability rush through me. I trembled and pulled him close. 'Never stop,' I whispered. 'I don't think I'd cope very well without you.'

James kissed my cheek again. 'Never in a million years.'

Once our clothing was straightened and final kisses had been exchanged, James and I made our way back into the house. As we reached the hallway, James took my hand and kissed it. 'Never worry Frannie,' he said. 'I am still as besotted, if not more so, with my little lady in britches… although you do tend to be wearing a lot of dresses these days!'

'I know it,' I replied, eyes twinkling and inner vulnerability well hidden. 'But then I haven't ridden a horse in years either. The world is changing us Jamie.'

The Black Marshes

'It is, but my love is constant, please don't doubt that. Do you have plans for the evening?'

'Yes,' I said, then took a deep breath. 'I'm going to go and speak to Henry on how he'd feel about splitting our assets and going separate ways.'

James chewed his lip and I thought I saw a flicker of sorrow in his eye. 'I should be doing that,' he said.

'I know, but I can take this one. If you are sure this is what you want?'

'It is, I'll be upstairs when you're done.'

Tentatively, I walked down the corridor and flight of stairs which led to the big wooden door of the basement. I paused there a moment and took a deep breath. Over the years, Henry had distanced himself off somewhat from James and I. That he was our leader, the alpha male, as it were, was at once obvious and as he'd seemed to drift further and further from the mischievous but lovable boy he'd once been, I had begun to feel a little – not afraid, but cautious of him. With a trembling hand, I pushed open the door and slipped in to the cold, dank basement. Before me were four doors on each side, and one at the end. I walked slowly into the corridor and stopped at the third door on the left. Henry's room. I took another deep breath, steeling myself, and then turned the door handle. Even as the door opened, I heard the sound of Henry's cooing, and glancing in, I saw he was about to feed. I stepped back and watched through the door, not wanting to disturb him.

Henry sat in a big comfy chair, legs up on a footstool and his shirt open. A little blond girl, she looked about my age, was knelt on the bed beside him. His eyes went down to drink her in, her long hair was matted with blood and her creamy pink skin was almost as pale as his. She tried to move, to raise herself up but she was too weak and I saw the fear in her eyes. I was repulsed. He'd probably kill her, I thought with a sinking feeling, he didn't like it when they feared him.

As I watched, he tapped a cigar on the wooden box he kept them in, flattening out the end, and then put it to his lips. He looked back down at the girl and for a moment I saw a glimmer of compassion in his eyes, but it was quickly quashed.

I moved to push the door again, presuming he wasn't going to feed after-all but then paused as he sighed and lit the cigar, and then moved to the bed and stroked the girl's blood-stained hair. The girl had been a barmaid, had come to the Orchard estate on a whim, I recognised her from before she'd vanished. Young blond girls had a tendency to vanish in the Orchard house. I wondered if she had acquiesced or whether he'd taken her by force. The very thought made my heart drop a little lower.

The girl sniffed a few times and tried to look upon Henry bravely as he touched her. He caressed her little round face and then used a nail to break the skin on his wrist, allowing her a few mouthfuls of his blood. Healing her up so that she didn't die. As you know, I guess, when the demon manifests itself in a host's form, the blood becomes the carrier for the disease, but when it is repressed, the blood is a salve for both humans and other drinkers alike. Within minutes, the girl was looking healthier again. Her little cheeks turned pinker and the skin on her naked arms and legs too seemed to lose some of their anaemic paleness. Henry pulled her into his lap and nuzzled her throat.

'So, Ethel,' he said, his hands running over that sweet little face. 'It's decision time.'

The girl looked frightened and did not reply.

'I have two choices, I could keep you here and let you die slowly day by day as I drain you dry, or I could kill you now. Which would be kinder? I do so want to be kind to you Ethel.'

Even I gasped at his cruelty. The girl cried out and flew from his arms but Henry was ready for that and simply

The Black Marshes

closed his hand about her hair, jerking her back to her knees.

'Go on,' he urged. 'If you can break free, I'll let you go.'

His eyes moved to the door but I was safely concealed out of sight, I was trembling though, shocked to my core. I had known he was cruel but this was an unexpected low.

After a few moments, the girl began to cry again, slumping down in despair.

Henry chuckled. 'What? Giving up already?' he asked.

A footstep sounded on the stair behind me. I started, not wanting to be caught eavesdropping and stumbled into one of the side chambers. These little rooms stank of blood and I retched, even as it brought back the hunger in me. So many lives lost, so much pain! I could almost feel the screams of the dying.

The footsteps passed without and I glanced through the bars at the door to see Phina gliding down to Henry's quarters.

'Henry?' Phina's voice

I watched as she moved into the room and then slipped back out to my spot by the door. I had to see what they were going to do. I had a feeling that when he heard of this, James might be more eager to leave. I hoped so, I felt sick to my stomach.

'Decided to have a bit of fun did we little brother?' Phina asked quietly, surveying the room before her. For some time after Henry had killed her last lover, Phina had been cold and hateful to him, but in time that had passed. I suppose the bond between them to have been very strong.

'You are intruding, yes.'

Phina raised an eyebrow at the struggling girl, and then smirked. 'Not a bad likeness,' she said with amusement. 'Quite like her.'

Henry's face turned several shades of red before his eyes darkened and he glared at Phina. I had no idea what was wrong but I shuddered at the sight of him in his ire.

'Get out,' he snarled, all good humour gone. I readied myself to return to my hiding spot again but Phina seemed unphased.

'Now, why would I do that? When it looks like the party is in here.'

Gracefully, she dipped her head and licked some of the blood from Ethel's neck, then bit deep into the girls armpit, just beside the breast whilst her white fingers began unpicking the buttons of her own shirt.

'Come, Henry,' she whispered. 'Bathe me in the blood of your companion here.'

With a self-assured grin back on his features, Henry laughed and approached the bed too. I could barely understand what I was witnessing. Phina's lips touched Henry's and his hands came to caress her breasts, like a lover rather than a sister. His tongue ran over her face, and then he looked down on poor Ethel and smiled a smile which chilled me.

'Come, Ethel,' he whispered. 'Come and please my sister and maybe I'll let you live another day.'

I could not watch and stumbled backwards. Henry's head shot up at the clutter of my retreat and for a moment, we looked straight into each other's eyes.

'Frannie?' Finally, there was remorse in his eyes, guilt and regret. Phina's eyes met mine too and with a gleam in them, she stretched out a hand to me; an invitation.

I could not reply, could not speak, instead I turned and fled.

20

The memoirs of Frances Orchard, 1912 (The Ending)

In the end, James and I never did have that conversation with Henry, never did leave. I first heard the name Hugh Haverly, some two years later, a name brought to my attention in a haze of murder and blood. A name I would never forget.

Amongst the young'uns was a man named Michael. I didn't really know him but then I didn't really know many of the younger ones. Still, the killing was shocking.

It happened on a Friday night, in the early hours. Amongst the younger brethren, I had noticed a tendency to bring strangers into the house. It was not a tendency I particularly approved of but one I tolerated and I knew that James at least felt the same way about it. That night I heard the footsteps in the corridor just below where I lay awake with a sleeping James lying in my arms. His head lay on my shoulder and my arms were tight about him. The footsteps were obviously of more than one person but I just sighed and tried to ignore it. For some minutes, I just lay, my hand on James's chest and my eyes beginning to droop. Then, perhaps fifteen or twenty minutes after the sound of the footsteps, I heard what sounded like a scuffle happening. I sat up a little more, hearing the sound of a cry and then more scuffling.

'Jamie?'

James opened his eyes, 'Hmmm?'

'Jamie, I… I think something might be happening downstairs…'

James sat up a little too, his arms still around me, then he sat forward, releasing me as more noises sounded below. 'Could just be a reluctant human?' he said doubtfully.

I shook my head. 'I have a horrible feeling,' I said quietly. 'I'm going to go down,'

'You're not going alone,' James said and stood up. I threw on an old shirt and a pair of James's trousers and turned back to watch him getting dressed, when his eyes lingered on me they glowed and I too could not help but grin.

'There she is,' James echoed words he'd not spoken in many a year. 'My little lady in britches.'

I felt my colour rise but still a grin broke onto my lips. 'Come on,' I said. 'We don't have time for this,' but my heart was gone from the need to go down and explore what the young'uns were up to. There had been no more noises since the ones which had awoken us and I was beginning to feel a little like I was over-reacting. James's hand went to my waist, and roping around it casually as he drew me in and put his lips to my breasts, just where they met at the top button of his shirt. 'They're probably all right downstairs,' he mumbled, undoing buttons. I laughed. James and I phased in and out of sexual intimacy over the years, but at that time, we were firmly back to it.

Then the screaming began.

I gasped and pulled away from James at once. He too seemed shocked and grasped my hand. First one long scream, then two other short gasping ones.

'Come on!' James said and grabbed my hand pulling me with him out of the attics and down into the sleeping quarters of the house.

Downstairs, the door to one of the rooms stood open and I pushed my way through the young'uns who had gathered there to look in at the gory scene. Sat in the doorway was another of them, a girl I recognised but couldn't name. She had dark hair and pretty eyes but they were red from sobbing and her skin was ashen.

I glanced quickly into the room. The window was open, swinging a little on its frame and the bed-sheets were rumpled. The body lay on the floor, the eyes closed and a steak-knife protruding from his chest. Some of the skin around his chest was soft and it looked as though it were melting. For a moment I didn't understand but then I saw the silver hallmark on the blade... the blade was of pure silver. I put a hand over my mouth and turned into James's waiting arms.

'My god,' I whispered. 'What is this?'

Before James could answer, I heard the voice of Henry behind us and spun around. He was dressed only in his trousers and a white button down under-shirt. His hair was ruffled and his eyes bleary. He moved roughly into the bedchamber and for a split second, I saw the worry and fear in his eyes as he looked over the room. James released me and turned to his brother.

'What the hell?' Henry asked, still looking shocked, dazed.

'No idea,' James replied, his expression not much different from his brother's.

I took a deep breath, and then sat next to the sobbing girl. Most of the younger drinkers were present by then, talking amongst themselves and peering in. Phina too had arrived, standing back from the family and just watching with cold eyes. Two of the older members of Henry's brood moved forward to speak with Henry who still looked a little lost and frightened.

I laid a hand on the younger drinker's arm. 'What happened?' I asked. The room seemed suddenly to be becoming a buzz of noise as the shock lifted and the younger drinkers moved into the room with the older ones and I really had to strain to hear the girl's reply.

'I… I don't know,' she whispered, frightened. 'Michael and I… we are lovers… I am… was… not alone in that but sometimes I would… would go in… join him with his… his…'

An image flashed in my mind of Phina's outstretched hand, that invitation to join her and her brother, and suddenly my heart felt heavy. My home was more of a pleasure-house than anything else these days, I realised– they were all at it.

I put a hand on the girl's arm, 'So what happened tonight?' I pushed.

The girl looked up at me, confused, 'I have no idea…' she whispered. 'I came to… to see if my company would be welcome tonight, and I… I… found this…'

I sighed inwardly, I'd hoped for more from the girl, but still I patted her arm and mumbled some words of comfort before I stood and walked back into the room. James was knelt by the body, a sheet in his hands and I guessed that he was going to dispose of the victim. Henry was stood at the window, looking out. I moved to his side and put a hand on his arm. Henry looked up in shock at my touch on the thin cotton of his shirt.

'What do you think happened?' I asked, 'Think he bought home a human and they over-powered him?'

Henry's thick-lidded eyes took me in for a few moments, pondering my words, but then he shook his head. 'No,' he said. 'Whoever did this… they weren't human.'

'You're sure?'

The Black Marshes

'Yes. For one, no human could over-power Michael. He might have been young but he was the oldest of this brood and well, humans are no match for us. Secondly, no human could jump from a second-floor window, onto hard paving stones, and then just get up and run away.'

'You're sure the attacker did that?' I asked, thinking that perhaps a human could have overpowered the drinker in the right situation, all they had actually done was stab him, after-all.

'There's blood on the stones,' Henry observed and when I looked again I saw he was right. Worried, I turned and saw that James and two of the brood had managed to wrap the body in a sheet and the younger ones were now carrying him down the stairs. I had no idea what they did with the bodies, they must have a secret stashing place, I thought grimly, between them all they killed enough.

The attack came less than a week later.

Even in my memory, the whole day is nothing but a blur. I awoke the same time as always, close on four in the afternoon, and after lazing an hour in James's arms, I stood and dressed myself. James lay on the bed, his eyes glowing as he watched me dress.

'Come on you,' I smiled, holding out my hand.

James burrowed further into the blankets. 'Too bright,' he complained.

I walked to the window to check the level on sunlight without, ammunition to scold him with for his laziness but as I glanced out, I froze, fear draining me of all strength.

'Frannie? What is it?' James asked, standing and wrapping he blanket around himself. As he joined me at the window, James's eyes widened too and I watched as he wet his lips with his tongue.

Outside, walking slowly towards the house was a man. He was too far away to make out any real features but I could see he was dressed in a white shirt and black trousers and waistcoat, his hair brown, the style undistinguishable and his demeanour confident but angry. At his heels though, were the reasons for my real fear. Wolves. Eight of them, all running alongside the man, snappish and playful about his heels.

'Jamie…' I whispered, beginning to shake and he stared at me, his eyes wide with fear. Trembling, I held out my hand for him and he grasped it hard.

'Oh,' he whispered. 'What… oh, god!' He moved quickly back, running into the room and pulling on a pair of trousers and a shirt, his fingers trembling almost as much as mine.

'Jamie?' I whispered, 'What…'

'His name is Hugh – Hugh Haverly,' James said, 'Ghost… Ghost warned us all those years ago to keep our noses clean, or else this would happen. Frannie, I don't have time to explain, we have to go!'

My eyes were glued to the window, unable to really believe what I was seeing. James came back to my side, putting a hand on my arm and I looked up at him stupidly, unable to clear the fog in my mind that the fear had caused.

'Who is he?'

'Death itself to our kind!'

'What…'

'Come on sweetheart, let's go!'

I nodded, James took my hand in his and pulled me away from the window so I could no longer see the changer and his pack approaching the house. James threw open the door and then we were running.

The screaming started as we passed the second floor, using the service steps to avoid the main house. James's palm was sweaty as he dragged me with him. I just followed. Inside my head I was barren, blank, like an idiot. It seemed somehow that sanity was leaving me, the fear taking over, but instead of releasing adrenaline, it made me malleable and placid.

James glanced at me as we arrived at the bottom of the steps, next to the door to the kitchen, worry apparent in his eyes. 'Fran?' he asked, touching my face. 'Fran? Are you all right?'

I shook my head, my fingers trembling. I was normally the strong one, normally the one who took the lead but inside me I had an odd sense of dread and I couldn't repress it.

'Jamie,' I whispered, stopping dead, somehow afraid to open the door and run through the kitchen.

He pulled me to him, kissing my forehead. 'It will be all right,' he whispered. 'You'll see, but we have to leave now. Please, stay with me here.'

'I love you,' I whispered and then kissed his cheek. He nuzzled me a moment and then threw open the door.

The house was in chaos. As James and I ran into the kitchen, Henry, who was just coming in from the other door, stared at us. Quickly he ran into the room, dragging Phina behind him in very much the manner that James was dragging me.

Henry slammed the door and ran to his brother's side. 'What…?' he gasped, and I saw he had blood on his shirt.

'Hugh Haverly,' James hissed, furious at his brother. 'It's him, the man Ghost warned us about… this is your fault.'

I expected retaliation but Henry just stared at James a moment and then nodded. 'I've been a fool. Berate me later…' he said, and then turned to Phina who looked almost as shocked as I did. 'Come on sweetling,' he said to her. 'We just have a little further to go…'

Phina nodded and raised her face to look at me, moving so that the left side of her face was in the light; I gasped. Phina had obviously been attacked. The side of her face which she'd been concealing was knitting back together, the muscles pulling tight and the skin re-growing but I could see the extent of the damage. It looked as though one of the wolves had ripped her entire cheek off. At once I ran to her side to embrace her but Phina threw me off and turned away.

'Phina!' both James and Henry cried out her name as the girl turned and fled back into the house.

James moved to go after her but Henry grabbed his sleeve. 'What the hell are you doing?' he hissed. 'You can't go in there! There are bloody wolves everywhere!'

'I have to get Phina,' James hissed, pulling free.

'What about Frannie?' Henry said and indicated me as I watched them both argue, still in a dazed state of shock.

James came back to me and kissed my lips, holding my face in his white hands, and then looked into my eyes. 'I love you,' he whispered. 'I love you so very much. If I don't make it out, look after my little brother for me, stop him from going off of the rails completely.'

I nodded dully, suddenly realising why James had never made any real pains to leave Henry's flock. 'I love you Jamie,' I whispered, almost already knowing that I would never see him again.

The sound of smashing glass came to my ear, and then another set of screams and I realised that another of the young'uns had fallen.

'Get her to safety,' James said to Henry, and then he was gone and Henry was pulling my arm.

'Let's go!' he said, and I saw the dash of beige as one of the wolves passed the open door. Going after James, I realised with a sinking feeling. I bolted, running towards the door but Henry seemed to anticipate the move and tackled me to the ground. Lifting me easily, he threw me over his shoulder and ran from the house.

Hours later, I sat mindlessly in a room in the little inn in the town where I'd grown up, the same one I went to just days ago, and there began this journey I am now on. My body just felt numb, my eyes dry and refusing to give me any tears. Henry was gone too, he'd run back to the house after locking me into my room in the inn, gone to look for James and Josephina. My hands shook and my bladder felt full and uncomfortable but I was too frightened to move, too frightened that I might really be alone in the world.

Finally, the door flew open again and there was Henry.

'The orchard estate has fallen,' he whispered. 'Frannie, I'm so sorry...'

'And James?'

'James is...' He paused and then lifted the item he had clutched in his fingers, offering it to me. I reached for it but as I realised what it was a wail escaped from my lips. It was James's shirt. The very same one I'd clutched at just hours earlier when I'd pulled him to me. The item was torn to shreds, and the front was drenched with blood. His blood. I put the wet sticky item to my face and inhaled the scent. Definitely his blood.

Oh god no, I whispered. No, not this please Henry, not this!

Frannie...

No, no, no, no! Not this! Please? My voice rose to a pitch, my hands clutching in horror at the ripped bloody shirt as my eyes ran over it, placing it in my mind onto a broken bloody body. A scream was building within, a pain which was so salient it was almost physical burning in my chest. My fingers clenched, so tightly that my own nails dug into the flesh of my palms.

'Phina too,' Henry said, and his voice sounded more tired than anything. 'I... I buried them together, out in the rose garden. I know they weren't close but they were family at least...'

I couldn't comprehend, couldn't take it in at all. The tears brewed, and then fell unheeded onto my cheeks. My whole body suffered with almost spasms, jerking twitches which I couldn't control.

'Frannie, dearest Frannie,' Henry's voice filled with sympathy, an emotion I'd never heard there before. His fingers tried to take the torn cloth of James' shirt from me but I snatched it back with almost a growl.

'No!'

Henry paused, but then nodded. He seemed awkward for a moment but then sat beside me and laid an arm about my shoulders. Just the touch, the scent of him – so like his brother – was enough to bring on the sobbing. The tears hurt as they fell, burning my eyes as the weeping caused a judging in my chest. Henry pulled gently and I lay my head down on his chest. He was all I had left, and I suppose that is why I allowed his embrace, allowed him to pull me down into his arms. He cried too, for his brother and I think that softened me further, allowing me to relax my form enough to allow him to hold me. Together we lay on the bed and sobbed, out limbs locked together in the grief of our loss.

That was the start of the chain of events which led you to find me as you did. It is almost shameful to say it now, but weeks later, when Henry and I first fucked, it was I who initiated it, not him. It was me who kissed him, me who pulled his hands to my blouse buttons. I would say then, "how was I to know the monster he would become?" but I suppose in all honesty, I can see it even in the writing of this account. Call me feeble then, I was – for some time. I was weak and tired and broken and he was all I had.

21

Frannie,
2016

Frannie broke off. That was the end of the tale really. Nothing which had happened since really impacted anything, and yet now that she'd opened up the wound, the idea of stopping there, putting down her pen and getting into bed seemed the most undesirable thing she could do. William's bed, she reminded herself, his scent and his things all about her. Frannie looked down at the papers in her hand. Poor James. It had been so long since she'd really allowed herself to remember him; as Henry's lover, it felt somewhat disrespectful to James's memory to think overlong on him.

'Jamie, I hope you understand why I did it,' she whispered, then stood. The clock read just gone 4am and she was starting to get tired. She really should sleep but first there was something she needed. She moved quickly from William's room to her own and pushed open the door. Inside, the room was dark but Frannie clicked on the light and then pulled the bag from under the bed. Inside, were James's things really, more than her own. They'd gone back for some of their belongings a week or so after the attack and collected up what they could carry. Frannie rummaged in the bag, under the folded still-bloodied shirt and a pair of soft white gloves, was a bundle of papers. Frannie pulled them free and pulled off the elastic band which held them together. Most of the papers were letters, written in the raw pain of his demise, and then later almost as a journal. Letters to a dead man. In the middle of the bundle though, were three old brown and white photographs. The first was of her, taken in about 1900. The second was of James and the third was of the pair of them together. Frannie touched the fragile old paper. The photos were cheaply produced and already they were fading. Frannie had never taken a copy of them but she thought she might have to soon or lose them forever. Perhaps William would allow her to scan them in – there had to be a computer here somewhere. She moved to the bed and sat down with the photographs. The two with her in she put aside and instead lifted the one of James alone.

'You handsome thing,' she whispered, trying for light-hearted as the tears fell from her eyes to look on him again. 'You always were too handsome for your old good though, weren't you? I'm doing ok now, Jamie… I've left Henry and I'm starting again! I might even be falling in love again…'

She paused and allowed another tear, then wiped her eyes and put the photos down. Sitting cross-legged on the floor, she began to unfold letters and cast her eyes over the words. Without James life was more of a blur and she had to remind herself of it, before she could finish the story.

22

The memoirs of Frances Orchard, 1912 to the present day (Survival)

That, as written above, is our origin. It contains all I know of where we came from, and how we were made into what we are. With James gone, things changed for me in a manner so dramatic I cannot think how to describe it here. In some ways I am but halfway through the tale, and yet from here-on-in, I struggle to find the memories, to know which tale to tell and which to leave out. I cannot write it all, for to do so would take me days, weeks even. Such a long life to record – and yet, in many ways, there is little to say.

Henry and I became nomads, after the cull of our family. We went back to the Orchard estate just once, before our permanent return, to collect our belongings and for me to stand above the disturbed earth in the rose garden where my darling lay. There was but one grave for both James and Phina, Henry had tumbled them in as one and so they were forever locked together. The image of that brought me again the image of Henry and his sister together on a bloody bed. I locked it away. Who the hell was I to judge them? – I'd been lucky, I'd ever had my James – I knew nothing, until he was gone, of what it was to be alone.

And so I stood, looking down to where the peaty earth lay disturbed and remembering my first encounter with James, where I had pulled him up from a similar grave. How I wished I could have dragged him up again, pulled him to freedom from death's slimy fingers. I would have done anything to see his face again, to kiss his brow and tell him how very much I loved him. At least he'd known though, ever he'd known.

'James was ever too soft for the lifestyle we lead,' Henry said, appearing at my elbow and looking down at the disturbed peaty earth, 'he was too good, too kind-hearted.'

'He never even drank from a person,' I agreed, tears falling – I think that time in my life was the last time anyone ever saw me cry – 'he was a gentle soul trapped in a monster's body.'

It was true, never once had James put his teeth into a person, choosing to feed from the jugs of blood his brother left, than to feed himself. Truly he was a purer soul than the rest of us.

'I have to tell myself that it is a blessing in disguise,' Henry said, 'he never was one for this life.'

I nodded, and allowed Henry to take my fingers. We stood solemn for a few moments, but then I allowed him to pull me away, upstairs to pack away what was left of our life into my two suitcases.

From here-on, things were very different. Rather than a nest, Henry and I had only ourselves. Neither of us had a heart to reproduce, either, and so we travelled alone. We went over to America and so I have had the privilege of seeing New York in the 1920s, and then in the great depression of the 1930s. Europe next – we travelled from

The Black Marshes

Spain to Italy to France where we stayed until the outbreak of the big war, and there fled back to the states where it seemed safer. I could write tales indeed of those times, and if I ever get the hang of this writing malarkey, perhaps I will.

Henry's temper worsened as time passed. The changes in him were so slow though, so subtle, that I can almost claim to have barely noticed them. As the 1950s dawned and we returned to England – to London of all places – I found him sullen often, snappish and short with me. He didn't hit me then, though, that came later – after I left him for another man.

Andre was a drinker, probably a little older than Henry and I. He was a nest-leader, and probably the most intelligent man I ever met. Henry and I stumbled upon him in the 1980s out in a little town close to Bristol, on the Welsh border. He was Russian, originally, dark of hair and of eye. Not what a person might call attractive, perhaps, but charismatic enough that he did not need to be.

Andre saw through Henry straight away – I suppose that much is to be expected. Henry is sly but not intelligent. He is a disciplinarian, but without the cleverness for authority. He and I arrived at Andre's nest in about 1983 or so, I think it was the July or August as it was very hot and sticky. I was in the pangs, we'd travelled too long without sustenance – something Henry liked to do as it often pushed me past the point where I could stop, and therefore ensured I killed rather than merely drank. Andre's house was an old five-bedroom country house. It was run-down but not completely dilapidated, grey stone with a modest garden surrounded by a green fence. I paused without as Henry looked in through the windows and then beckoned me over.

'Look, there's definitely a group here,' he said. 'Can't tell if it's changers or drinkers though…' Henry's hatred of changers had not lessened over time, in fact I think that the lack of a place to take them, and his own private army of children behind him, was the only reason his torture had ceased.

'Drinkers...' a voice came from behind us.

I spun about and looked up into the face of the man I would come to love. Taller than both Henry or I, with dark hair, cropped fairly short and black eyes. He was dressed in plain black too, and wore trainers and a plastic wristwatch. Andre appraised us slowly, but then smiled. 'And I offer you the sanctuary of my home, kin.'

I nodded and smiled but Henry lingered.

'Who are you?'

'Alexandre Petrov. I am the leader of this group and owner of this house. Either come in, or leave...'

Henry stiffened at once but I looked up to Andre and spoke. 'I need to feed, urgently...'

'I have people here you might drain...'

And so we were accepted. Andre was not a humane man, not like the house here at Haverleigh. He kept humans to be killed, but he at least was picky about who he took – not the dark-eyeliner wearing teens who Henry favoured, despite that the 1980s were pretty rife with wanna-be vampires. Andre was a... I suppose you would say he was an inquisitor.

'I am no man to judge,' he once said to me as sat together out in the meadow behind the house, 'and yet to kill we must, yes. And so I take those who would to harm others, a murderer – yes but those are rare, and so others too. A rapist, a person who beats animals.'

I sat quietly allowing the wind to ruffle my hair. Secure for the only time ever in my life, that I was free to speak as I would.

'I think that is how it must be done. Henry gives me little choice in who I take, but when I do take that choice, I will chose those who wish for death, or those who are terminally ill. I find it sits easier on my soul.'

'Your *Henri*, he has some control over you, no?'

'Somewhat, but it fades since we came here.'

'I am pleased for it,' he smiled 'Pleased that you have come here to join with us.'

Andre's little group of followers were less disciplined – the very worst of them was a guy everybody just called Rat. Rat was a mean one, cruel and hard. It's no surprise that he and Henry became firm friends very quickly. Rat is one of the men who resides with Henry still, and he is one to watch – he's cleverer than Henry is, and he likes to wind Henry up.

There is a temptation in me now to fall again to dwelling, ruminating on those early times. I want to speak of my love for Andre, my slow move to understanding that not all leaders were as Henry was – cruel and unkind. Not all drinkers wild and carefree. Andre taught me many lessons; that we should not kill indiscriminately, that we should maintain discipline, that we did not have to give in to impulse. I took on his teachings and tried to live within them. Andre and I became lovers some three years into mine and Henry's stay there, in total we remained with Andre for five years, so for two of those, I guess.

I suppose I should have seen the signs. That haunts me now. Andre and I were never officially what you would think of as "together". We did not share a sleeping quarter, nor did we hold hands, speak of love and all those little things. Despite that, he knew of my love for him, and I knew he felt the same way. Henry could never have tolerated that, any more than he tolerated Andre having the leadership of the pack. It started with little incidents.

One night, as I sat reading, fully satiated on the blood of an old man Andre had brought home a week earlier. The night was a chill one, late in October, and Henry had refused the offer to feed from the prisoner, choosing to go out instead and find somebody more to his own tastes.

Andre was out that night but had returned shortly thereafter, coming to sit at my side.

'What are you reading?' he asked.

I showed him the book.

'War and Peace, you read Russian literature, eh?'

'I am. I am inspired to it – I don't know why…' I grinned, the foolish smile of a girl in loved despite by then being almost two hundred years old and was rewarded with a chuckle.

'It is a dry book,' he commented and then moved to the window. Andre was fairly young to lead a nest, younger than Henry and I by quite some years, and as I watched him, his confident movements and his thoughtful eyes, I could see how he had won his place as such.

'Will you come to me tonight?' he asked, 'I…'

We were interrupted by the sound of the door, an occurrence not overly unusual, but then the muffled sound of a woman crying. I was on my feet at once, with Andre close behind. Henry stood in the hallway. At his feet was a woman, well – more of a girl I suppose. Blond, curvy, about seventeen or eighteen.

'How's that for a meal…' Henry said, 'don't mind if I savour this one, do you?' his eyes flashed dangerously, daring Andre to disagree – a look which would have won him the respect of our previous group.

'No.' Andre said, 'You might do as you like but not under my roof!'

'And who are you to dictate to me?'

'I am the owner of this house and the leader of this group. If you don't like it, leave!'

'Henry, don't…' I whispered.

'Shut up Fran,' Henry snapped, then glared at Andre, 'perhaps it is time things changed, around here…' he said.

'Perhaps it is time you moved on…'

The girl Henry had brought in struggled throughout this exchange, held in place by her hair by Henry's fingers.

She screamed suddenly, and made a bid for freedom. Henry kicked her back down.

'I will not have you torture your victims in my house!' Andre said again, his eyes turning black, 'Kill her now or get out!'

The girl screamed again, trying to claw Henry's hands with her nails.

Henry held Andre's gaze for a moment too long, but then knelt and put his teeth to the girl's throat. She was panicking, as often a human will when taken thus, and I screwed up my nose as her hot piss covered the floor. Andre watched a moment longer, then shook his head,

'You can clean that bloody mess up too, when you're done...' he said, and then turned to me, 'Come, lets go elsewhere, Frances.'

I took the offered hand and together we walked around Henry, leaving him glaring after us.

There I suppose you begin to see why and how Henry's tolerance of Andre whittled away. Andre saw him as inferior and Henry could not bear to be seen as such. It made him feel small, like the child he still is in so many ways. Still – I think I was the final nail in his coffin. Andre could have survived, if not for me, if not for our love. But then how could I have ever not loved him? Where Henry was angry and full of venom, always, Andre was serene, kind and collected. Where Henry was rough and caused me pain in our previous sexual encounters, Andre was a gentle lover, showing me the dizzying heights of passion before plunging me into the very depths of pleasure. Ever he was kind, ever he was gentle. Oh god how I miss him – almost as much as I miss James. Writing this brings him back so vividly, I don't think I have ever been able to really grieve for him.

Henry killed my darling Andre – I guess you already realise that. A struggle for dominance, and a fight for me too. I know it is not my fault, I honestly do, and yet ever a part of me will blame myself for Andre's death.

It was the turning of five years, maybe a little longer but certainly not six, when Henry turned the nest to his leadership. Again, there were warning signs! Henry pushed and pushed at Andre's boundaries, and in time he began to get others involved too – Rat for certain, and then another, Christopher. The three would kill indiscriminately and often in the house despite how it was forbidden. I suppose though, that I was still lost in happiness, and so when I heard the shouting, one evening when lying in my bed, I still did not see the danger. I sighed and rolled over, sensing already that Andre's naked body was gone. That was nothing new though, for even if we had shared passions, he preferred to sleep alone. The shouting came again, and I frowned, sitting up. Then I heard my name called – Henry's voice.

'Frances, get down here now!'

My palms went sweaty, my head hurt as though I already knew what was about to happen. I dressed quickly in jeans and a tee, and almost flew from the room, to the top of the stairs. There I froze, gasping.

Andre was knelt in the hallway, god knows how they'd caught him. He was bound with his hands before him, his neck secured to the silver cuffs with a chain. He looked up at me, just once, and in his eyes I saw only confusion and fear. Henry stood behind where Andre was bound, surrounded by our new family. He grinned up at me.

'I thought it best you see this,' he said, 'you most of all, and any of you,' he indicated the rest, 'who would dare to challenge me.'

He turned and lifted an axe from the chair behind him. It was no giant battle-axe like you see in medieval movies, nr was it an executioner's axe, but a simple tool, designed probably for chopping logs.

I moved to descend the stairs, to stop this madness but

The Black Marshes

I'd neglected to notice Rat's absence below. He came up behind me and grabbed me about the middle, pinning my arms. At once I was like a mad creature, fighting and struggling but despite that he was younger, he had me at a disadvantage and managed to hold me as Henry swung the axe down on Andre's neck.

I screamed, tears exploding from my eyes as the blade hit flesh and I heard Andre's grunt. He did not scream though, didn't speak, holding his dignity as Henry swung the axe again and again. Two, three, four blows and the head was nearly off. A fifth severed it entirely and thus my lover was dead. He'd not made a single sound but for that first grunt.

Rat released me as Andre's head was severed, and in a fit of panic I ran down, as though it were not too late to save him. I have little memory of what followed, but I have memories of sitting sobbing in a pool of blood, Andre's head in my lap.

I need write very little more, and I find my heart closes now to the stream of words which bubble within. After Andre died, I gave up. Henry took us all back to the Orchard estate – now a ruin – and installed us there into the basements. He never forgave me for loving Andre, and so I became his punching bag just as William can attest to. There, for the past twenty years, he has plotted and seethed and planned the destruction of this clan. Have a care, do not underestimate him again!

23

William Craven,
2016

Upon their return, William took his leave of Hugh and of Sam, who had accompanied him back to Haverleigh House, and headed straight out to look for Frannie. It was five o clock in the evening, so he knew she would be up, or at least getting up soon. He came home laden with stuff for Frannie and a tired head which needed to lie on his own pillow. Ella's gentle tones told him she was in the living room and so he went there and scanned the room. Karen, one of the pups, was sitting in the corner with her laptop whilst three of Sam's humans were playing cards but at first, he didn't see Frannie. When he did, he paused. She was sitting with her feet up on the sofa, wrapped in the arms of a young human. A pang of jealousy ripped through him as he saw her lips go to the boy's neck but then he realised what she was doing and the jealousy faded. The boy gasped as she began to feed but he was one of the donors who lived in the house and he knew better than to pull away at the pain. From what William had heard, it was only fleeting anyway and then it felt good. Quietly, he stood in the doorway and watched her as she fed. She drank for a few minutes and then pulled back. Blood had dribbled down her chin and he found it almost endearing the way she wiped it away quickly before the boy could see it.

'Here,' he heard her say to the boy, 'take some of mine, it'll heal your wound.'

The boy took her offered wrist, his eyes showing the honour Frannie obviously didn't realise she bestowed on him, and put his lips to where Frannie split the skin there. William had never known a drinker besides Sam to offer up their own blood to one who was not bound to them in some way. The boy drank a few sips and then pulled away and whispered what William presumed was a thank you to Frannie. She nodded and then looked up and saw William for the first time, standing in the doorway watching her. A mixture of shock and shame coursed over her pretty features at the realisation he'd watched her feed.

'William? I didn't… didn't see you…'

William smiled and shrugged, 'You seemed preoccupied. I didn't want to disturb you.'

Ryan, the human she'd fed from, stood then, and moved away. The boy was actually a man, William realised, nineteen or twenty years old and handsome enough with it – one of the goths, the ones who glorified the drinkers and got some weird thrill out of being bitten. Another wave of jealousy overcame William but he repressed it, inwardly swearing at himself.

'Something going on there?' he asked as he perched beside her on the sofa.

'No. Nothing, I met him ten minutes ago when Ella brought him to me. I am tender because that is how I want to be to my donors, now. Like the others. I have spent so long being a monster, I want to feel like a good person again, I want to be gentle and kind.'

William's heart swelled, and a bead of shame coursed through him for his jealousy. 'I find it hard to believe you ever were anything but kind…'

'And yet, I was.'

'Then your kindness makes your apologies for a past you cannot change. You bestowed a real honour on the kid though, he'll be bragging…'

'I… really?'

'Yeah, your kind don't normally part with their own blood on a first feeding.'

Frannie shrugged, 'Ghost used to feed me his blood to heal me back when I was still human.'

'Ghost?'

'I was once somebody's human too. I know how it feels to be the donor.'

A strange chill passed through William and he had to bite down on a fierce urge to shield her again from… what? From a past which was gone, which happened before he was even born? He tried to find the words but found himself at a loss.

'I have my story for you… for you to read, if you will? The story of my life.'

'You want *me* to read it?'

'Unless you prefer not to?'

'I'll read, if you want me to know the content…'

'I do. Perhaps later?'

'Of course…' he indicated the bags on the floor by his feet, '…I got you some bits and pieces whilst I was out.'

'Oh! Thank you. Shall we go upstairs then?'

William felt a stirring within him at her words but he dismissed it with a slight warmth to his cheeks, she just meant to unpack the clothing, he told himself firmly, *pull yourself together Will Craven!*

'Sure,' he said, hoping his voice was calmer than his brain, 'yeah, sure…'

Inside Frannie's chamber was as bare as it had ever been and William smiled to think of the gift he had for her in one of the bags, it would brighten the dresser at least.

'Right,' he said, trying to sound authoritative and not to look at the bed where it would be so easy to throw her down and have her. He doubted she'd push him off if he tried but he also had a feeling that if he did that, he'd lose her mind, her heart, in favour of her body and he didn't want to do that. With a dry mouth, he wet his lips and then tried to sound neutral.

'Right, I got you a pile of plain black t-shirts, two pairs of jeans, under-things and a jumper. I picked out an evening dress too, Rosa – my late-wife – always used to say every girl needed a cocktail dress so I took her advice. I am a man and one of little taste however, so if it is hideous then I apologise. There's a hairbrush in that bag, some other bits and bobs as well as a veritable rainbow of hair-colours... I thought you might like a choice…'

Fran laughed and William decided he liked the look of her smiling. He handed her the bags, aside from the one in which he had his gift.

'Thank you, William,' she said softly, in much the same manner as she'd thanked the boy downstairs for his blood, 'I don't have an awful lot of money right now but if I owe you anything I…'

'Nah, don't worry. I'm not a rich man but I'm good for a couple of quid to clothe the girl who lost everything saving my life.'

Frannie took his hand, the touch startling him and sending a tremor through his skin.

'You're really sweet William, you know that?' she said suddenly, and then blushed a pretty pink colour. William's eyes moved from her eyes, to her cheeks and then down to the white of her neck, the swell of her breasts under his shirt which she still wore. Not wanting to linger there, he moved back to where her pink lips were just parting, her eyes searching his monstrous countenance. She took in a deep breath, her breasts swelling under the shirt, and he wondered how it tasted, how her lips would soften to be kissed properly.

Don't kiss her! he told himself. *Don't do it! Get a fucking grip on yourself old man!*

Frannie's eyes bored into him almost as though she could read his mind, perhaps the thoughts were apparent on his face. He wet his lips again, and pulled his mind to matters at hand, and then nodded, somewhat curtly.

'Frannie I... I also got you this...' he said, handing her the plastic bag with his gift in it, 'As a gift... I mean a thank you for what you did for me...'

Frannie's lips set together, 'What I did for you? You mean watch my lover torture you and then get myself caught trying to rescue you afterwards?'

'No Sweetheart, I mean how you gave me a drink and the hope to keep going, even in the face of what Quinn did to me. Because of what you risked... what you have lost... to try and save me.'

Frannie's face seemed to soften again at once, 'I failed though... I didn't save you – Hugh did that! I merely...'

Her fingers danced up to touch the mottled scar from the silver on his face. William put his fingers over hers, stilling the exploration. He wasn't ready for her to touch his face yet.

'You merely gave me the hope to keep going when I was on the verge of giving up. Yes, it may have been Hugh who dragged me out of there, but it was you who saved me.'

Frannie blushed again and looked down at the bag in her other hand, 'I can't remember the last time anyone bought me a gift. I hardly know what to do.'

'What? You're telling me Henry Quinn didn't buy you presents?'

Even as he said it, William chided himself for the ill-timed humour but Frannie's lips parted to let a chuckle escape. She didn't reply, but her smile was firmly back in her eyes. She sat down at the desk and opened the bag.

He'd asked the store to gift-wrap it and so he had to watch with a pounding heart as Frannie's slender fingers pulled away the brightly coloured tissue paper. Inside was a cardboard box and inside that was the gift. William had seen the little music box in a shop window as he'd been on the way home. It was only small, modern rather than antique and was designed for holding rings. The box itself was circular and decorated with images of horses galloping. He hoped she'd like it, it wasn't a gift you'd normally buy for a girl like Frannie but as he'd passed the shop he'd known he had to buy it for her.

Frannie didn't speak, just sat the box on the table and opened it. William moved closer as the little strains of the song played. The little plastic rider within went around and around as the tiny thin strains of Beethoven played their reedy tune. Frannie's lip quivered and he saw a tear well up in her eye.

'Frances?' William said softly, 'are you all right?'

'I'm fine,' she said and then, with a sniff, she brushed away the water from her eyes. Not a single tear had actually spilled. 'It's just that… well… this reminds me of when I was human… my father owned a farm… god that seems so long ago now,' she wiped the tears away again. 'I used to care for the horses, they were my babies… Silly really.'

'No, it's not silly!' he insisted. 'I understand… and I'm glad I inadvertently bought you something meaningful.'

Frannie smiled and William moved to kneel at her side.

'There's a ring in there too,' he smiled. 'Just a token of my thanks… I don't even know if you wear rings but… well …'

Wordlessly, Frannie opened the ring compartment of the box and pulled out the ring. A gold band with an amber coloured stone in it. 'It's beautiful,' she said.

'I'm glad you like it. You have pretty hands. They ought to be adorned in rings.'

'Thank you, I... I love it.'

With a smile Frannie slipped the ring onto her hand, it fit the middle finger of her right hand perfectly and she held it up to show him.

'Pretty.'

'This is a time in my life for change, for rebirth,' she dipped her hand between her breasts and pulled out the wedding ring she still wore on a chain about her neck. This she deposited in the box.

'Quinn...?'

'No, Henry called me his wife but we were never married. No, my ring is from James. Ninety-seven years I have been a widow in mourning, and do you know the sad thing?'

'Hmm?'

'In truth, I can't even remember what he looked like. Whenever I try to imagine his face, all I see is my own memory of a portrait of him that I once owned, and then from later, a photograph. I can't remember him, in the flesh... I stopped missing James a long time ago and missed the memory of him instead. Writing my life-story today brought that home more so than I realised. Already I feel more alive than I have in many, many a year.'

'Good.' William said gently, 'And I do know how it feels, I'm a widower too remember,' he paused, and then put his hand on her arm, 'Look, I know the world seems cruel right now but it doesn't have to be. I'm here Frannie, if you need me... I... what?' he paused as she shook her head.

'I think you should stop being so nice to me,' she said, her eyes filling up again. 'You're making me feel things I haven't felt since... but I can't, William!'

A surge of adrenaline made William's heart pound. Surely she wasn't reciprocating his feelings... he put a hand out and she gave him hers. William gazed into her eyes a moment, and then caught himself imagining how

The Black Marshes

she would feel naked in his arms again.

'I ought to go. My thoughts are bordering on uncivilised and if I stay much longer I cannot guarantee that I will be a gentleman. I don't want to do anything I shouldn't.'

'I don't understand…'

'You too, make me feel things,' he managed, the best explanation he could muster up.

Frannie looked at the floor, but then back up to him. God the girl was pretty – so pretty! He tried to bite down on his impulses again but by his very nature, William had always been impulsive. He took in a deep breath and wet his lips again, then slowly he moved in, scooping to wrap an arm about her and half-lift her to meet him. Her lips were soft, very much so, and her kiss shy, tender. William allowed his eyes to close, his body to tingle, as the kiss deepened, but then, with trouble, he pulled free. For a few minutes both stood in silence, but then Frannie pulled away from him again.

'I want you to know me,' she said, and moved to the bed. As he watched she rummaged there and came up with the notebook. 'Here. Read this. It is my whole life…'

'This is so personal to you.'

'It is, but you have to know, you have to know what I am before you… before we… I mean, before anything happens. More too, Henry… Henry murdered the last man I… I cared for. I want you to know what you're getting yourself into.'

William nodded, pondering how he was going to go about telling her of his own past, his own deeds. That could wait though, just for now. He took the book from her fingers and smiled. 'Ok, I'll read it later, when you're sleeping… are you sleeping in the day or night?'

'Night, I'm trying to re-socialise myself to regular hours.'

'Ok, cool. So what are you going to do now? Have you

eaten? I mean…'

'No,' she smiled, 'No, not yet…'

'Come on then, let's go and find some food and then maybe I'll show you around the house and grounds a bit?'

24

Hugh Haverly, 2016

Hugh sat quietly in the small room at the back of Haverleigh House which he had claimed as his own. The room was decorated with greens, and held dark stained oak, and green leather furniture. Night had pulled in, casting shadows in the corners but Hugh didn't mind that. His hand rested gently on the silky fur of a little spaniel who he kept always at his heels. The house was not the same as when he'd lived there as a boy, not even the ruins of his old home remained, aside from the basement… that damn basement where this whole mess had started. Hugh pushed the thought aside and looked tiredly at Sam, his brother. Sam was strangely quiet too, his old eyes seeming less alert than normal, hands neatly folded on his tailored trouser leg. Sam was a wealthy man, owner of several trusts which in turn ran several businesses out of each. Hugh, without Sam, had very little and yet Sam financed it all without complaint – well, it was the least he could do.

'Pensive?' Hugh asked his brother.

'Somewhat. I am… surprised as this turn of events, indeed. You say the girl is here?'

'Yes, she is calling herself by a different surname, but I

am 90 percent sure that the Quinn boy is Henry Orchard…'

'And the girl, Frances, was his wife?'

'So she says.

'Frannie Hodge cannot still be living,' Sam said, 'it's impossible. I know she was still aging, and I forbade them to return for her… she must be dead, long dead by now.'

'You forbade them? You never checked that they obeyed you?'

Sam looked somewhat shocked that such a question would even be asked of him, 'you think they disobeyed me?'

'If they loved her… love can be stronger than fear…'

Sam's eyes gleamed with silver and Hugh backed off. Frances Hodge, the first hybrid. Not human, not drinker, but an odd merging of the two. His brother had spent years watching over her, observing her and then, later, feeding from her. It was he who had inadvertently led the stray changer to her, and in guilt for that he'd created the first children he'd made in hundreds of years, since the beginning. Hugh understood well how he must be feeling, but that didn't change matters.

'I suppose they might have gone back for her,' Sam eventually said, 'I didn't want to interfere any more, the poor child suffered enough because of me.'

'Shall I go and bring her down? She's probably asleep by now but…'

'She's sleeping at night?'

'She's rather enamoured with William, I think she's trying to keep his hours. He feels somewhat that she saved his life.'

'I know, he told me… multiple times. No, let her sleep, I'll speak with her tomorrow. Now, what are we going to do about this little bastard, Quinn?'

As he spoke, the door opened and William entered. Hugh allowed his eyes to fall on his friend's broken face.

The Black Marshes

Fury bubbled again. Hugh was fiercely protective of those he considered family and to think of what that little brat had done to William pulled at something deep within him.

'Come in,' Sam said to William, 'grab a seat, we're just planning ahead…'

'Quinn?' William asked.

Hugh nodded. 'Quinn was always high on our list, ever since he rekindled the Orchard nest,' Hugh replied, taking a long sip of brandy, 'What with the killings, kidnappings… torture… he couldn't be allowed to live. Sam wants him dead. I want him dead.'

Hugh watched the emotions rage through William's face, his good eye glowing with a little more than just fury. The man would need to run again soon, he mused. He looked like he was barely holding his shit together.

'I want him dead too,' William said at last, 'but we have to be more careful. Last time we walked into an ambush, you realise that?'

'I do,' Hugh said, and then sighed, 'I'm getting too old for this…'

'*You're* getting tired of this? Then really, I am worried,' William said. Sam's eyes came to his face too and Hugh wished he'd made no mention of it.

'It's different now Ellie is here,' he said, 'The old fire is dying. Damn the woman, I knew she'd make me soft.'

'You have something to lose now,' Sam observed, 'it's made you cautious and caution is no weakness! I always thought you were too rash, before.'

Hugh took another swig of his brandy, his mind on his girl also sleeping above. It was true, he had something to lose now, and so did she. He'd place her happiness above his own survival.

'So,' William spoke, 'do we have a game-plan?'

Hugh shook his head, 'not yet.'

'I'll speak to Frances tomorrow,' Sam interjected, 'and we'll go from there. If this Quinn is an Orchard, then we need to be on alert, he's my own direct offspring and that makes him one of the most powerful drinkers on the planet.'

25

William Craven,
2016

William walked slowly back up to his chamber and sat bemused in his ragged old chair for some time. It wasn't overly late really, about 2am, but he felt he needed time to be alone with his thoughts. He allowed himself to think of Frannie, telling himself that he was just trying to analyse his feelings for her but finding himself dwelling on her smile, on her blue eyes. He had no illusions of how she'd been treated in the hands of Henry Quinn, no illusions about how badly she had suffered and he knew he had to cool off a bit, take things slowly. He also knew he didn't want to, though, as pathetically enamoured of her as a schoolboy. At the thought, his mind turned to a door he liked to keep firmly locked closed. Rosa, his first love, his wife. The thought pulled him back to reality as the guilt set back in. Rosa his love, his life, his victim. He'd killed her, and his grandmother, and his children. Not consciously, but with the wolf-form upon him for the first time. Hugh had tried to intervene but it had been too late.

'Come on Will Craven...' William muttered to himself, pulling out his ponytail band and running his fingers through his hair, 'Pull yourself together!'

Emma Barrett-Brown

With trembling fingers, he went to the desk and picked up a piece of paper and a pen. When he'd been a mortal man, he and his grandmother had often sat together with a pen and paper, his grandmother had been a poet, he a musician and so together they'd written songs, musical poetry.

"Write," she used to urge him when he was bitter or melancholy, "Write it all away," and William would diligently take up her pen and write. Always she'd applaud his efforts even if the writing was poor; he'd loved the old lady for that. For a few moments, William chewed the plastic lid of the pen, thinking of another life, another time and then suddenly he laid the nib of the pen on the paper and began to write.

A stronger one than I, walked across my barren heart,
Although I know you tempt me so,
My empire's nought but dirt.
I see your sorrow smile for me, affection fills your eyes,
Although I know you tempt me so,
My empire's nought but lies.
Even as I look at you, intentions become overt,
Temptation beckons in deep blue eyes,
But you risk so much hurt.
I cannot but to long for you,
A beckoning I can't deny,
But although by god you tempt me so,
My empire's naught but lies.

William was no more known for crying than Frannie was, but as he wrote, his own eyes welled up and tears spilled gently. The tears were not just for Frannie but nor were they for Rosa, but in a way, also for his grandmother who he missed terribly: this was the first poem he'd ever written that she would not read, the first time he had ever written anything without her. He'd found himself dry from the moment she'd died and until that night had never felt the urge to write. Suddenly he missed her, more than he thought possible. William's father, David, had been a rake and his mother a fainthearted, gentle woman who allowed his father to do as he pleased. David Craven had fathered over ten children but only two of them on his wife: William and his younger sister, Kathy, named for his grandmother. In the end, his mother had passed into sleep and he'd been delivered at the gates of Haverleigh to be raised.

After that, life had become easier, Katherine Craven had taught him to block out the anger, she'd told him a little of her life and of her sister who had died at the hands of a murderer. She spoke of seers and gifts and ghost and spirits, without even a glimmer of scepticism. In some ways, it was she who had allowed him to accept Hugh for what he was, when he had come calling. When he married, a clairvoyant Jazz singer named Rosa Smith, Katherine had welcomed her too with the same open arms.

Then he'd lost it all. Hugh the Huntsman had come for him in the night and inadvertently sent him home to massacre his wife and children… and Katherine Craven herself, the mother he'd never really had, dead with a snap of his jaws. After that, William had not gone home again. Years later, he had claimed his inheritance and upon entering the study, he had thought he'd seen the image of his grandmother standing there, just for a moment looking as she had in her younger life. She'd smiled and then faded out. That had been the only spirit he'd ever seen since the changers had taken him, despite that before then they had been abundant – a seer's gift.

William wiped the tears away angrily, crying solved nothing, and spilling tears would not bring back any of his dead. Grandmother and Grandfather were gone, his babies were gone and Rosa, poor Rosa. At least Frannie wasn't going to die on him, at least he couldn't destroy her the way he had his first wife and children.

As he often did, William lit the candle on his desk and turned off the harsh electric light. He'd actually been born in just the right generation to have grown up with electricity but the lights then had been so much dimmer and the modern ones just hurt his eyes after a while. He sat back in his chair and rummaged in the drawer until he found the little miniature portrait his grandfather, an artist, had painted as a wedding gift.

'I'm so sorry Rosie,' he whispered to the picture, 'But I think I am falling for that little drinker in there.'

Somewhere deep inside, the thought tried to raise its head that he'd been faithful to Rosa for longer than most mortal men were to their dead wives, and that she'd want him to move on and be happy, but the guilt washed over the feeling and quashed it.

Tiredly he undressed and slipped into bed, blowing out the candle as he did so. He couldn't sleep again though. His mind raved on and on, refusing to rest for even a moment. Thoughts of Rosa, thoughts of Frannie. As he pushed the feelings away, his mind brought him instead the horrific memories he'd been trying to repress for days. The feeling of helplessness as Henry's goons had strung him up, the anger at them, then the pain of Henry's own twisted fun, the agony of losing his eye. Fear too, he thought grimly, as hard as it was to admit it he'd been utterly terrified by that man who still looked like a boy.

As with the last time he'd lain in that bed, it was not long before the sound of footsteps came, and then the door creaked open and there she stood.

'Hey Frannie.'

'Do you mind? I keep having the worst dreams...'

'Come and I'll hold you.'

Frannie nodded, murmured something William didn't catch and then got into the big bed and snuggled herself into him, pulling the covers about them both. She was wearing just panties and t-shirt and, despite himself, William revelled in the smooth skin of her cold legs as they slipped into the bed next to his. Gently he put his arms around her, no lust stirred, other than the normal prickling he felt when she was close by, but instead he felt a tremendous closeness to her as she curled into his embrace with her back to him and her behind cuddled into his groin. Her little fingers clutched his hand, pulling his arm about her as she lay her sleepy head on his pillow. William watched her until she seemed relaxed and then he kissed her softly on the cheek, holding her tightly to him. Sleep came easily then for them both.

26

Frances Orchard,
2016

Frannie awoke to the feel of William's weight settling on the bed. She mumbled and opened her eyes. The drapes were tightly closed to protect her from the sun's rays but from the colour of the light she could tell it was late morning. William was dressed already; black combats, boots, his customary sleeveless shirt over a long-sleeved tee combo. His hair was pulled back in a band and frizzed slightly at the bottom where a good brush had sent static through it. There was a towel on the back of the chair, and the scent of William's sea-scented soap filled Frannie's nostrils. William had the book in his hands, open to about half-way. Frannie's gut tightened but she pushed the emotions down. William had to know, had to know it all. At her movement, he glanced down at her face.

'Good morning,' he whispered. The words were just words, dry and plain but even then, Frannie could hear the husky emotion in them.

'Good morning, William.'

'What they did...' he indicated the book and Frannie's eyes scanned it to see that he'd just passed the time of her turning, and was reading of the life of the nest in the 1900s.

'It was done with good intentions, on James's part anyway.'

'Henry wanted you for himself, even then, didn't he?'

'I think so.'

'Shall I continue?'

'Yes… there is so much more to go. I hope you don't mind reading about… about James?'

'He was a big part of your life, Frannie, and I have no jealousy for your dead husband. If anything, I think perhaps I see him in a clearer light than you do… he seems to have… but never mind…'

'No, what?' Frannie asked, her innards churning.

'He seems to have been very… easily led… by his brother…'

'He was, at times, but not all of us are blessed with a strength of character. I never saw James as weak, just innocent.'

'I guess. I didn't know him.'

'No, but I can... I can see why you might… think that. In some ways, I think he's better in the other world where he cannot see what Henry has become. He loved Henry, ever he did.'

'That much is obvious too. Why don't you go shower and get dressed? I'll finish reading…'

Frannie nodded and then put a hand on William's arm briefly, squeezing and then withdrawing.

The water in Frannie's on-suite shower was not as hot, nor as fast as William's, but it was enough to take away the grunge of having slept another night in a hot bed. Frannie had no soap, but yet the water refreshed her, it's sting on her face chasing away and semblance of sleep. For shampoo, there was a little sachet in amongst some cosmetics Ella had donated, and Frannie used this to soap up her hair, using some of the run off to wash too, and then stepped out of the cubicle. The tiles beneath her feet were cold, the breeze from the open window soothing after the heat of the shower. Frannie picked up the towel which had been left for her, and dried her skin thoroughly, then went to lay on the bed for a long moment, blissfully naked, with hair still damp from the shower, half-wrapped in a towel. It was years since she'd had such freedom without fear of Henry's molestation, and so for a moment she simply lay, eyes closed and body being caressed by the breeze.

When Frannie finally dressed and returned to the other room, William was just skimming through the final pages. He looked up and nodded, 'I'm done.'

'And your thoughts?'

'That you have committed atrocities, but that I have, in my time, done at least their equal, if not, worse. Redemption comes next for you, just as it once did for me.'

'What... what did you do?'

'I will tell you later, for now Sam wants to meet with you. Bring the book as it might save you a long story.'

Frannie nodded. 'Anything I should be aware of?' she asked, standing again.

'Nothing, other than that Sam is the eldest of your kind that I have ever met. Perhaps *the* oldest of your kind. Be respectful just as you would to Hugh, he's kind at heart but he doesn't take any crap.'

Downstairs, the house was empty but for the sound of voices coming from a room to her right. Thankfully, most of the drapes were closed, with just a few windows by the front door giving off light. William took Frannie's hand again and led her into the corridor there, and then pushed open the door. There Frannie felt her heart stopped beating in her chest, as she came face to face with a man she had all but forgotten.

The Black Marshes

'Oh my god! Ghost?' she whispered.

27

William
2016

William's eyes darted from Frannie to Sam, and then back again. Sam? *Sam was her "Ghost"? Sam!* His eyes moved to where Frannie stood rooted to the spot, her expression flickered from fear, to confusion, back to fear and then a beam of affection. Sam didn't move, didn't speak, just cast his eyes over her in the same way.

At the edge of the room, Hugh's dog thudded its tail against the floor next to his master's feet but did not move. Hugh sat in silence, watching events unfold in that quiet way he had, whilst Ella moved to stand, but then paused, uncertain. The only other person in the room was Reuben, brought in for his prowess as a fighter, William imagined, and the fact that he was Sam's own blood-child… that made him Frannie's kin, then…

The room was dark, shadowed for Reuben and Frannie's sake, William could bet, rather than Sam's, Sam was so old now that even the sunlight barely bothered him. In the time William had known him, some hundred years, he'd never seen him in a thirst, unlike some of the younger ones. Sam was ever calm, ever collected.

For the longest moment, the atmosphere in that room

was almost tangible. Sam stared at Frannie and she at him. Neither of them spoke, and nobody else did either

Finally, William spoke, just to break the silence. 'Frannie?' he said softly.

'Ghost?' she whispered again.

Sam Haverly wet his lips and then nodded. 'Hello Frances,' he said quietly, 'it's been a very, very, long time…'

Frannie nodded and then stepped forward, releasing William's hand. Sam stood and moved from his chair by the fireside to take her hands in his. He glanced around the room at the stunned faces and then barked out 'A minute, if you don't mind?'

Ella moved to withdraw at once but Hugh didn't move, other than to grab her wrist, and nor did William. He wasn't going anywhere. Reuben, however, nodded and slipped out of the room with just a nod to the others. Sam glared at the rest of them but did not challenge their presence. He led Frannie to the chair beside his and sat her down.

'Well, there we are then, mystery solved' he said at last in a tone quiet enough that it was obviously intended only for her, and then looked to his brother. 'Hugh, this is Frances Orchard…'

'I thought it might be, but didn't I already kill you once?'

'Hugh,' William snapped, his eyes darting to that man. He couldn't believe Hugh could speak so blasé of it. Frannie seemed nonplussed though and shook her head.

'You tried. You killed Josephina and… and James…'

'When was this?' Sam asked.

'1912,' Frannie said, 'August 1912'

Sam seemed surprised but as always, he kept himself in check. William wanted to go to Frannie, to wrap her up and tell her she needn't rehash it all again, but he didn't quite dare and besides, Frannie was holding her own all right.

'I presume then, that the family Orchard returned for you? You were a half-breed, but you were aging last I saw you.'

'I was,' Frannie whispered. 'I'm no longer a half-breed.'

'No, and yet still not quite… but never mind, we'll cross that bridge later. Was it James?'

Frannie nodded, 'and… and… Henry,' she said. 'I didn't want them to but it was the only way. I have come to understand.'

William found himself looking from one to the other during the conversation. He was exhausted, body and mind, and if it weren't for Frannie's fingers tangled in his, he might have got up and left.

'And so the man calling himself Henry Quinn, is in fact Henry Orchard? The younger brother?' Sam asked.

'He is,' Frannie confirmed.

Sam stood and moved to the window. He was dressed in a tailored suit and expensive shoes. A wealthy man beyond doubt and much less ragged than the pack of mingled changers and drinkers William was used to at Haverly House.

'Tell us about Henry. It's not often anybody gets one-up on my brother… I want to know everything.'

'That can be summed up easily. He's clever but he's a coward. If you get close, he will run. He hides behind tricks and cameras because he's deathly afraid of wolves.'

'He didn't seem overly afraid of me,' William could not help but comment.

'No, because he had you in chains. It is easy to be brave when your enemy is restrained,' she paused a moment, her eyes resting on him, and then turned back to Sam. 'I was never as Henry is, I swear it. If you believe nothing else, believe that.'

'I believe you. I had no idea this had happened,' Sam replied. 'I left the others to their own and forbade them to return. I left you because I had already caused you so much loss. I wish I could say it was for your benefit, but you were in as much danger as you ever were… I think it was guilt, Frances, I'm sorry.'

'It's done now,' William interrupted. 'Frannie's with us now, and we have that fiend to deal with.'

'Agreed,' Hugh said. 'I'll not make this mistake again.'

A silence fell, broken only by Ella's murmuring to Hugh's dog, stroking its ears. The atmosphere thickened again, but then Hugh spoke, catching William's attention back from where it was wandering again.

'Sam, I suggest you and I go in alone. Frannie can draw us up house plans and mark on the cameras we know of but I'd rather she stay here. The boy will pose no threat you either of us if we can just catch him. Rather than trigger his defences, we could just go in as I did when I took William out.

'I'll come,' William volunteered at once, 'I wouldn't mind showing that boy just what he has to be afraid of, in us.'

'No,' Hugh shook his head.

'Why not? Because I was captured? You were nearly captured too, it was a damn trap…' he paused and let his gaze settle on Frannie, 'I want to… to help in any way I can.'

'No because you are too angry,' Sam said. 'and no longer… objective…' the man glanced at Frannie, then back to William. His point obvious.

William nodded, 'Fine, you have a point, although I'm unimpressed you think I'd allow that to better me.'

'Will, it would, it would anyone,' Ella said, speaking for the first time. 'Stay? It's not worth the risk.'

William sighed, and then stood. 'Fine, he said, 'Fine. I'm going home though, I'm not going to pace around this house wishing to know what was happening. Frannie, Ella will show you where I live, if you want me. It's walkable for a drinker during the day if you're quick.'

Frannie looked shocked but merely nodded. William glanced from her to Hugh, then back to her. He let out a long breath, trying to calm himself.

'Ella will show Frannie over in a few hours… after you have run…' Hugh said, firm.

William nodded again, bit back a retort, unsure even of what was angering him so badly. Without another word, he stood and stalked out of the room, through the corridor, and out of the front door.

28

Frannie, 2016

The cottage was somewhat lost in the woods, just as William had once described it to Frannie. The trees nearby let off a scent of honeysuckle and the odd pine smell of evergreens. It was an old structure, as old as the house at least, two storeys but they must have had low ceilings, and old brick-work which crumbled a little. The rain had rendered the ground beneath Frannie's feet a little slushy, but not enough to make a mess of her boots. The sky was darkening too, not just with clouds but with the pulling in of the dusk.

Frannie knocked and stood nervously without. Her day had not been easy, trying to hold back from coming to find him. She'd sensed his pain well enough, but didn't know how to abate it. Finally the door of the little cottage swung open and William stood in the doorway. He'd obviously not long showered and his hair was still loose and damp around him in a long honey mane. His chest was covered only by a thin black workout vest and he was wearing black jeans, bare feet. Different clothing to earlier and the second shower in a day; Frannie guessed he must have heeded Hugh's words. William's gaze ran over her, but he still looked tired, didn't smile. Frannie's eyes drank him in eagerly but with caution. It was hours since he'd stalked out of the study and she wasn't sure of his mood. She tried a smile, and he stepped back, still wordless, to give her access to enter.

'Am I welcome?'

'Always,' finally he spoke.

Frannie took a long breath, a hidden sigh of relief, and used the moment to survey the house. The evening's rain still glistened on the doorframe but within was warm and dry. As she entered, Frannie could hear the crackle of a fire and thought she could see the glow of it through the open door to her right. Before her was a dark corridor with a staircase and another door hidden behind. To her left, was another door and from beyond this came the smells of food cooking.

'I hope I haven't interrupted your cooking?'

'Not at all, in fact, if you haven't eaten I've plenty for two.'

'Thank you. I brought wine,' she said, showing the bottle that Ella had given her before showing her the way. William took the wine and then re-entered the house, bidding her to follow him. Inside the door from whence the fire crackled, Frannie found a pleasant, homely little nest. There was an overstuffed couch against the wall, opposite the fireplace, and a table in the corner set up with two chairs. At the wall above the fireplace to either side of it were two painted portraits, a man and a woman of probable Victorian dress. The woman was red of hair, and the man darker. Both had smiling and friendly countenances.

'Your parents?'

'Grandparents,' he corrected. 'I was brought up by my grandmother and grandfather.'

'Beautiful work.'

'It is. My grandfather was an artist, and my

grandmother a writer. I have a few bits and pieces I appropriated from the house.'

'He was very talented then,' Frannie smiled. Then her eye lit on another picture, this time a photograph, which was mounted onto the far wall, opposite the door. This was late 1920s perhaps. Blurry and brown-led colours as would be expected for the era. It was of a woman and a man who for a moment Frannie did not recognise. Then suddenly the face became clearer, joltingly so. William's hair was short, clipped neatly about his ears. He was dressed in the height of the fashion for the time, with a black-tie suit and a shaven face. He looked perhaps thirty in the picture. The lady by his side had a wide smile as she clutched his fingers. Her hat sat on her head cockily and her bobbed hair beneath was shiningly dark. Frannie turned back to William and saw him wet his lips.

'Rosa,' he said. 'And I.'

'Your wife?'

'Yes.'

'She was... was very pretty.'

'She was.'

'What happened to her?'

William shook his head, 'I can't... not now. I'm tired Fran.'

Frannie nodded, compassion filling her, and put a hand on his arm.

'I'm ok, just... just tired,' he said again.

'Ok,' Frannie whispered and sat herself at one of the little wooden chairs by the table. William popped the cork on the wine and poured them both a glass. Frannie stepped further into the room and took a seat on the sofa, wine in hand, whilst William served up the food.

They ate in almost silence, every conversation dying quickly. Frannie sighed at last. 'Look, you said I am welcome but I don't feel it. Should I go?'

'No, please, don't.'

'What then? This morning we were… and then Ghost… and now you can barely look at me and I don't know what I have done.'

'You've done nothing.'

'Then what?'

William sighed and sat back in his chair. He looked up at her and then sighed again. His fingers fidgeted with the ends of his hair.

'Frannie, I'm just overwhelmed,' he said at last, 'Back there, Hugh said I was too lost in anger to be any use to him, and he was right. The control you saw, when you saw me change, is hard worked-for. Not many can master it and in such a heightened state, I can't. I lost myself, just now, when I ran. I've not done so for many years. I am clouded by my anger and the feral in me is fed by it.'

'Because of what Henry did to you?'

'No! Because of what Henry did to you, Frannie… I'm dangerous when angered and the more I come to know of you and your life, the more angered I become. Us changers need to be disciplined to remain non-dangerous to those around us! I know that better than most and I am losing my grip on myself.'

Frannie sighed and laid back against the sofa. 'William,' she said, 'I'm going to be really honest now. Really, really honest.'

'Go on.'

'Until I met you, no, not just you, but all the good people here – Hugh, Ella, my Ghost, all of them… my intention was not to go on, anymore. Oh, I'm not talking suicide, but I wasn't going to fight either – Hugh, when he got to us… which I fully believed he would do, was supposed to take me too. I never asked for this. I was just a little girl when Ghost did what he did to me, and it has all spiralled and moved on in ways that I cannot fight. I've no strength left in me, where once I had so much. I was a farm-girl who secured the hand of the wealthiest heir in the county. I had gusto and self-assurance. I've lost that. I still don't know if I can find that again but when I'm with you…' she allowed the words to hang a moment and then spoke them, 'when I am with you, I feel something again other than crushing misery and regret.'

William leaned forward suddenly and pushed his lips to hers. Frannie mumbled in surprise but it was lost in the kiss. William's tongue probed hers and his body moved to wrap itself about her.

'That's just how I feel,' he whispered, pulling away just long enough to speak, 'just how I feel.'

'Then let us stop all this pussyfooting around and just say it. I want you, William. We've not even known each other a week yet, but I want to be with you. I want to lie in your arms and kiss you and fuck you and let go of what was. You said you don't want to be my bandage but it's not that, it's more than that! I knew something was changing the minute I set eyes on you!'

'And I you, Frannie, I wish to call you mine.'

'I am my own, but I will let the world know that no other can have me, if that is enough?'

William's arms tightened and his lips sought hers again. Frannie felt somewhat like she was melting inside, all of the tensions pent up so long beginning to spill. William kissed her for a long, languid moment, and then stood and offered her his hand. Frannie took it and allowed him to lead her out of the door to the living area and up the old wooden staircase. Above were two rooms, a bathroom and a bedroom. Frannie's heart pounded as he led her into the latter. The bed was old, wooden, and steady in the way old furniture is. The bed-set was plain black, with soft looking pillows and a black fleece bedspread over the bottom of the bed. A gas heater stood in the corner of the room letting out a little heat so that the room wasn't too chilled. William's hand clutched Frannie's gently as he led her to the bed.

'If you are sure?' he asked softly.

'Surer than I have been for some time.'

The bed was warm and soft where William lowered Frannie into it, so soft that she guessed the coverlet was more likely an eiderdown than a duvet. William stood above her for a moment, and then stripped himself of his t-shirt. Frannie allowed her eyes to take in his form, covered in a downy coat of hair, and felt her body responding to him. She sat up but rather than embrace her, he slid his hands up her top and pulled it up off of her skin, leaving her in just her bra and skirt. He moved in then, running kisses along her throat and shoulders, touching every inch of exposed skin he could find. Frannie's fingers slid into his hair, tugging slightly on the thick locks whist his lips pulled her closer and closer to losing herself in the oblivion of pleasure. The feeling of oneness was closer than even the bond she had shared with Andre, more like that of she and James. William went into her and Frannie moaned. Her body was sleek with sweat and her limbs limp from exhausted pleasure. William's love-making was slow, unhurried. He thrust deeply, but without haste, until Frannie felt the orgasm rushing over her limbs, followed shortly by his own gasp and stiffening. Together then, they fell into a heap. For a long moment, they lay thus, and then gently William removed himself from Frannie and pulled the covers about them. Frannie rolled in so that her face was buried in his shoulder and closed her eyes.

29

Henry Quinn, 2016

Henry Quinn was sitting alone in the chamber he'd once shared with the bitch when he saw the two figures enter the house on the CCTV. He started, moving to view the tiny figures on the blue screen, and his heart pounded. That was Ghost, there was no doubt of that, Ghost in the company of his enemy, Hugh Haverly. Henry sucked in a deep breath, his mind darting about from one idea to another. He had nothing in place, no plans for this lone attack. He'd guessed the bitch would have given away half his secrets, but she'd not known them all. Only a fool would give somebody who hated them as much as Frannie did the keys to their destruction... but he'd expected word of the imminent attack at least.

As the figures entered the house and slipped down through the back door, Henry moaned aloud. He was at a loss of what to do. He could run, now, just like before, or he could stay and try to defend his children. In another world, Henry had had a lot more to lose, and a lot more to fight for. Everything was spiralling out of his control now. He'd lost her, he was losing hold of the nest, slowly but surely, as the younglings turned against him. He'd lost his sister, and in many ways, he'd lost James too. His mind tried to take him to the sad ruin which had once been his brother, but he couldn't bear to think of that, not in his panic.

For long wasted minutes, Henry sat staring at the screen, He was surprised that they would have the gall to come alone, and then the thought took him, where were the rest of the pack, if not entering with their leader? Another wave of panic tried to take him as the memory returned of those dripping maws, jaws of steel tearing off half of Phina's face, more so earlier in his life them ripping out his own belly and leaving him hanging onto life by a thread. Henry moaned again and put his hands over his temples, pressing there. A glance at the clock on the mantle showed him that it was close on 5am. It would be dawn soon, they must have done it on purpose, left it so late that his children would be retiring. He glanced back to the screen, they were gone from it now, but at a guess, they were probably close to entering the cellar. There was, of course, another way out, Henry's bolt-hole, but if he wasn't careful, they'd catch him before he could get to it.

Quickly Henry jumped to his feet and pulled on a jumper. He never felt tired, never felt lost, but suddenly he realised he was done with it all. Let them clear out the house, god they could burn it to the ground for all he cared, he had already lost everything. Almost running, he opened the door to his chamber and peeked out. In his mind, screams echoed, although in truth there were none yet, just the memories of the children he'd lost, of the sister he'd left to die and, before that, the family he'd lost.

Henry stifled a sob, trying to harness the anger which he normally employed to keep him going. He missed them all suddenly: Frannie, Phina, his human family, his undead family, even James – but Henry pushed that aside, of all the faces he must forget, James's was the worst. A tear ran down from his eye as he slipped through the secret door and up the stairs. Feeling like the worst coward on earth, he looked up the stairs to where some of the brethren lived, to where Hugh and Sam must have gone, and then turned tail and ran towards the back of the house and escape just like he had before.

30

Samuel Haverly, 2016

Sam felt rather like a murderer as he put his knife through the last of the sleeping drinkers whom he'd found in the rooms just below stairs. He'd expected resistance, had expected them to be prepared, to fight, but they had all obviously given up for the day, gone to ground and he'd simply had to walk between them with his knife. It felt cowardly and ungallant to do it this way but he soothed himself by thinking that at least they died without pain. This was Hugh's territory, Sam normally didn't get involved in culling and the brief taste of the life he'd thrust his brother into all those years earlier was enough to leave a bitter taste in his mouth. Sam wiped his knife clean on an old rag, and then jumped as the door opened. It was just Hugh.

'Quinn's not here,' he said quietly. 'And my wife just discovered we're gone and sent me a rather… blunt text message explaining how she feels about this.'

Despite it all, Sam couldn't help but smile. His younger brother had shocked them all when he'd finally brought home his tiny little wife but Sam could see how she'd changed him and it made him feel a little more optimistic that somebody so set in their ways could still change.

'You're in trouble then?'

'She'll soften as soon as I get in.'

Hugh smiled and Sam would have hardly believed the activity that his brother had just been engaged in if he hadn't known better. Sam never reminisced about the time before the curse, but just briefly he had a flash of a memory of his much younger brother in a time when all he had hunted was boar, and the sadness set into his old heart again. This curse was his fault, the result of his idiocy. Hugh had grown accustomed to killing people, and that too was his fault.

'So what now? This was the last one sleeping here. There are one or two still outside but other than Henry, I guess we're done.'

'There are... people down in the basements,' Hugh said.

'People? Other drinkers?'

'No...' Hugh sighed heavily and for a moment Sam saw a glimpse of softness before it was covered up. 'Food...'

'We should go and let them out I suppose.'

Hugh nodded. 'You do it Sam, they'll all need to be... and I... can't... not tonight.'

'I know, little brother, I know...'

'Good. I'm going home, home to my wife,' Hugh said.

Sam put a hand onto Hugh's arm. 'Go, take my car. I'll rent a cab to get home.'

'Nah. Going to walk into the village and call a taxi myself, I don't feel much like driving. Besides, I plan on taking out any of the stragglers we've missed on my way.'

Sam nodded again and left a hand on Hugh's arm. 'Go... go and bury your anguish in that pretty little woman of yours... and let the others know what has happened here if you will.'

Hugh nodded again and then left, knife sheaved safely

away in his belt. Sam took a deep breath and then made his way down to the lower basements of the house. Hugh was right; there were five humans, all bound and in various stages of being bled, locked into rooms down in the basement. Sam untied them quickly and sent them, stumbling and confused, on their way. They were all dazed, ill-looking but made their way out of the house slowly, thinking that they were just members of a party which had gone wild. Sam wasn't as good with the mind control as Hugh was, it was a changer trick really, but the elders blurred those lines somewhat anyway. Sam was pretty sure it would do. Most had come of their own accord anyway, drawn in by the appeal of the drinkers which was born in their mind by the mainstream media outbreak of romantic vampires. There were few of those, Sam thought bitterly and even those in his care who tried to do good were so broken and damaged that they were more likely to cause hurt anything else. His mind flickered to Frannie and William, and he allowed a smile to come. He wished them luck, they'd both been through hell, but inside him the cynic still believed that time would bend them. At least Hugh had Ella, he thought, at least there were some constants to love amongst their kind.

Sam sat in the dark basement for some time, just thinking, and then stood to leave. As he did so he caught the scent of another, not a human but a drinker like himself. He frowned. Was Henry still hiding down there somewhere?

Warily, he pulled out his already stained blade and began a second search of the basements. Nothing. Confused, he sat back down again and tried to concentrate, it was definitely a drinker, he thought bitterly, and it was definitely close by. It was the third search of the basements where he found the drain-cover, under some boxes. With trepidation, he pulled up the cover and peered down. It was pitch black below and Sam felt his heart pound. There wasn't much left in the world to frighten Sam, but the idea of climbing down into that darkness filled him with unease. Leaving the cover open he went back up into the house looking for a torch. He found nothing but a box of candles and an old jam-jar. It'd have to do.

The first few steps down into the peaty earth were the worst, after that it was easier although Sam couldn't lose the thought that Henry was still lurking somewhere, waiting to trap him inside. It wasn't so though, and soon Sam found himself at the bottom of the rusty old ladder which hung there. He lit his candle and found himself in a hidden annexe, a large room with a corridor running off of it. All around him were boxes and a quick examination showed him it was just tat, rather like the stuff most people kept in their attics; old clothing, rotten books, some chipped and faded ornaments. All going mouldy and half of it broken. Sam looked about him with apprehension which was fast turning to curiosity. In fear of losing himself down in the hidden basement, he placed the candle in the jar at the foot of the ladder and lit a second one from the wick of the first. Then, hoping that the ground was well encased in mud rather than the more flammable peat which made up the marshes, Sam set off down the corridor. If he had thought to explore though, he was disappointed for the corridor simply led to another door, old and heavy. Sam pushed it, expecting it to be locked but to his shock, the door rolled open.

Sam stopped short. In the corner of the room was a crouched figure. Sam felt his muscles tense but at once he realised he need not worry, this one was another prisoner. The man's hands were chained to the floor and his long stringy hair was tangled and matted with dirt. He was clothed but the clothing was ragged and torn beyond recognition.

'Frannie?' the old creature whispered. Its voice cracked,

dry and rasping. 'Is that you? Henry? Frannie. Dead – all, or none. Don't know… maybe… maybe…'

'Who's that?' Sam murmured. 'Who's there?'

'Frannie? Who is that? Ghosts? Henry?'

Sam stopped sharp as he began to recognise the voice of his youngest offspring. He'd not heard it in so long but the familiarity was unmistakable.

'What? No, it can't be…' Sam muttered, stepping into the room, using his knife to wedge the door open.

James Orchard lifted his head painfully, wincing at the light spilling from the candle in Sam's hand.

'Ghost?' he whispered again, 'Ghost…'

31

William,
2016

The cottage was very quiet but for the whispers of the forest which surrounded it. The room was dark too, lit by a candle in the window, despite how a single click of a switch would have flooded it in bright electric light. William sat on the edge of the bed. He'd half-dressed again, wearing his black jeans, but topless.

Frannie lay naked behind him, wearing only the duvet about her form. Three times, since they'd fallen into the bed, they'd made love, enough that his muscles felt strained and sore, and Frannie's eyes had taken on a deep, satisfied glow. He hoped he was not about to remove that glow from them for good. It was close on 5am. The darkness was soothing though, as was the sound of the wind murmuring through the trees outside.

William looked up at Frannie who was still waiting for him to speak. 'I killed my family,' he finally said, allowing the words to echo, 'my wife, my grandmother and two of my three children….'

Frannie didn't react, not even a glimmer of surprise. William watched her face in the darkness for a long moment, waiting for her to speak but she didn't. He wished he could read minds. He didn't want to lose her affection, but he knew he had to go on now.

'I was born in 1900,' he said. 'I was brought up by my grandparents, as I told you earlier, and that was for a reason. I was a seer – you'll know more of that word if you spend more time here…'

'Like seeing the future?'

'No, like seeing the dead. Apparitions, phantoms, ghosts. My grandparents were like me, my father wasn't. He went off when I was a kid and I had very few friends. I was a musician, I didn't play anything particularly well – a few tunes on the piano – but I wrote music, songs, words. I think I would have been destined a poet, like my grandmother, had it not been for the jazz explosion in the twenties.'

William looked to Frannie again and she nodded, encouraging him to go on.

'I met Rosa at a bar, not far from here,' William continued. 'She was pretty as a picture, modern and feisty. Where my life at home was still very much lost in the last century, she was so modern, so brave with her bobbed hair and knees on show. She made a living as a Jazz singer, but she was also clairvoyant and gave private readings… I went to her, to see if she could tell me anything more about the spirits which plagued me and I loved her almost as soon as I saw her. Somehow, for reasons I never did understand, she loved me back. We were married in 1925, and the babies came quickly after. Rosie, Jack, and then Alice. By thirty years old, I was settled and happy and I could not have asked for more.'

'So what happened? You said you killed them? I presume you mean… figuratively?'

William moved his eyes to her face, he hoped she could see his reply in his eyes because he couldn't find the words to correct her. 'I met Hugh,' he said at last, 'That's what happened. It wasn't his fault though, not really. Hugh had

The Black Marshes

always kept half an eye on us, we were the main line of his descendants and I guess any man would be interested in what happened to his family after so many years. I never knew what he was, I could never have guessed it, but he was introduced to me as a distant cousin and we became friends. Hugh rested here for a time, then. He was tired of the world and I now know that this was because he'd been working too hard, with no end in sight. You know what he does… it's not easy for any man to carry such a burden and he didn't have Ella then, to comfort him. I suppose this was about 1930ish'

'1930? That was only twenty years after he'd cleared out the Orchard Estate,' Frannie said softly. 'When James died.'

William shifted on the bed so that he could take her fingers in his. A million emotions rushed through him, his condolences and sympathies but he knew that to express those would be to change the subject and he needed to finish his tale. Instead of voicing the thoughts, he kissed her fingers softly, then laid them back down.

'Hugh and I became friends,' William continued. 'It was against his better judgement, I know that now, but it happened anyhow. Then I became ill. I still don't know what it was but I was burning up, lost in the agony of a gut which felt on fire. I was feverish and hallucinating wildly. I have no memory of the events which followed, but I know from talking to Hugh that he came for me and he took me away from my home by claiming he knew of a doctor who could save me.'

'He turned you?'

'He did. There used to be another house, right on the edge of the land here, which was built in part by my grandmother's family. It was destroyed in a fire in the fifties but still stood then and was by then in Hugh's possession. He took me there, and he locked me in the basements so that when the change came upon me I would be safe. I was insane, Frannie. He'd changed me whilst the hallucinations were upon me and afterwards, they didn't go away. I half-believed that what was happening to me was just another hallucination. I had no grasp on reality. I think Hugh realised then what a mistake he'd made, but the true danger didn't show until the day one of his offspring came to feed me, and didn't lock the door behind them.'

'Oh... oh god...'

'I don't think it was a conspiracy against me,' William said. 'I don't think it was done on purpose, just pure clumsiness... there was a small group there then, some of Sam's tutees and they took it in turns to care for me. As night fell, I escaped and I went home...'

'You don't need to tell me anymore,' Frannie said gently, leaning forward to touch his hand.

'No, I don't suppose I do, but now I've started... I... I killed Rosa first. Then Jack – my boy, a servant next, then Grandmother and finally my eldest daughter, Rosie. I was still... I was still chewing on Rosie's carcass when Hugh found me.'

William looked up into Frannie's eyes and silently pleaded for her understanding. She seemed to be processing this information and did not speak.

'I was suicidal,' he said, 'I think any man would be after doing what I had done. Hugh stopped me. He said if I truly wanted to die, he'd end my life, but before he did, he had a counter offer – he told me about his work here, how he rids the world of those who cannot live in harmony with humanity. He offered to train me to help him and in the ight of redemption, I agreed.'

'Oh William, I am so sorry for...'

'Don't! of all things, I cannot abide sympathy! There's more, too. In the spirit of openness. I have another child...'

'You had an affair? Then?'

'No,' he shook his head. 'No, I'm still… I mean I can still…'

'You are still… fertile?'

'Yes, it's not unheard of in my kind, and sometimes it happens. None of us know how or why. I fathered a little girl not so very long ago, really. There was no relationship to speak of with her mother, just a casual affair which led to the birth of a child – my little girl. I sent money for the child and as I am sure you can imagine, Hugh kept an eye on her, but she was simply human. She had offspring too, humans, so I have descendants.'

Finally, he stopped talking and looked up at Frannie. She was sombre and quiet but there was no disgust in her eyes, simply tiredness.

'I suppose this is us done?' he asked, unable to contain it. 'You won't want me now…'

'Of course I still want you William. I…' she was interrupted though by a knock at the door.

'Who the devil?' William frowned. Quickly he pulled on a t-shirt and waited for Frannie to throw on her clothes, then they moved to the door. Ella was without. Her hair was ruffled and her eye-makeup smudged. She looked very grave. Newton was at her heels.

'What? What is it?' William asked, alarmed.

'Hugh and Sam went after Quinn… alone, whilst we were sleeping. I've just spoken to Hugh on the phone – the nest is gone but Henry escaped. I thought we'd all be safer in the house.'

32

Sam Haverly, 2016

Sam stared at the broken man before him. His hair was long and thin from malnutrition but still it curled and still it held its dark pigment. He had no beard and, as Sam moved closer, he realised that he had no eyelashes left either. His frame was so thin that he looked skeletal. His eyes were dim, uncomprehending and the flesh of his jaw and cheekbone emaciated to the point that the skin was stretched tight. He was dressed in rags, old clothing which was hanging off his form. He was chained to the floor in a manner which stopped him from even being able to stand.

'Oh Jesus,' Sam whispered. 'James?'

The man looked up at him again in shock and Sam fancied he saw a glimmer of recognition again, just for a moment, and then the man began to gibber again. His eyes shone an odd shade of red and his teeth were extended but it was definitely him.

'Ghost in the corner, ghost, ghost,' he muttered. 'Ghosts always but never Frannie, Frannie. Henry,' then suddenly he looked up and his eyes widened. 'Not a ghost?' he said. 'but a ghost…I know you?'

'You should,' Sam said, kneeling down beside James so

The Black Marshes

that the man could see his face. James started violently.

'Oh god,' he cried out, trying to shuffle to the end of the chains. 'No! No! Not again... don't! No more... Henry, kill me for god's sake! Stop this, stop it,' the man began to sob and Sam felt his heart go out to him. Gently, he laid a hand on James's trembling shoulder.

'Frannie?' James whispered suddenly, looking up as though he had forgotten Sam was there already. His eyes dimmed a little and then raised to the ceiling. 'God, if you're going to send me tormenting visions then send me Frannie.'

'What the hell happened to you James?' Sam asked, and then he realised another darker, more hideous truth: Henry had told Frannie that James was dead, that he himself had buried the body, but that was obviously a lie. Sam's lips twisted in disgust. 'James... did... did Henry do this to you?'

'Henry?' James muttered, fear written all over his face. 'Henry's here? No Henry! Please! Why?'

'James?'

'Henry... what? Who are you? Where's Frannie? No Henry please!' James stared at Sam again and then anger shone on his face. 'Let me out! Now!' he hissed. 'This isn't funny ... not funny, not funny...shush! Don't let him hear!'

The anger faded and then James began to cry again, dry hiccupping sobs which tore at Sam. His hands went to his face and Sam realised he was holding his lips closed. His hands were scarred beyond belief and Sam had to avert his eyes from the old bloodstains around him. Then he saw it. The pile of finger bones by James's side. There must have been ten at least and something else too, rotting old meat. His stomach contracted suddenly and he had to move back a step. What the hell had been going on down here? Sam stood in silence for a moment. In five hundred years, never had he seen sadism of this magnitude. Never could he have imagined it, even of his own kind.

'We can figure out what to do about Henry later,' he said at last, 'For now, we need to get you... to get you out of here.'

'Are you really real?' James whispered.

'Yes James. I'm really real. How long have you been down here?'

'Maybe one hundred years, maybe one. Maybe twenty, maybe none,' the man began to sob. 'Hungry,' he whispered.

Sam felt the anger twist in his gut. It was more than likely that the poor guy had been here since Henry had told Frannie he was dead. 1912. A hundred years... it didn't bear thinking about. He gripped the thick chains in his hand, and pushing all of his weight against his bent knee, he snapped them. The exertion made his hands hurt, his muscles pull, but the anger fuelled him. 'There,' he said when the man was loose. 'There can you stand?'

'Home now? To Frannie?'

'To Frannie, after we've fed you.'

Sam watched in silence as shakily, James stood and tried his legs. He was incredibly unsteady and stumbled as he tried to walk. Sam put an arm out to him to help him steady himself but he fell again. Sam sighed and slid his fingers about the knife he carried.

'James, I am going to need you to drink something,' he said, and he slid the blade into his hand and held it out. James all but leapt on the blood, a snarl in his throat. Sam did not pull away, no fear at all, just pity. James drank until the wound was fully healed, then bit deeply into Sam's wrist, opening the vein like an animal. Sam winced but tolerated the pain. Finally, he pulled away. James sat slumped again for a few minutes, but already Sam could see the healing beginning. As they sat, the younger man's eyes didn't leave Sam's face, searching him intently and suddenly he spoke again, his voice was clearer now, and

Sam could see clarity returning to his eye.

'Frannie's ghost,' he said.

'Frannie's ghost, yes.'

'Frannie's dead?'

'No James, Frannie's alive,'

James frowned. 'Still?' he whispered and Sam felt his heart breaking for the broken creature.

'Still. Always. Now come, if you can walk now we need to leave this darkness.'

Together, Sam and James walked up the old dark passageway, James still leaning heavily on Sam as they went. The candle Sam had left at the foot of the ladder still burned and Sam led James to it. When they reached the ladder he nodded at it.

'You're going to have to climb it,' he said, hoping that the tiny amount of healing James had done so far would be enough.

'Here, like this,' he added, gripping the ladder with his hands. James's eyes moved up and down the metal structure, and then he nodded. He couldn't do it though, there was nothing left of him to power his old bones. In the end, Sam half-dragged, half-carried him up.

Upstairs, James stopped and looked about him in amazement. Sam didn't speak, letting the shock of the modern world encompass his blood-child. So much was different now. Even if the man regained his mental faculties, the whole world was a much different place than when he'd left it.

'What…?' James asked with awe in his voice and turned back to Sam.

'A hundred years is a long time. You will adjust.'

Darkness still pooled from the window, albeit dimly fading darkness and Sam was glad of the winter month, glad he'd not had to drag James out of the basement in the bright sunlight.

Telling the awestruck James to wait there, Sam headed

back into the used rooms of the house, looking for some modern clothing. The first room he tried was a woman's room but the second was better and he pulled from a drawer a pair of trousers and a hooded sweater. That would do, he thought, the hood would hide the man's skeletal face at least.

The journey home was a long one, longer than it should have been. One filled with James's terror and the churning emotions that man's emaciated state put within Sam. Before, he'd been happy to simply know Henry Orchard had run off again but now he knew he'd do anything to find him and put a silver blade through his heart himself. At home, the lights were all on, despite the beginnings of the morning. They were all still awake, waiting for him, he presumed. Unsnapping his seatbelt, he turned to James.

'Wait here,' he said, 'just... wait.'

Sam strode up to the front door and paused a minute, trying to untangle his thoughts before he went inside. Several long strides took him to the living area and there his eyes sought out little Frannie. There were several people lounging about the room. Ella in her normal chair, Reuben at the window, William on the sofa and another girl he didn't know playing with her phone in the corner. Human. Probably donor.

Frannie was sitting quietly at the corner of the sofa on which William sat. In her hands was a book and Sam almost smirked to see she was reading a romance novel. Her hair was bright blue but she wasn't wearing any makeup and her clothing was casual. Her feet were bare under soft cotton pyjama trousers. She wore a tightly fitted t-shirt under what looked like a man's shirt and her hair was pulled to the sides and braided prettily. William was also reading, but had a hand on Frannie's foot, just gently touching her. Damn, this was a right mess.

'Frances, I need to speak to you,' he said, 'a matter of

urgency.'

At once Fran was on her feet and Sam noticed that William too looked like he was about to rise. Sam was just finding the right words to tell William to stay behind, when suddenly he felt himself pushed aside. *So much for waiting in the car...*

'Frannie!' James whispered, 'Frannie!'

William stood and made a move to go to Frannie's side but Ella stopped him with a gentle hand to his arm. Frannie was oblivious; her eyes were stuck fast to the figure in the doorway. Sam went to speak again but was interrupted by the man pushing past him and half-running, half-stumbling into the room. Sam wondered grimly if it were possible for someone of his kind to faint, certainly Frannie was swaying slightly.

'Jamie?' She whispered, obviously overwhelmed.

Sam's eyes went to William who seemed to lose all his breath as he realised what was happening. Frannie's eyes moved back to him and Sam saw her anguish there too.

'Fran?' he asked in a trembling tone but she just stared at him for a moment and then back to James.

'Frannie?' James said again, moving closer.

'Jamie? But... but... you're dead!' she held out her arms and James fell into them, pressing her as tightly to him as his emaciated arms would allow.

'Am I?' James asked, shocked. 'Am I dead? Is this heaven? Frannie why is your hair blue? Is it because you are an angel? Are you dead too Frannie?'

Frannie reeled. Sam came to their side and gently pulled the two apart.

'Frannie?' James whispered again, taking her hand. 'Why are you sad Frannie?'

Suddenly the door swung open and his brother, Hugh, entered the room.

'What the devil is going on?' he snapped.

Sam watched as William's horror-struck face set to

neutral suddenly and he looked to Hugh.

'Frannie's husband is apparently not dead,' he said and then, with two slow, deep breaths he turned and left the room.

At William's departure, Frannie wailed and detached herself from James's embrace, running for the door in such a panic that she barged Sam out of the way. James looked to the door with forlorn eyes.

'Frannie,' he whispered again, and then there was silence.

33

Frannie,
2016

It was with a frantic, almost panicked gait that Frannie ran out after William. He was far enough ahead of her to leave her behind but as a sob broke through her voice, he paused, allowing her to catch up with him. He didn't turn though, not until her hand went to touch his arm. All at once all her senses were rife with a bombardment of emotion, the scent of him, the feel of his taunt skin under her fingers.

'Don't,' he almost growled.

'It's not my fault…'

William turned and showed her the pain in his features, the tears welling. 'I know it's not your fault, but I also know what it means.'

'How can you, when not even I know that?'

'I know how much you loved him, and I know what he was to you… I've read your story.'

'Yes, and you also know how I recovered from his death, how I… I moved on.'

'And now he's back…'

'He is, and I don't know what's going to happen now. I… for fuck's sake! I want you, William.'

'Only me?'

'I... can't answer that...'

William moved closer and cupped her face. Frannie looked up, willing him to understand, to accept that she was going to need time. William's good eye examined her for a long moment, and then he seemed to just deflate.

'William, don't...' Frannie whispered again, 'please, don't...' she broke off, she didn't even really know what she wanted him to not do.

William's thumb rubbed a tear from her face, then he leaned in and kissed it away. 'What do you want of me, Fran?' he whispered.

'I don't know,' she whispered, her heart hammering. 'I... fuck!' William's sighted eye roamed her face again and Frannie clutched his arm. 'I love you,' she said softly, 'I shouldn't say it yet, not when it's been such a short time, but I've never been so sure of my heart.'

'You love me?'

'Yes.'

William kissed her again but did not say it back, Frannie could not help but to wonder if he might have, in other circumstances. Pulling herself together, she pulled away from his kiss, but gently, and spoke again, 'I need to go in there now and... Jesus! I need to find out what the hell is going on but you and me are solid, ok?'

'Ok,' he murmured.

'Please don't go away.'

'I won't... let me go Fran, I'm going to go and run. Being human isn't overly appetising right now.'

'Ok,' Frannie whispered and let him go, her eyes running with water.

The light in the living room seemed suddenly dimmer as Frannie re-entered. Hugh and Ghost both sat quietly, watching events unfold as they were wont to do. Ella sat on the edge of the sofa where she had been when Frannie had fled. Her eyes were filled with concern. James, now next to Ella on the sofa, was feeding, a female, blond, donor in arm and blood trickling down over his wasted arms. Frannie just stared a moment. In the two hundred years she'd known James, she couldn't recall ever seeing him feed from the source, as it were. After a few moments he looked up, pulling away from the human donor in his arms, and shot Frannie a look of pure shame.

It's all right, Jamie,' she whispered.

'Fran,' he seemed less disoriented, more calm.

Hugh stood and put out a hand to the donor and she stood, grasping it gratefully. Hugh handed the girl to his brother who soothed her, holding her and kissing away her tears. James stood, hesitated, and then held out a hand for Frannie. She took it.

'What happened to you Jamie?'

'Henry…'

'Henry had him locked down in the basement, under your catacombs,' Ghost filled in quickly, 'he's been starved and tortured.'

'Oh god,' Frannie breathed, gripping James a little tighter, feeling the softness of his skin under her fingers. Smooth too, less human than she'd expected.

'Dark,' James said, 'kept locked there. Away from… everything, rats and bugs.'

Frannie's breathing turned ragged.

'Chained,' James added, 'chained to the floor. Don't dare cry, don't dare shout.' He wriggled his hand free of hers and showed her the scars networked over his fingers. 'cut them off,' he whispered.

'Why don't you take James upstairs?' Hugh said softly to Fran, 'Go and be together up there, Sam and I need to chat…'

Upstairs, it was some relief to be alone with James. Outside of the pity and sympathy of the others. The room was dim with the drapes closed, the electric light not quite giving off enough light to really illuminate the corners of the old dusty room. James sat on the bed, and Frannie noticed his fingers curl to touch the soft cloth, curling around it and caressing it.

'Are you tired?' Frannie asked.

James nodded. 'like I haven't slept in a hundred years.'

'I'm so sorry, Jamie, I thought you were dead.'

'I think I was.'

Frannie paused. 'In a way, I suppose, but now you are reborn.'

'Reborn, broken.'

'Not broken!'

James sighed, 'it clears and clouds. This smog inside of me.'

'It'll clear properly, in time.'

'Hope so,' he muttered and then fell quiet again.

'James, I have some of your things,' Frannie whispered, 'I managed to grab them when I fled, here…' she picked up the bag and removed the letters, then upended it onto the coverlet beside James. Out tumbled a mixture of keepsakes and suddenly Frannie was annoyed that she'd not kept more of his belongings. A shirt, some gloves, a few knickknacks. James touched each item with his long fingers. He was silent and Frannie couldn't even really tell if he recognised them. At last he looked up.

'Thank you.'

'You're welcome, Jamie,' Frannie paused, awkward. It was like talking to a stranger, the ghost of a person she'd once known. She moved to sit beside him and put a hand on his arm. James frowned, then looked up at her.

'Frannie – gone,' he whispered, 'my Frannie…'

'Yes, I'm afraid so, I am still her but time has changed me… I'm not your Frannie anymore.'

'My lady…' he smiled a painful cracked smile, 'my lady in britches.'

The Black Marshes

Frannie felt a tear fall and allowed it, not brushing it away but allowing the salt of it to tickle its way down her cheek. The sensation surprised her and she put up a hand to touch the water. 'I was… her… once.'

'And now?'

'And now I am just Frannie.'

'His Frannie – the wolf?'

Frannie paused, her hands felt suddenly clammy and her heart pounded. 'Yeah,' she whispered, 'I guess so. His Frannie now.'

James began to sob, his emaciated shoulders juddering with the force of it. He put his hands up over his eyes, hiding the tears from her, but Frannie slid an arm around him and laid a kiss on his forehead. 'Ever will I love you, darling,' she whispered, raw herself, 'time changes us and life has moved on. I can't be your wife now, but I can be your friend.'

'There's nothing left of me.'

'There's plenty and you too will move on from this, from all of it. You too will be happy, you too will learn to look back with ought but nostalgia.'

James still sobbed but the violence was lessened. 'So alone,' he whispered.

'Less alone than we ever have been. We have a family now, we are family to each other.'

James sighed and sniffed again, then moved his hands from his eyes, 'I'm hungry,' he whispered.

'Again? Already?'

'Always. Constant.'

'That too will pass, I'll ask Sam to send someone up, you sleep for now.'

James lay down, obedient as a trained dog, but his hand grasped hers a moment longer.

'Glad to have found you,' he whispered.

'Glad to have you back,' she replied, and it was the truth.

Emma Barrett-Brown

34

William,
2016

He had to run, had to! His anger and frustrations were too far gone to resist the pain which overcame him. Frannie's voice came again and again to his memory, tearful and pleading but William didn't stop, didn't falter. He almost tore the front door from its hinges as he swept out of it, repressing the change only until he was free of the house, off the drive and in the edge of the forest. Then he let it come, tearing the clothing from his form as the fur began to force its way through his skin.

The Haverleigh estate was safe to run in, it was designed to be so, and so William had no qualms as he fell to his knees, allowing his bones to click and grind, allowing his mind to let go of his humanity. Despite the worry of doing so, he let go of William and allowed the wolf – and the demon which controlled it – to fully encompass him.

At last, consciousness dimmed. The wolf stood, shaking free of the last of his clothing. He stood, and shook his body so that all his fur fell into place, and then padded towards the wood. Somewhere, deep within, William still held a semblance of control, although it was just by a thread.

Footsteps approached, and then the girl stood there, the tiny girl with the blond hair. Pack sister. If he thought hard enough, he could even have found her name, but he didn't. The girl paused, standing firm and calling something. Calling his name. Maybe. The wolf made to growl, but the fine thread within which was William stopped him. His bright eyes held hers, the feel of the wind calling, and then with a grunt, he turned and fled into the trees.

The trees were vibrantly alight, a crispness that no human eye could ever imagine. The grass beneath his paws was wet still from the rain, and the dew soaked into his fur. William, or the creature which had once been him, pushed itself further and further, faster and faster. He almost didn't see the danger until he was in it, and even then, it was too late. The boy stood, waiting, somehow knowing. The wolf tried to stop, to avoid the danger, but then a crash sounded, echoing all around him. He squealed and then, not realising yet, tried to continue to run. Then the pain exploded within him as the bullet entered his heart. The wolf squealed again, it's legs crumpling. Within, the being known as William screamed out, wanting to clutch as the wound as the molten silver coursed through him. With a crash, he fell.

35

Frannie,
2016

The clock above the living room fireplace ticked on and on relentlessly, screaming the ever-passing minutes like a doomsayer. It was close on three in the afternoon, and William had been missing for nearly a day. No word, no note, nothing. Half-convinced that he'd left on his own accord, Hugh and Ghost had half-heartedly looked for him until they found the blood. Then suddenly it was chaos, and panic.

Frannie sat sobbing in the living room. James, now rested, fed, and beginning to look more human, sat by her side, a hand on her shoulder and blue eyes examining her face. His own face was emotionless, his lips pressed closed and his eyes blank. Frannie didn't even know how to process all that had happened in the last day and so she allowed James to comfort her as she sobbed for William.

'I'm so sorry Frannie,' Ella whispered. 'We will get him back, I swear.'

Ella too had cried when they realised he'd not come back, when they had found the blood in the grass down by his cottage. Less hard and stern than the Haverly men, she was not afraid to show emotion.

'I just can't believe that Henry managed to take William down,' Frannie whispered. 'He's so scrawny and William is so… well, big.'

'William is also a hundred years younger than Henry,' Ghost reminded her from across the room. 'Remember, we are not dealing with humans here. Yes, William is very strong but Henry is no petty drinker, he carries my blood. That makes him one of the strongest currently in existence… and he's your sire…'

'I don't care… I will kill him for this.'

'Better to overpower him,' Ghost said, musing, 'I think that he seeks death, and that means that death is no punishment for what he has done.'

'We don't have the time or resources to play games,' Hugh interjected, appearing at the doorway. 'Revenge is a petty man's sport, brother.'

'But is justice?' Ghost snapped, then pointed to James, 'What justice is death for this? Poor James wished for death daily.'

James said nothing but looked at his hands.

'What do you suggest then?'

'A taste of his own medicine. He is my offspring, I'll take responsibility for his deeds if you allow me to intervene in my own manner!'

'Very well,' Hugh snapped, then sighed, 'That's if we can catch the bastard at all.'

'I think we should just go over to The Orchard Estate and try to reason with him,' Ella said softly. 'Henry's got nowhere else to go and he's no match for Hugh, Sam or… or even me! I don't see why we are all still waiting?'

'Because Henry is expecting us to do that,' Hugh said.

'Yes!' Frannie said hoarsely. 'Exactly. Henry is not to be underestimated. He's a trickster and a coward. If he hasn't planted some sort of trap I'd be very surprised! He has cameras all over the house, and he's a madman, not afraid of anybody. I'd imagine that the moment he sees us,

The Black Marshes

William will die. He wants me, don't you see that? He wants me back. Don't you people understand? Henry has the mind of a seventeen-year-old boy. He never grew up, he never matured! He is thinking like a teenager and he's playing games with us. All Henry ever wanted was me, look what he did to Jamie to get me…'

James glanced over at her. He still wasn't right, his face was ashen, still so gaunt, and his eyes flashed madly, moving from person to person, sometimes just staring into space. Feeding him and letting him sleep had helped though, and he no longer seemed completely bat-shit-crazy.

'Frannie, you can't just give yourself back to Henry though,' Ella said softly. 'You can't go back to that hell.'

'No! Won't let you!' It was the first time James had spoken in over an hour. His voice was returning too, to what it had been, despite that it was still somewhat gravelly.

'I don't intend to! I intend to make sure he releases William, and then turn him over to Ghost. We can.. can trap him! We can… he's not likely to see through a rouse if we… oh god!'

'How?' that was Hugh. 'How exactly are you going to trap him?'

'I'll find a way…I'll… I'll find a way.'

Hugh stepped further into the room and looked hard at Frannie. His lips pressed together but his grey eyes shone.

'You say Henry Quinn is playing games with us…' he said 'I say, let's play one back.'

Ghost's brow furrowed and Frannie watched as he frowned at his brother. 'Hugh…' he started but Hugh raised a hand to shush him.

'It'll work,' Hugh said simply.

Sam shook his head and Frannie saw that his brow furrowed with worry. Ella looked mystified.

'What is it?' she asked quietly. 'What are you thinking

Hugh?'

Hugh examined Frannie a little longer and then looked back to Ghost.

'You can try it, but I personally don't think it will work,' Ghost said. 'and it's a huge sacrifice, for dealing with one lone drinker.'

'What? For Christ-sakes, what?' Frannie exclaimed.

Hugh paused again, and then moved to sit at Frannie's free side. 'Frances,' he said, 'You are not completely, one hundred percent drinker... just like before. There's something in you, in your blood which is hanging onto a thread of humanity. I didn't sense it at first, but Sam and I have spoken of it, and I do see it now. You're still a hybrid, you always have been. The blood James put into you triggered the drinker side of you which Sam started, but it didn't destroy what was left of that human girl.'

'That's... impossible.'

'I know,' Ghost agreed, 'and yet...'

Hugh nodded again, and then put his hand on her arm. 'This is dangerous, and if it were not for the danger to William, I would not suggest it, but what if we... if I... tried to turn you, now? The human side of you might take on my blood...'

'What!' James exclaimed, shock in his tone but Ghost looked at him warningly and he lapsed back into silence. Frannie took his other hand, holding it tightly.

'Surely that's not possible?'

'I don't know, but what I do know is that it will hurt, it will be painful and almost impossible to bear. You see, when a drinker drinks from one of us, it is as though they merely drank human blood... until the change comes upon us. They... your kind that is... cannot digest the blood once the demon shines through, Frannie. If you seemed, to Henry, like a normal drinker, and if you let him taste you... you might be able to shock him for long enough to overpower him. You are already his equal because he's not actually your sire, as far as I understand it, Sam is. It is only through bullying and fear that he subjugated you. With my blood too you will be stronger again – stronger than him.'

'Ghost?' Frannie turned her eyes to her mentor.

'I don't like it Frannie, I say look to the long-term consequence! There's never been a hybrid before.'

'But I could take on Henry, if I did?'

'Yes, I think so, if it worked at all.'

'How…'

'I'd drain you first – and then…'

'You want to drain me?'

'I will have to, else you will experience the pain of the two forced within you fighting. If we drain you of what you have, it gives the wolf-blood a fighting chance to take over your human form, whilst the other re-forms.'

James made a strange noise in his throat and Frannie just gripped his hand a little harder. Despite her love for William, she had no intention of hurting James any more than she had and she knew how abhorrent the very idea must seem to him.

'And you are sure this will be enough to take Henry down? Alone? Enough not to just kill him, but to overpower him?'

'Yes, Henry will no longer be stronger than you, and also you'd have the power of surprise. I guarantee that he won't be expecting this. I agree with you, if Henry sees us all, then the chances are he'll kill William and possibly trick one of us into a trap – but if you went in alone…'

Frannie swallowed. 'And if it doesn't work?' she asked,

'Then either you will just revert back to what you are, or… well… it could even kill you… I just don't know.'

'All right,' she said softly. 'So then how am I supposed to get Henry to bite me? If he thinks I am a threat, if he thinks I'm not cooperating, he is more likely to behead me than to bite me.'

Ella had been quiet for a few moments, her face pale, but suddenly she spoke. 'Yes,' she said. 'If he thought you were *not* cooperating.'

Hugh pressed his lips together and Ghost sighed. Frannie looked about them in confusion and then suddenly the penny dropped.

'You want me to sleep with him?' she gasped. 'Oh god.'

'No!' James interjected again, his hand gripping Frannie's shoulder. 'No... no Frannie... No! Don't...'

'Hopefully it won't get that far,' Hugh interrupted. 'If you can manage to not get lost in the blood, let him bite you and then pull on the change. Hold him to you as long as you can so that he drinks... too much.'

Frannie gently removed James's hand from her shoulder and moved to the window. Tentatively she lifted the edge of the curtain and peeked out. The sun was high in the sky, making the lawns of the house crisp and beautiful in their bright green luminance. Frannie looked out, ignoring the feel of the life sapping from her. Ghost and Hugh watched in silence, Ella too did not speak but her eyes were softer, more sympathetic.

'Do you realise what you are offering me?' she asked, turning back to Hugh. 'You are offering me a weapon, as you put it, to beat Henry and save William but there is more to it than that. You are offering me the chance – even a small one – of a life in the sunshine with him, a life of running together, of sharing a curse. You are offering me a life and I want it Hugh, even despite the risks.'

James made another odd noise in his throat but Hugh nodded. 'Perhaps that might be the case – we just don't know.'

'It's worth a try, surely.'

'I thought you would see it that way, I would feel the same, in your position. There is more to it than you are considering, of course, you will have to be careful, always. You are agreeing to give yourself up for a few nights a month. You are agreeing to the risk of the unknown. As far as I know, this has never been done before and god-knows what will happen.'

Frannie nodded but still her eyes were on the little gap in the curtains where the sun spilled in. James got up and moved to her side again, gently he put an arm about her waist.

'Love you,' he whispered. 'Always…'

'I know, I'm so sorry Jamie.'

'You want… this?'

'I do, I'm so sorry.'

'You want him?'

Frannie nodded, tears spilling.

'Then come,' James said, and pulled her into his embrace. Frannie acquiesced, knowing what he was about to do, and silently nodding to the poetic justice of it.

'Are you sure?' James whispered again.

'I am.'

James looked about the room, his blue eyes scanning all the faces, and then his demon shone through again. Frannie closed her eyes as James's teeth tore at her throat.

36

William,
2016

William gasped and opened his eyes. His entire body ached, hurt. All about him was darkness, a thick blackness which blanketed the room, wrapping itself around his body. For a terrible moment, William's heart thudded as he contemplated that he must have lost his other eye, lost his vision forever, but then his good eye picked up a movement beyond.

'Henry…' he managed. It felt as though a weight were on his chest, a crushing heaviness which prevented his breathing. He wheezed, then coughed.

'Oh, that will hurt for a while,' Henry said, stepping out of the darkness a little. A chain rattled against his foot as he moved in closer. 'I shot a 7mm silver bullet into your chest. Cliché, I know, but sometimes Hollywood really does get it right. Bit surprised it didn't kill you, but a happy surprise…'

William groaned and tried to put a hand up to his heart but he was chained, just like before, strung up by his hands. He was too weak to change, too weak to move at all. He moaned in pain and allowed his weight to fall down onto his wrists.

The Black Marshes

'Not long now,' Henry whispered, 'Not long at all and then you get to die. I might take your other eye first, though, maybe an ear although I guess you'd just grow that back, wouldn't you? Maybe I should cut your cock off? I wonder if you could grow that back? What do you think, wolf? Time for you to lose your balls like a good doggy?'

William growled something in his throat, and then pulled on the chains again, despite the pain in his chest. He rattled them, but already he knew he stood no chance of breaking them. Henry just laughed, and approached with silver knife in hand. William swore he wouldn't give him the satisfaction, wouldn't scream but as Henry began to cut off his fingers, in the end, he did.

37

Frannie, 2016

William's screams filled the hallway and echoed through the silent house. Frannie stood still, quiet, watching from her spot in the doorway for the right moment. She had to time this just right if she wanted to save William. Despite their worries, despite the Haverly men's reluctance to risk a trap, Henry didn't seem prepared at all for the invasion, driven mad with fury. Frannie didn't trust it at all though, if nothing else, Henry was clever. This was not the deep basement, not the place James had been held, but one of the ones on the level above. Henry's torture chambers. Still Frannie was glad she'd not allowed James to follow her down despite how he'd wanted to. Instead, he remained upstairs, with Hugh and Ghost, in case Frannie failed. Even if William couldn't be saved, Henry was about to die. William, brave darling William howled again and then there was the thud of flesh, a finger, hitting the floor. Henry's chuckled; he was really enjoying having William bound and helpless again. It was enough to make Frannie sick. Henry raised the blade to William's face, touching the point to the cheek, just below the eye. William flinched violently but he didn't speak.

The Black Marshes

'You gonna come in Fran?' Henry asked, not even looking over his shoulder, 'Or shall I blind the beast for good? I reckon if I cut the eye out, it'll die like the other one did…'

Frannie stepped into the room, 'No, don't!… here I am,' she said.

'Here you are…'

'You were expecting me?'

'I was.'

'What do you want, Henry?'

'You. I want you. You and me, like before. We'll go back to America, be Frannie and Henry Quinn once more.'

'Then let William go.'

William grunted from behind her and Frannie cast him a quick glance. Henry had hacked at him a bit but no more permanent damage. Relief settled within her.

Henry's fingers closed around hers, suddenly, and he pulled her to him. 'And then you agree to be mine again?'

'As long as you let William go, I will be the most loving, devoted woman you ever knew… as long as he lives.'

'Only for him? Not because you missed me?'

'We've both hurt each other,' Frannie whispered, trying to soften her tone. 'we can work on being together again, give it time…'

'Do you still love me?'

'I'm trying to, I want to love you again…'

'Say you love me, and I'll give you anything,' Henry whined and just for a split second, Frannie's eye moved to William. He was watching intently, perhaps already catching the strange new scent about her. She hoped he realised that this was just deception. Henry's hand went to Frannie's face and he kissed her lips. Twice he kissed her and then, suddenly and abruptly he threw his fist up, hitting her so hard that she was knocked almost off of her feet.

'Frannie!' William uttered his first word since she'd entered the room, she nodded to him and regained her feet. She couldn't worry about anything now but saving William.

'Henry, please...' she gasped, faking a few tears, 'please...'

'I'm no fool,' Henry snapped. 'I'm not a man who takes being lied to easily. I know you despise me Frannie, you have done for so long that I've grown used to it, this little farce would have served you better if you'd remembered to flinch when I kissed you. What sort of a game do you think you are playing?'

'Yeah, that wasn't easy either,' she said. 'Your breath still tastes like shit. When was the last time you cleaned the dead meat out of those fangs?'

Henry stared, but then chuckled, his lips falling into a more natural grin, and threw an arm around Frannie's waist, kissing her cheek. 'Now there's my little lady,' he said and the affection was back in his tone. 'Now come on, bitch, what is it that you're playing at? Why are you really here?'

'Him,' she said, nodding at William. 'Release him and you get me. I will never leave you again so long as he lives. I swear. I don't have to like you, do I? I haven't done for years and that never bothered you before.'

'No!' William cried out, 'No Frannie please...'

Henry glanced up at William then back to Frannie, new interest in his eyes. 'So, for your everlasting obedience and affection, all I have to do is release him?'

'Yeah.'

'You fucked him?'

'Yeah. Several times.'

'Oh Frannie, really?'

'I am sorry, but I...'

'You feel for him?'

'Yeah.'

The Black Marshes

'You love him?'

'I do.'

'But in return for his freedom you will cast him off? Really? Without protest?'

'Yes... forever. You can fuck me, torture me, lock me in a basement for hundreds of years. Whatever you like, I won't even fight you... unless you want me to. Just let him go. I'll do anything.'

William moaned again. 'Frannie, no!' he cried out. 'Don't you dare do this!' He pulled on his bound hands furiously. Frannie turned her eyes back to him and allowed a tear to run down her cheek.

'Anything,' she said again, turning back to Henry.

Henry's eyes ran over Frannie's form hungrily. 'And what's to stop him from killing me as soon as I release him?'

'We leave him here and make a run for it, Hugh will know where to look – or Ghost will, he found James after all, we'll be long gone by the time they get here.'

'Frannie no,' William wailed again. 'Please Frannie... please...'

'All right,' Henry said at last. 'All right. I can live with allowing one of them its freedom if it means your loyalty. But Frannie, and you too, wolf, if I'm ever betrayed by Frannie again, I'll kill you both. You know I can do it, you're both only alive because I willed it.'

Henry pulled Frannie to him again and kissed her throat. Then he glanced at William. 'You see this? She's bought your life, wolf-skin. Frannie's paid for you with herself... she is mine.'

'Over my dead body,' her darling snarled.

Frannie's heart felt like it would burst. Even William had bought into her trickery. She wished she could reassure him but his life depended on Henry's buying into her deception so instead, she drove the nail home. 'I get to choose, William,' she whispered. 'My choice, my life, remember?'

Henry laughed and his hands slipped around Frannie to cup her behind. Almost roughly, he pulled her lips to his and kissed her again. Frannie pulled away.

'Let's go upstairs,' she whispered, realising his intent.

'No, let him watch... if he can control himself, I'll let him go. This way I know that you are no longer playing games with me.'

Frannie all but winced but then nodded, her eyes flickering to William. Henry licked at her throat and then nipped it with his teeth, his hand sliding up the back of her shirt, then pausing to undo the buttons so her bra was exposed. William moaned again and then Frannie heard a repressed sob. She glanced up at him again, willing him to read the expression in her eyes. Henry's teeth grew, his eyes glowed, and then his teeth sank into her throat, even as he began to unbutton her jeans. William moaned again, pulling on his chains and Frannie knew that the time had come. She hoped that Hugh and Ghost were right, that the demon blood would repel her attacker. The agony when they'd put it into her was still raw, so it was a good bet that it would, she thought wryly. With a sigh of relief, she let the changer demon take her into the secondary form, the face of the demon before the change, and hoped that she could control it, the last thing she needed was to fall screaming to the ground. As she let the change take her she felt Henry shudder.

'Yeah,' she muttered, fury overcoming her as she held his struggling form to her, pressing his lips to the wound as his fingers tightened on her flesh. 'Choke on it you son of a bitch!'

Henry spluttered on the blood and threw himself backwards coughing and gagging on her blood. 'What...?' he gasped. 'What the fuck...?' his stomach heaved again and he fell to his knees.

Frannie allowed herself a brief glance at William. He

was staring at her with eyes full of confusion.

'Frannie?' he gasped.

'You're safe now, William,' she said, 'just give me a minute here…'

'You… what?'

Frannie smiled and turned back to Henry who was staggering to his feet.

'What are you?' he gasped. 'What the fuck…?' but he staggered again as once more his stomach heaved.

Frannie smiled. 'Tastes funny at first, doesn't it?' Burns the gullet. Trust me I know – they had to tie me down to force enough of it into me to turn me… and that was after James bled me almost dry of drinker blood.'

Henry retched again, his whole form shaking as she bent and pulled Hugh's silver knife out of her boot and unwrapped it from the silk which had protected her new, changer skin from the precious metal.

'Nobody deserves to die more that you do,' she said, lifting the knife, 'but Sam Haverly – that's Ghost to you – has asked me to spare you your life. He says he has a better plan, a more fitting punishment, for you. I think that's a damn shame.' Frannie knelt and put the blade to Henry's throat. She was tempted, so tempted. She'd dreamed of being his murderer for so long, and yet there was the difference. The Haverly clan, the pack, adhered to a system of law and order. Ghost had asked for Henry's life to be spared, and as his sire, he had that right. Frances looked into Henry's eyes and saw fear. Not insolence, not anger, but fear. She nodded, perhaps Ghost was right, perhaps this wasn't the right course of action. She inhaled a few more times, steadying herself, and then reached into her pocket and pulled out a thin cord. Like the stuff that bound William, the cord was laced with silver. At full strength it would not have held Henry, but injured it would do fine. This she used to tie Henry's arms and then his feet. He still retched, coughing up her blood in a frothy vomit. His skin was whiter than white, and his body limp. He was not a difficult prisoner to take. Once he was secured, Frannie pulled the mobile phone that had been given to her from her pocket and pressed Hugh's name on the contacts screen.

'It's done. Come get him,' she said and then hung up.

Frannie stood for a moment, taking in deep, ragged breaths, and then glanced up at William. His face was a picture: horror, shock, pride. She smiled, allowing the corners of her mouth to lift and he mirrored it.

'I suppose I'd better cut you down,' she said, rebuttoning her shirt.

'Aye, if you would…'

Frannie moved to his side and with trembling hands, she released the bonds holding William. His arms went about her as soon as they were free, holding her tightly, but then he stepped back, almost falling to the ground.

'Are you… are you ok?'

'Aye, well, not really, but better than the brat at least. What's happening… to him…?' William asked.

'I happened. Smell me.'

William frowned but then did so, his brow wrinkled in confusion… 'how…?'

'Hugh,' Frannie said. 'There was still something left within me that was essentially human, apparently. It's not any more…'

William rested his weight on her for a moment, and then allowed himself to drop to the floor. Frannie sat down beside him, her hand on his arm. She kept one eye firmly on Henry but he was losing consciousness, drowned in her changer blood. He was no threat.

'So now you're partly like me?' William asked.

'Now I'm mostly like you, I think.'

William sighed and looked down at his hands. 'How does… does James feel about such a transformation?'

'He's obviously not happy,' Frannie said, 'but

The Black Marshes

William... James and I aren't...'

William looked up into her face and Frannie hoped her emotions showed in her eyes.

'I love you, William Craven,' she said, slowly and firmly, 'and I want you. Only you, as you asked me. I am happier than I thought I ever could be to find that my dear James is alive – surely you must understand that. He will recover, and I will be there to help him do so, but as his friend and... if you will... as your...' she paused and wet her lips, 'as your girl?'

'As my wife?'

'If you want?'

Frannie's heart ached at the multitude of expressions which ran over William's scarred and broken face. His good eye examined her, and then he seemed to slump. Frannie put her arms around him and kissed the top of his head. 'if you want me?' she whispered again.

'Always... Frannie, always. I...'

'Then that's settled then,' she smiled. 'Come, Hugh and Ghost are on their way down to collect Henry. There's no reason to stay down here – he's not going anywhere.'

'I have silver lodged right on the edge of my heart... I can barely move.'

A shiver ran down Frannie's spine. 'If I cut that with my knife...'

'You'll kill me,' he whispered.

'If there's already silver in your heart...'

'I should be dead... unless it's only grazed... I think... I hope he's missed but it's close, it's sapping me...'

Frannie's limbs trembled, but she forced a calm, 'a non-silver blade, perhaps? If I am careful not to push it into your heart?'

William moved her hand to the wound, still open and oozing, 'your fingers...'

'My fingers?'

'Yes... pull it out! it's the least risky way...' Frannie

nodded, her fingers splaying over the wound.

'Fran?'

'Yes?' her voice was a whisper.

'In case this… in case… I… I want you to know that I… I love you.'

Frannie's eyes ran with tears but she nodded, not trusting herself to speak, and slid her fingers into he wound in his chest. The wound was hot, wet and slippery. Frannie steeled herself and pushed down past sharp smashed ribs and into the fleshy muscle of his heart. Her gut contracted, and her mouth filled with bile, but then she felt the metal lodged there.

'Are you sure this won't kill you?'

'No,' he wheezed, agony written in clenched teeth and closed eyes.

'Oh god…. William…'

'Do it!'

Frannie did so, unable to stand the pain on his face, gripping the slippery bullet with her fingers and pulling it loose. William screamed, a half-human yelp, and then slumped so that he was laid down on the ground, curling up around the wound. He was silent for so long that Frannie dared not roll him over, but then he moaned and put out a hand.

'William?'

'I'm healing it,' he whispered, 'thank god, it's healing.'

EPILOGUE

All about, a scent of decay permeated the air, an acrid, sharp scent of rotting flesh and damp rot. Henry groaned and pulled at his bindings, hissing where the silver burnt into the flesh of his hands and made his wrists bleed. The basement was dark, so dark, and if it were not for his half-blurred memories of being dragged down there by Ghost, he'd not have known where he had been taken. Two days, two long, terrifying days he'd been left alone, but then on the third a rattle of the door pulled him from his shock and anger. As well as he knew her, he half-expected it to be Frannie, but instead William Craven stood above him. The man he'd tortured twice, whom he'd been so close to killing, cast eyes upon him in his bondage. Henry said nothing, pressing his lips with distaste. William stood silent for a long moment, and then lifted a bent, broken silver bullet on a cord from his pocket.

'I wanted you to see this,' he said. 'I wanted you to know that you have not managed to end me.'

Henry said nothing, rage making him strong, almost strong enough to break free and throttle his enemy. Not quite though, Ghost – Samuel Haverly – had made sure that the chains were beyond strong enough to hold him. Besides, the more he pulled on them, the more his skin touched the silver which lined the outer edges of the chains and that was agony.

'I come here not to taunt you though,' William said,

'I'm not like you and feel no pleasure in seeing another creature suffer – even one as despicable as you. I have come here to tell you that I am going to marry Frances, and that from now until forever, she is under my protection and the protection of my pack. If ever you escape this place, if ever you come anywhere near us again, you will fail again. You think yourself strong but you are weak. You are weak and you are a bully.'

'Why not just kill me?'

'Oh trust me, if it was my say, I would! ...but I follow a higher authority, a law. That's what makes you and I so different.'

'Why does Haverly want me alive then?'

'God only knows but I think he considers death too easy after what you did to your brother. Hugh and I both wanted to destroy you for good.'

Henry's breath caught, and the shame of his actions towards James threatened to flood him again. He'd become adept though, at repressing such feelings and so pushed them back down into his gut.

William stood a moment longer, looking at where Henry's hands bled in their shackles. Henry tensed, hoping that the changer was fool enough to pity him and assist. He did not. Instead, he threw down the bullet, spent as it was, onto the floor and turned to walk away. The light which spilled in as the door opened was almost bliss for a moment, and then the darkness set in.

Time was tortuously slow and unfathomable in the darkness. Days turned to weeks and then it felt as though weeks turned to months. At first the anger kept the madness at bay, but gradually, over time, it began to creep in. Even knowing that above the house was an empty ruin, still Henry screamed and screamed, he begged, he bargained with the universe. When the hunger took him at first he resisted but that too overcame him, forcing him, as

The Black Marshes

it had his brother before him, to grasp at insects, rats and mice. Brought low, brought to nothing. Henry could feel his flesh wasting away on his bones, could feel the darkness pressing in. Even James had had the distraction of Henry's torture, but Henry had not even that, locked and bound in an oubliette more vile even than those of the medieval variety, for there at least the men could starve to death and be gone.

Then suddenly, there were footsteps again, it must have been years, surely, or was it mere days. Henry no longer knew. He opened his mouth to shout but instead produced a thin reedy murmur, like the groan of an old spook. He gasped and tried to cough but there was no saliva to moisten the dryness of his vocal chords. More footsteps, those of authority, somebody who knew where he was hidden, and then the door opened. Henry squinted at the sudden brightness of a torch, the light burning his eyes. He squinted and tried to see, but the figure in the doorway seemed purposely to flash the light into his eyes, keeping him blind.

'Well, there's a sight to see indeed,' came an unfamiliar male voice, 'are you sure he's the one?'

'Yes,' a female reply from beyond, 'I'm certain that that's Sam Haverly's blood-child, the one he exiled.'

The figure stepped closer, still pointing his light at Henry's face. 'Well, well…' the male voice again, 'Looks like today is your lucky day, Mr Orchard…'

TO BE CONTINUED…

ABOUT THE AUTHOR

Emma Barrett-Brown is an author and History PHD student from Plymouth, in the UK. Emma writes under two genres, Historical Romance and Supernatural Romance. As yet, her released novels are all in the latter genre but this is set to change soon. Emma uses her background in Psychology (being educated to MSc) and her interest in History (PHD underway) to inform and enhance her novels. She currently both studies and works her day job at Plymouth University.

Ella's Memoirs was released in May 2013 and after a short social media campaign, it was found to be a success, making it into the top 10,000 best-selling ebooks overall on kindle, and the top 1000 free ebooks on kindle during a free promotion shortly after release. This led then to the full proof and edit of novel number 2, The Blood of the Poppies. Unfortunately, due to the death of Emma's father, this novel was somewhat delayed. However, it was released a year later than planned in the May of 2016. Emma has a backlog of novels waiting now, and is looking likely to be a name which will become known in the future.

https://www.facebook.com/EmmaBarrettBrown/

Printed in Great Britain
by Amazon